W9-CEK-479

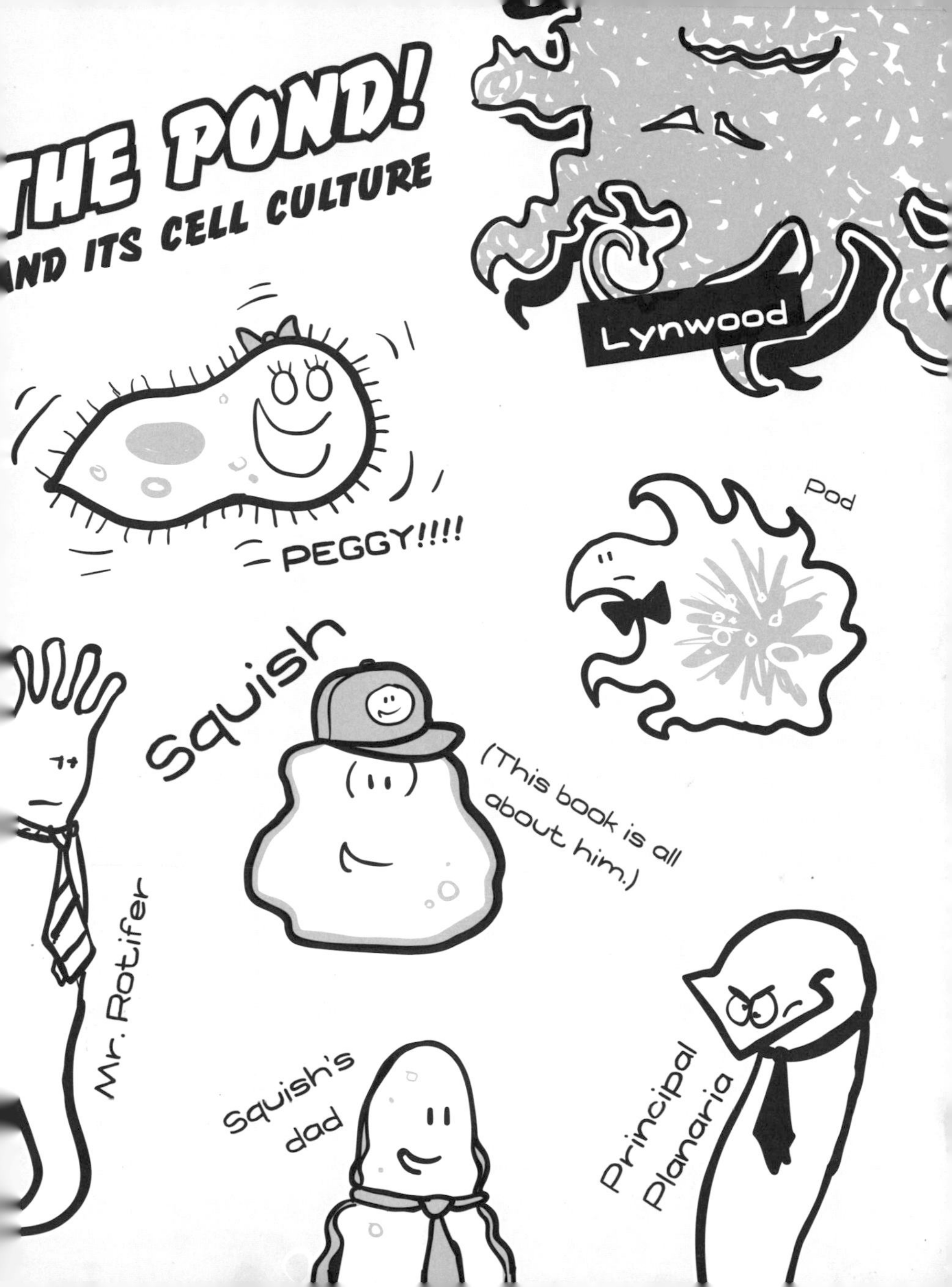
THE POND!
AND ITS CELL CULTURE
Lynwood
PEGGY!!!!
Pod
Squish
(This book is all about him.)
Mr. Rotifer
Squish's dad
Principal Planaria

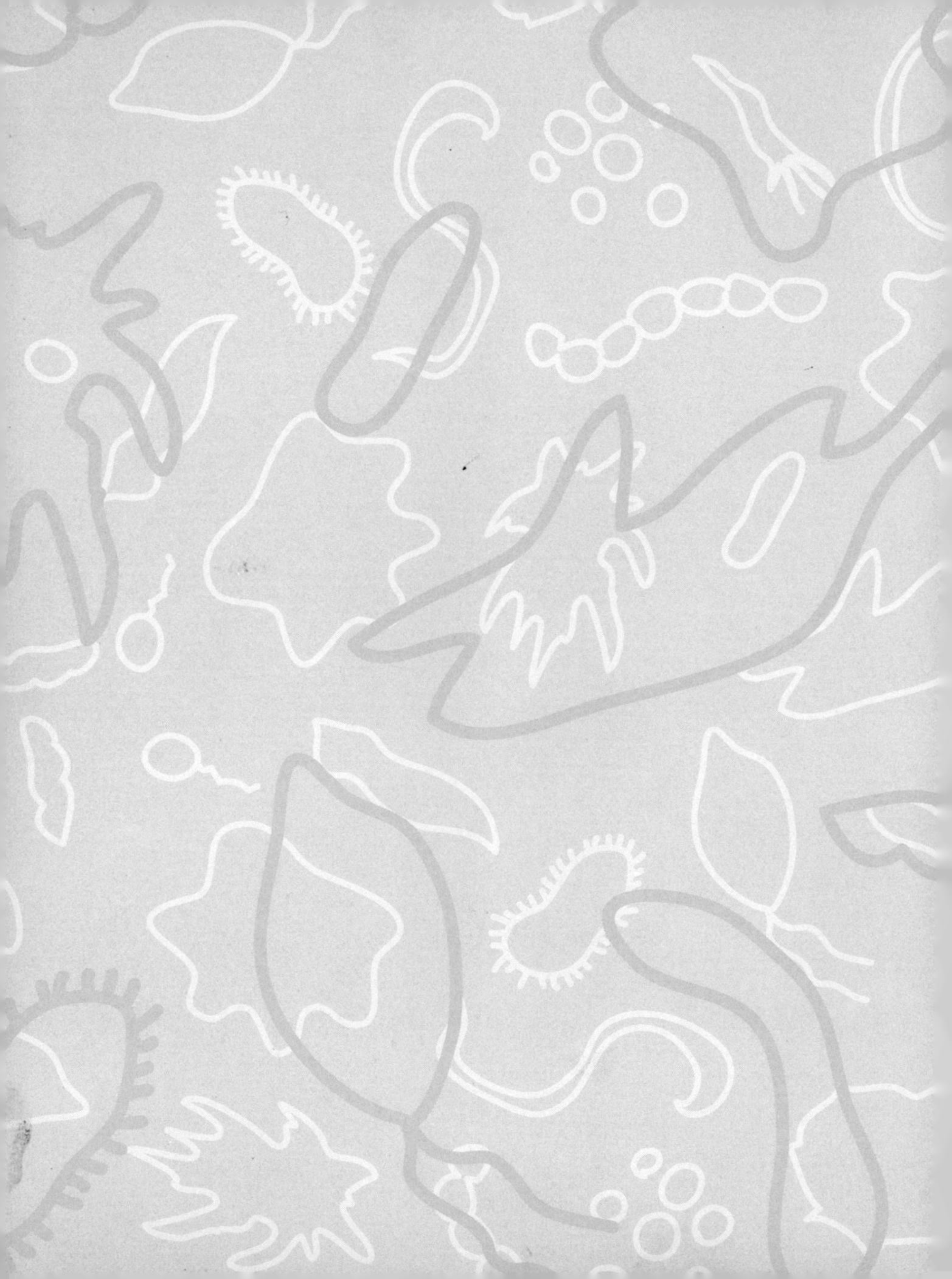

squish
SUPER AMOEBA

BY JENNIFER L. HOLM & MATTHEW HOLM

RANDOM HOUSE 🏠 NEW YORK

This is a work of fiction. Names, characters, places, and incidents either are the product of the authors' imagination or are used fictitiously. Any resemblance to actual persons, living or dead, events, or locales is entirely coincidental.

 Published in the United States by Random House Children's Books, a division of Random House, Inc., New York.
Random House and the colophon are registered trademarks of Random House, Inc.

Visit us on the Web! www.randomhouse.com/kids
Educators and librarians, for a variety of teaching tools, visit us at www.randomhouse.com/teachers

Library of Congress Cataloging-in-Publication Data
Holm, Jennifer L.
Squish, Super Amoeba / by Jennifer L. Holm and Matthew Holm. – 1st ed. p. cm.
Summary: Squish, a meek amoeba who loves the comic book exploits of his favorite hero, "Super Amoeba," tries to emulate him when his best friend is threatened by a bully.
ISBN 978-0-375-84389-1 (trade) –
ISBN 978-0-375-93783-5 (lib. bdg.)
1. Graphic novels. [1. Graphic novels. 2. Amoeba—Fiction. 3. Schools—Fiction. 4. Bullies—Fiction. 5. Courage—Fiction. 6. Superheroes—Fiction.] I. Holm, Matthew. II. Title. III. Title: Super Amoeba.
PZ7.7.H65Sq 2011 741.5'973—dc22 2010008004

MANUFACTURED IN MALAYSIA 10 9 8 7 6 5 4 3 2 1
First Edition

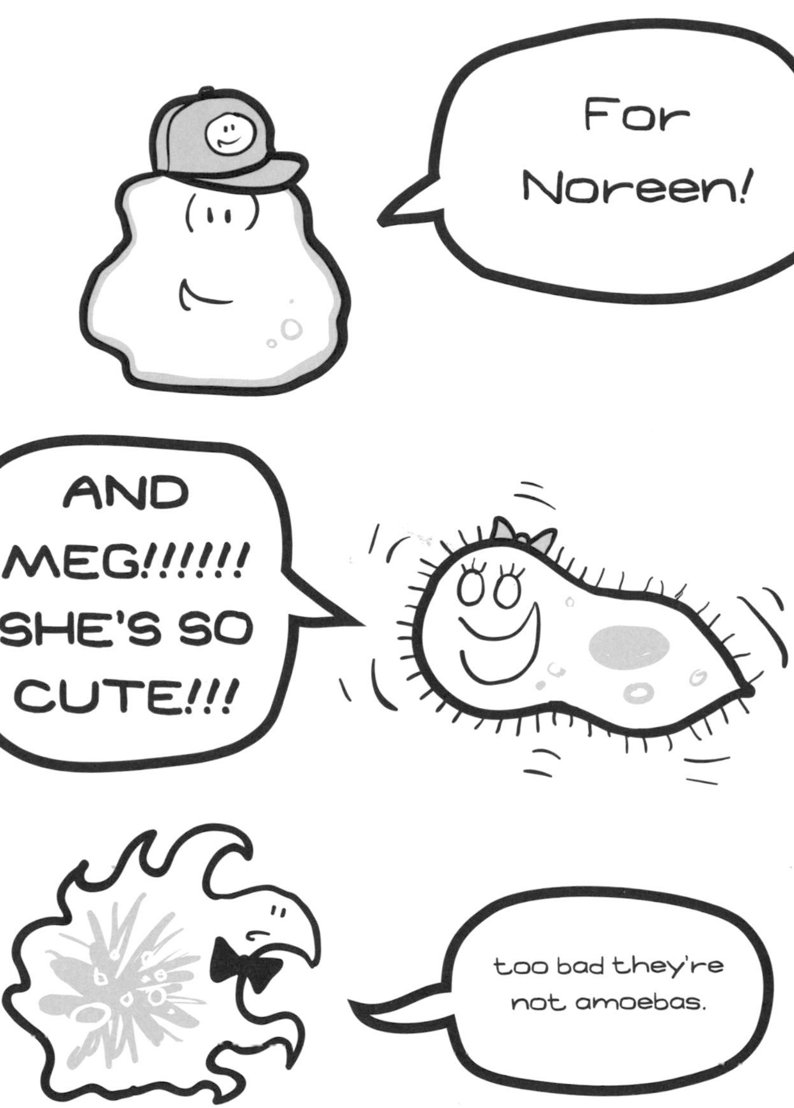
For Noreen!
AND MEG!!!!!! SHE'S SO CUTE!!!
too bad they're not amoebas.

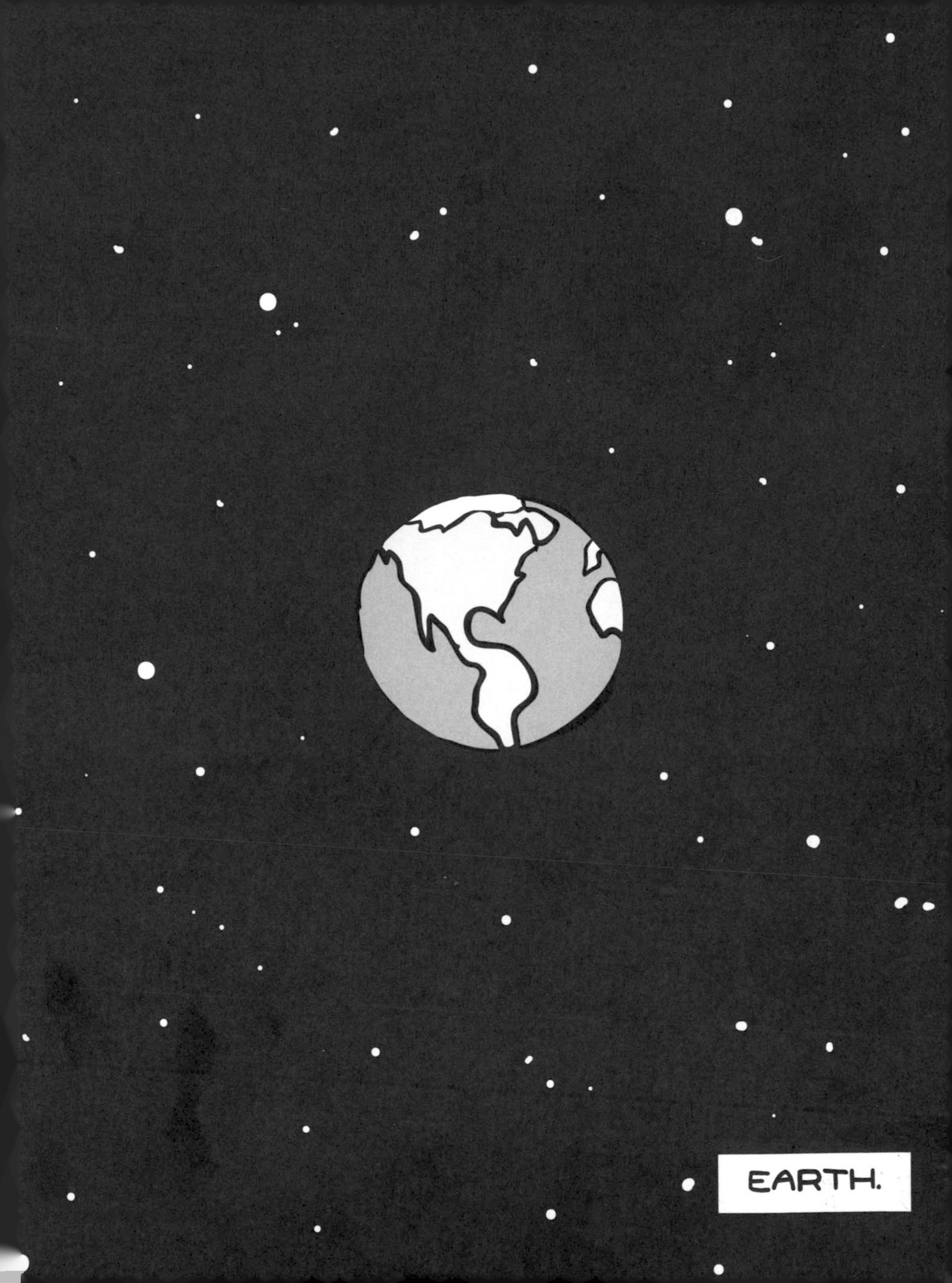
EARTH.

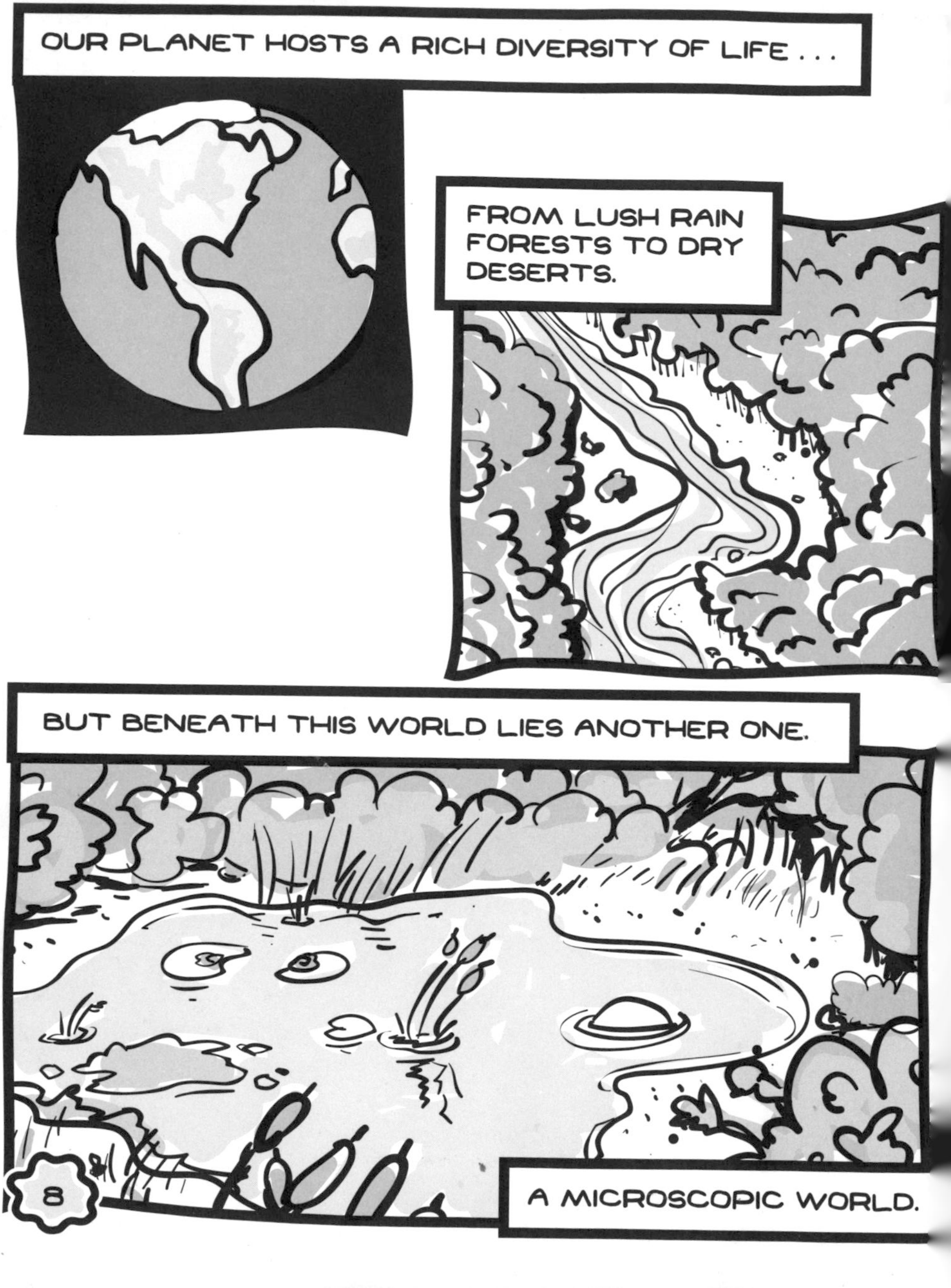
OUR PLANET HOSTS A RICH DIVERSITY OF LIFE . . .
FROM LUSH RAIN FORESTS TO DRY DESERTS.
BUT BENEATH THIS WORLD LIES ANOTHER ONE.
A MICROSCOPIC WORLD.

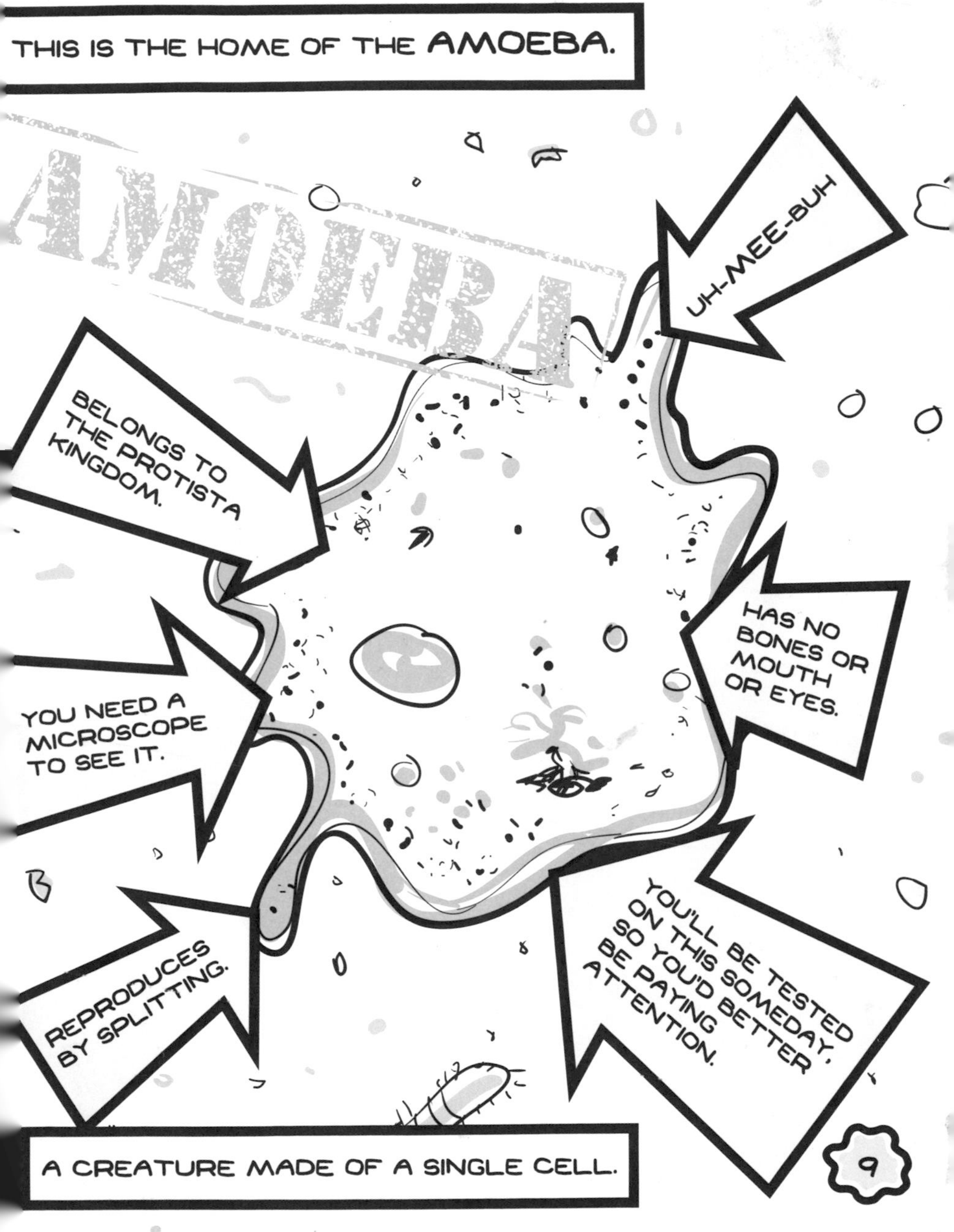
THIS IS THE HOME OF THE AMOEBA.
AMOEBA
UH-MEE-BUH
BELONGS TO THE PROTISTA KINGDOM.
HAS NO BONES OR MOUTH OR EYES.
YOU NEED A MICROSCOPE TO SEE IT.
REPRODUCES BY SPLITTING.
YOU'LL BE TESTED ON THIS SOMEDAY, SO YOU'D BETTER BE PAYING ATTENTION.
A CREATURE MADE OF A SINGLE CELL.

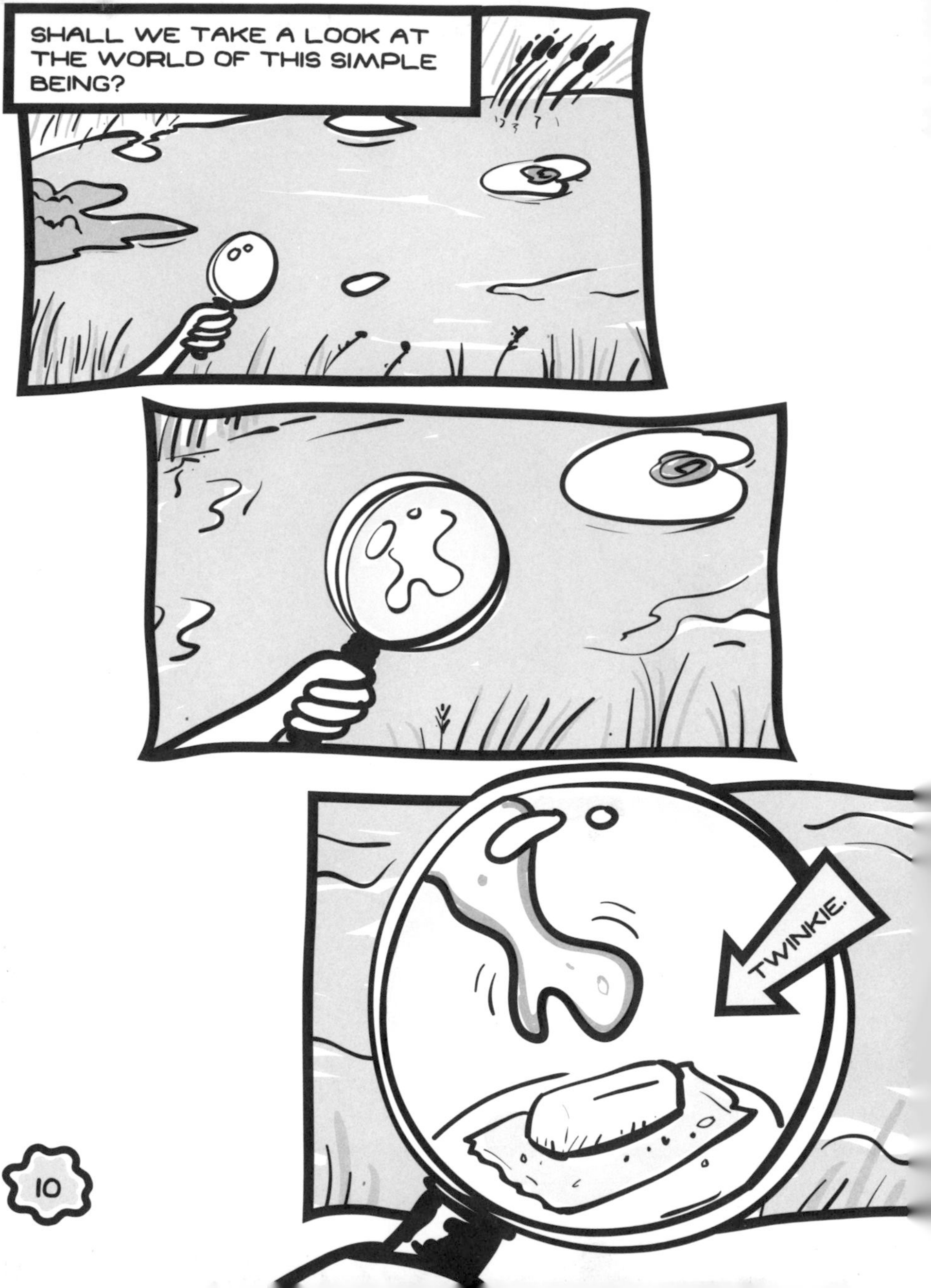
SHALL WE TAKE A LOOK AT THE WORLD OF THIS SIMPLE BEING?
TWINKIE.

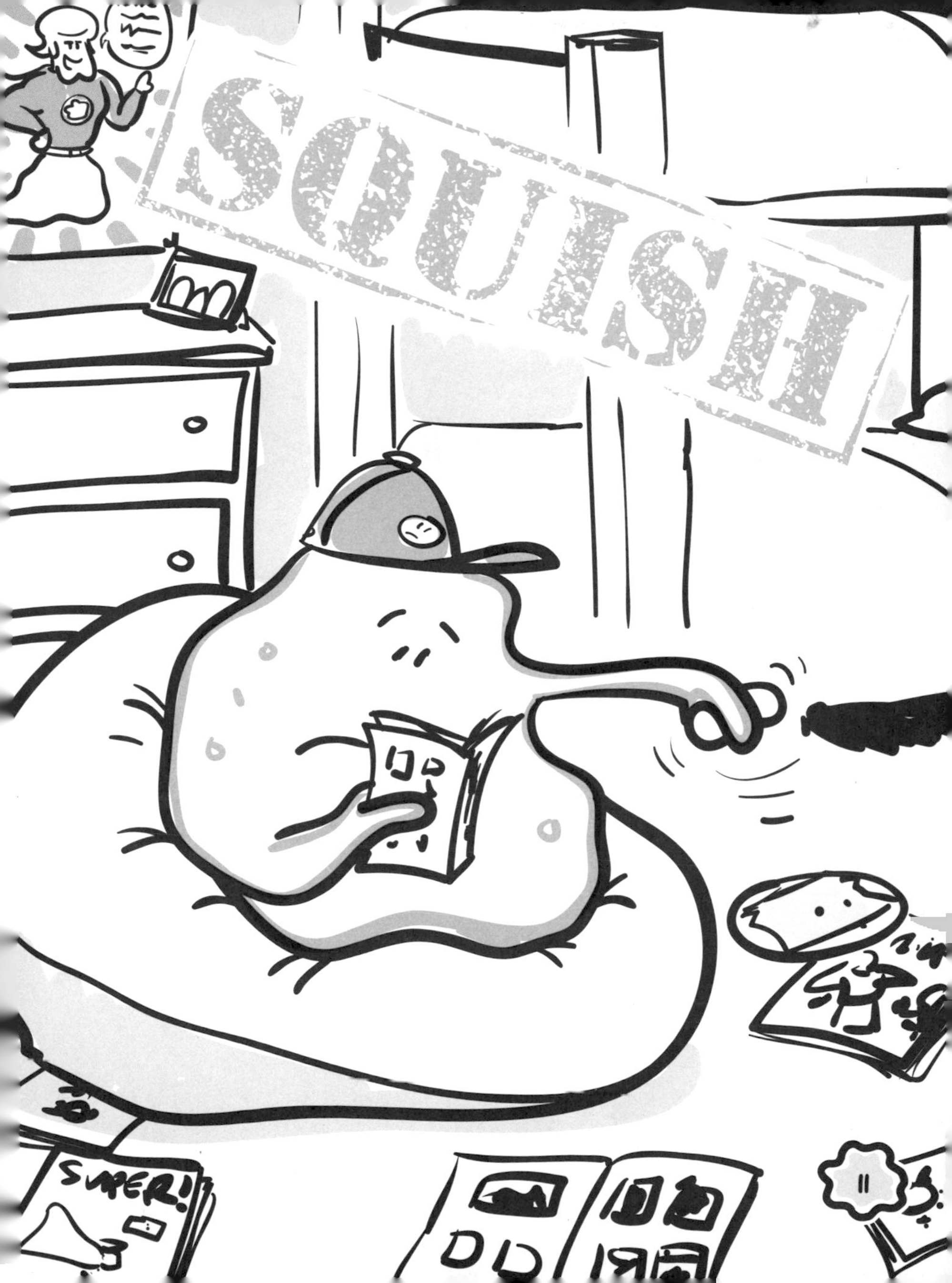
SQUISH
SUPER!

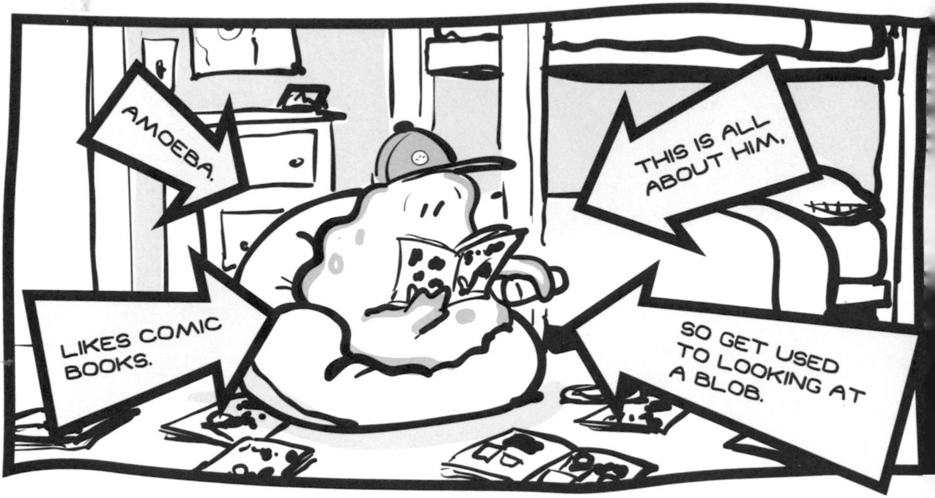
AMOEBA.
LIKES COMIC BOOKS.
THIS IS ALL ABOUT HIM,
SO GET USED TO LOOKING AT A BLOB.

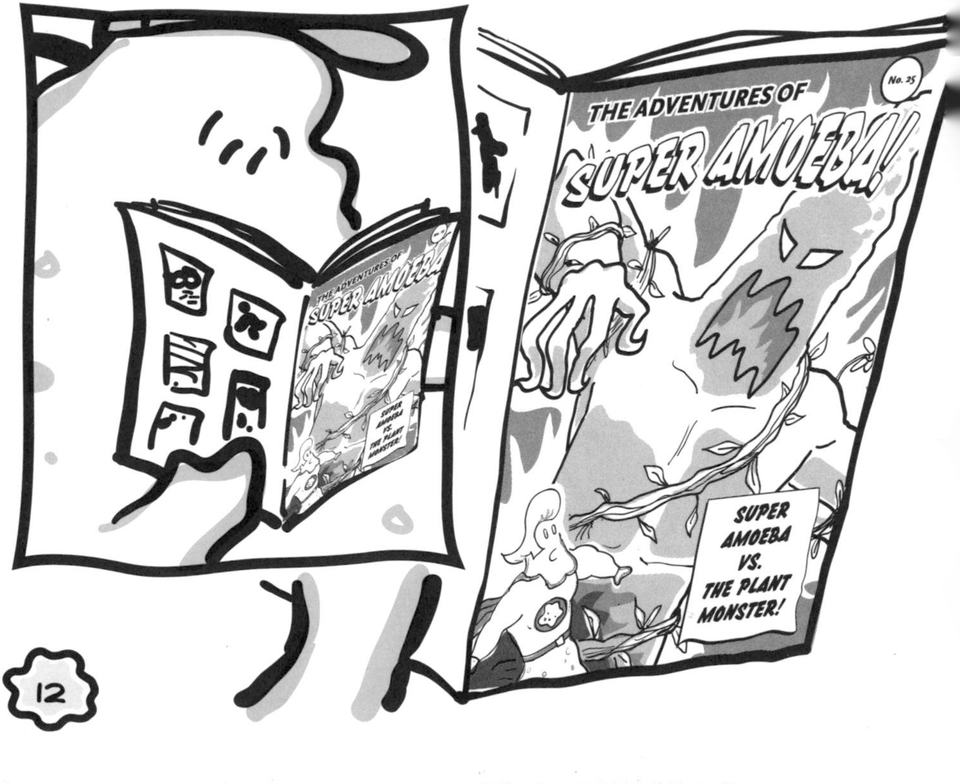
No. 25
THE ADVENTURES OF
SUPER AMOEBA!
SUPER AMOEBA VS. THE PLANT MONSTER!

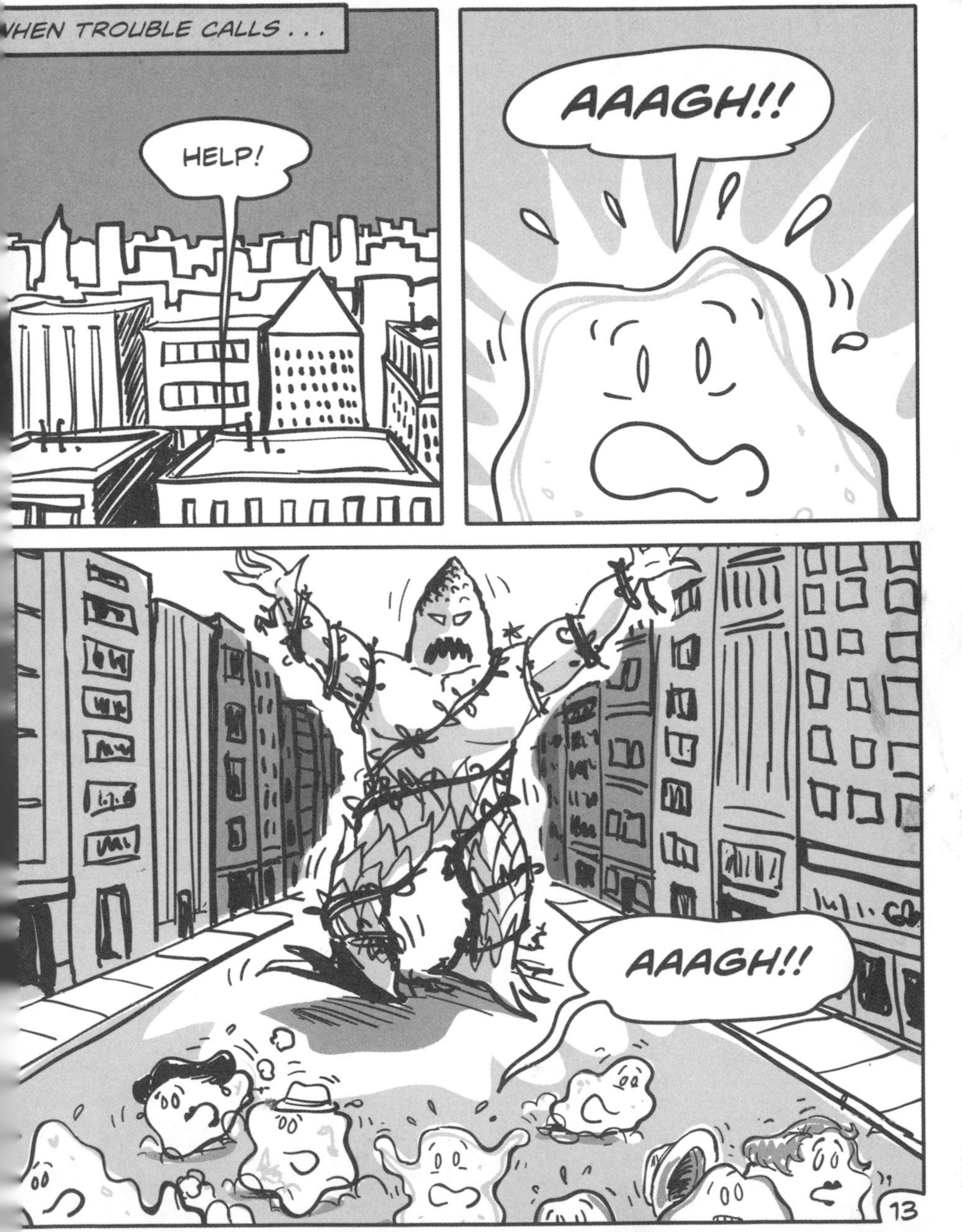
WHEN TROUBLE CALLS . . .
HELP!
AAAGH!!
AAAGH!!

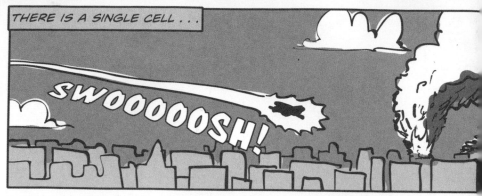

THERE IS A SINGLE CELL . . .

SWOOOOOSH!

PLUCK

WAUGH!

SLURP!

14

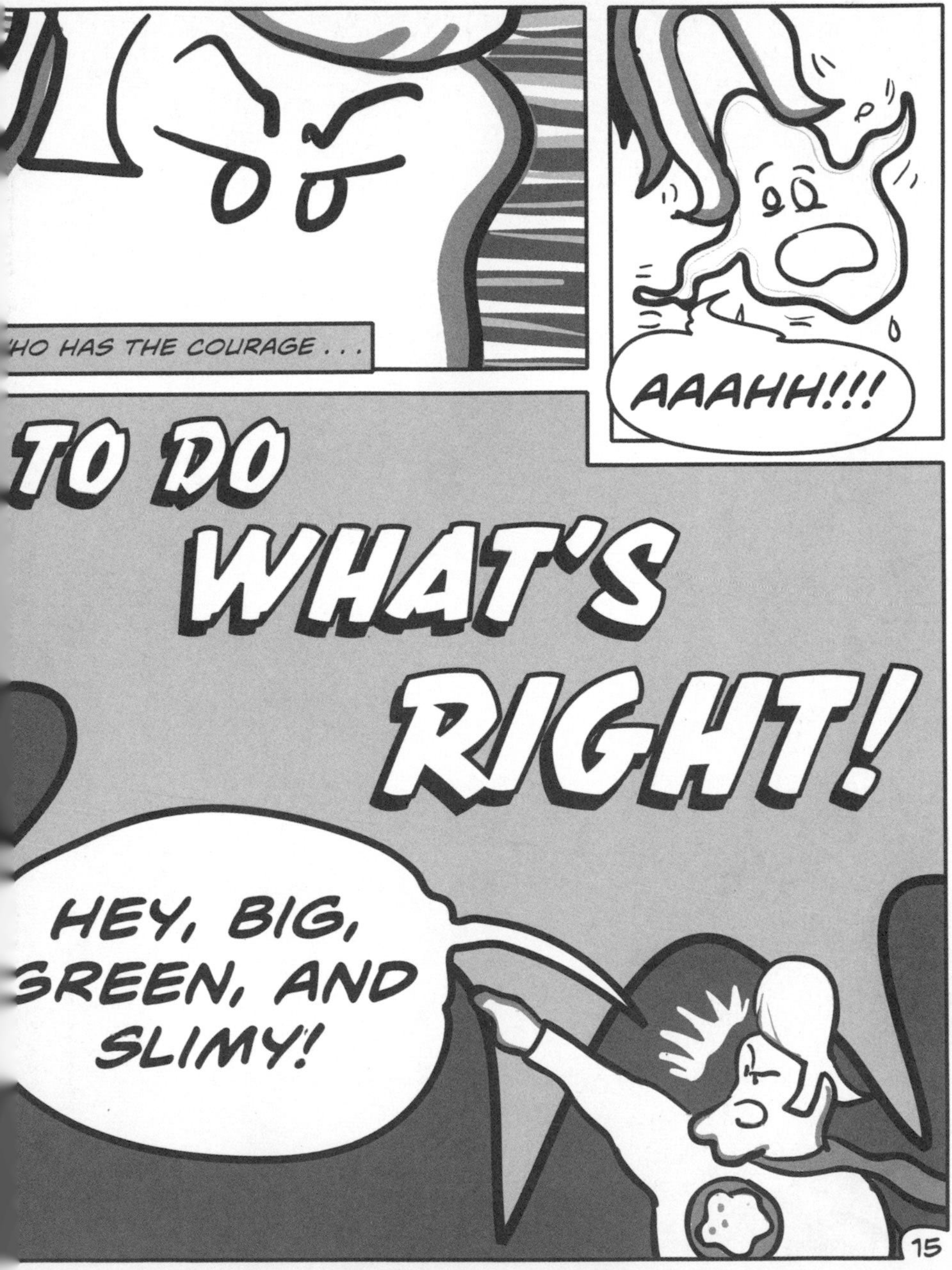

HO HAS THE COURAGE . . .
AAAHH!!!
TO DO WHAT'S RIGHT!
HEY, BIG, GREEN, AND SLIMY!

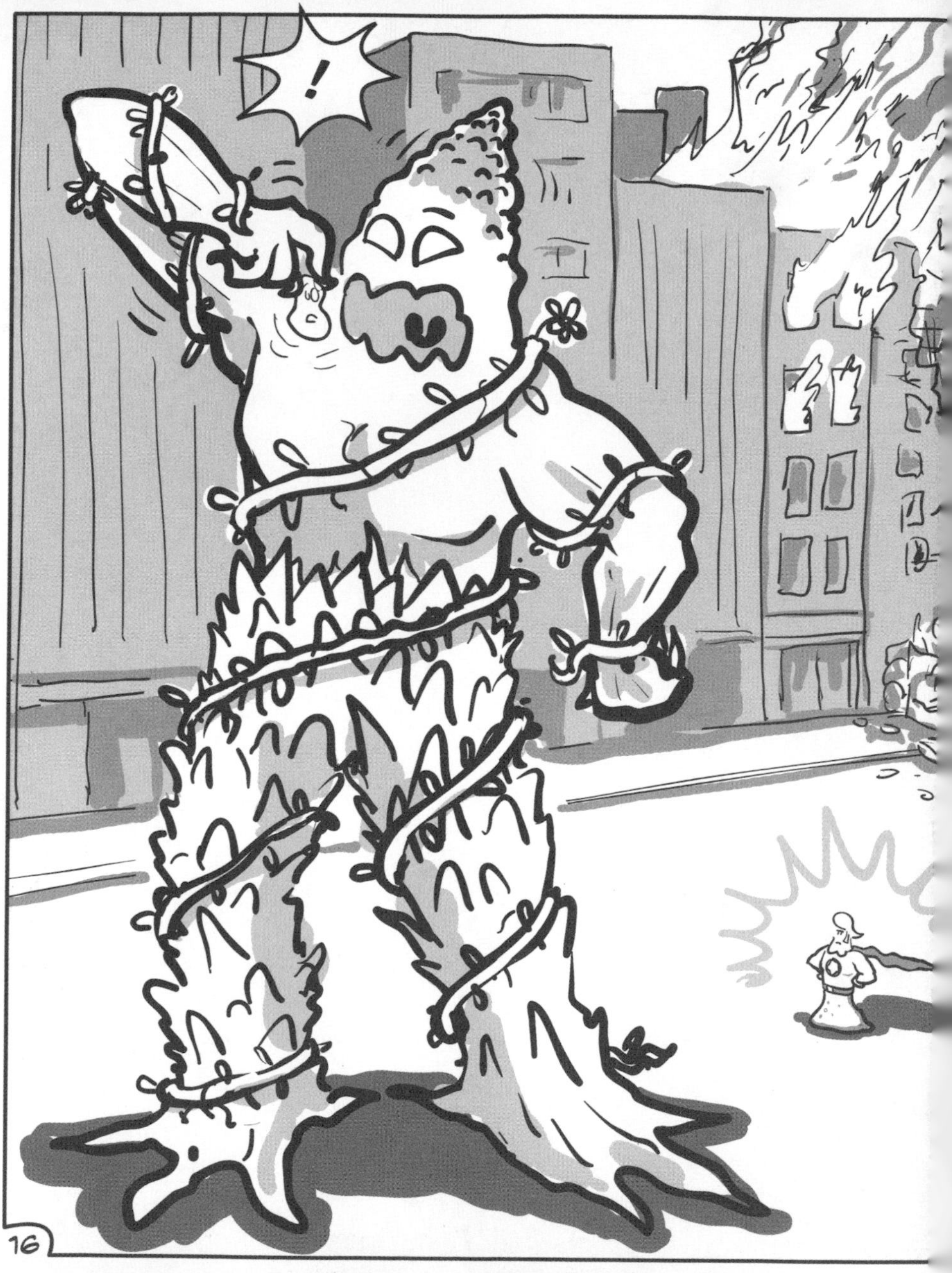
!

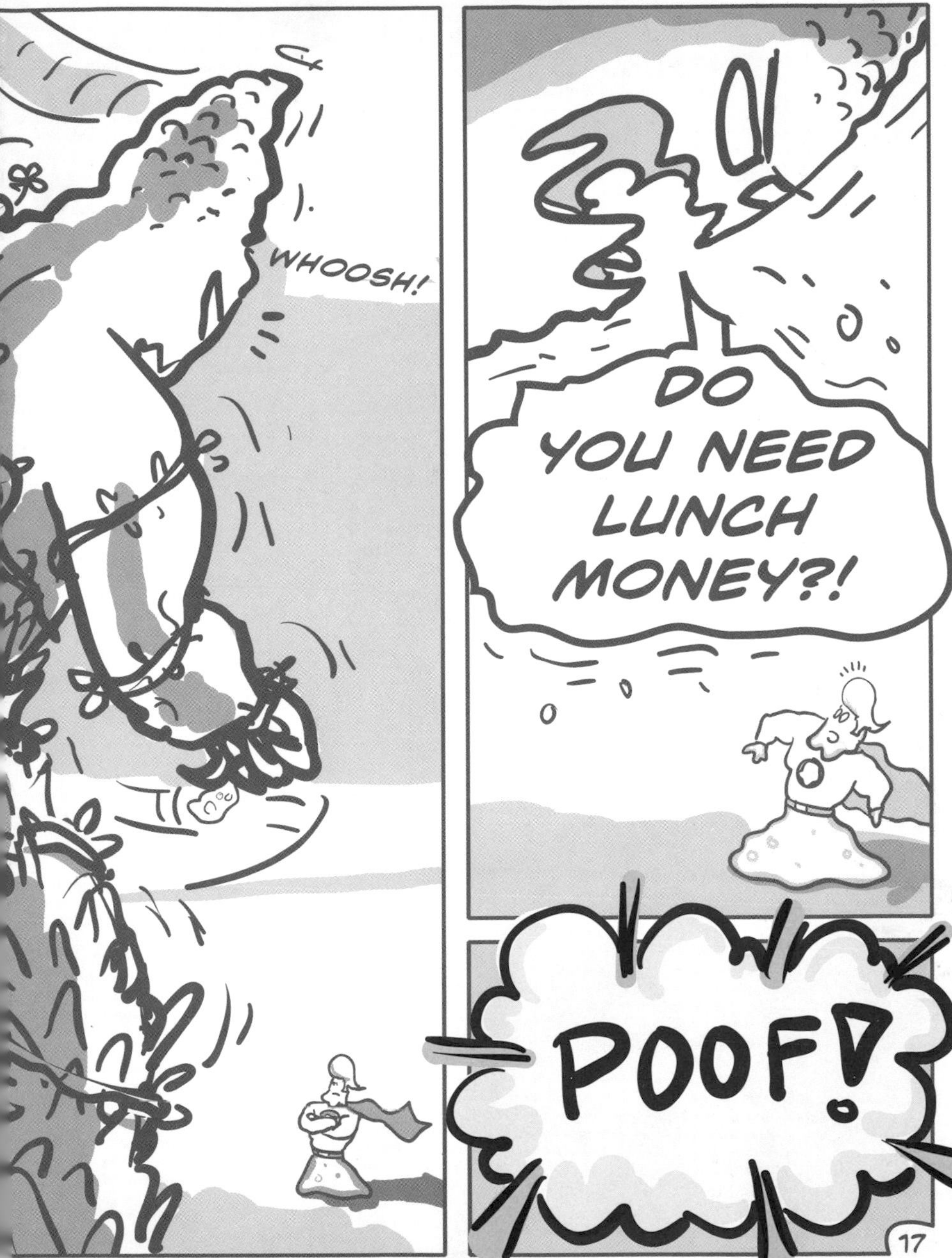
WHOOSH!
DO YOU NEED LUNCH MONEY?!
POOF!

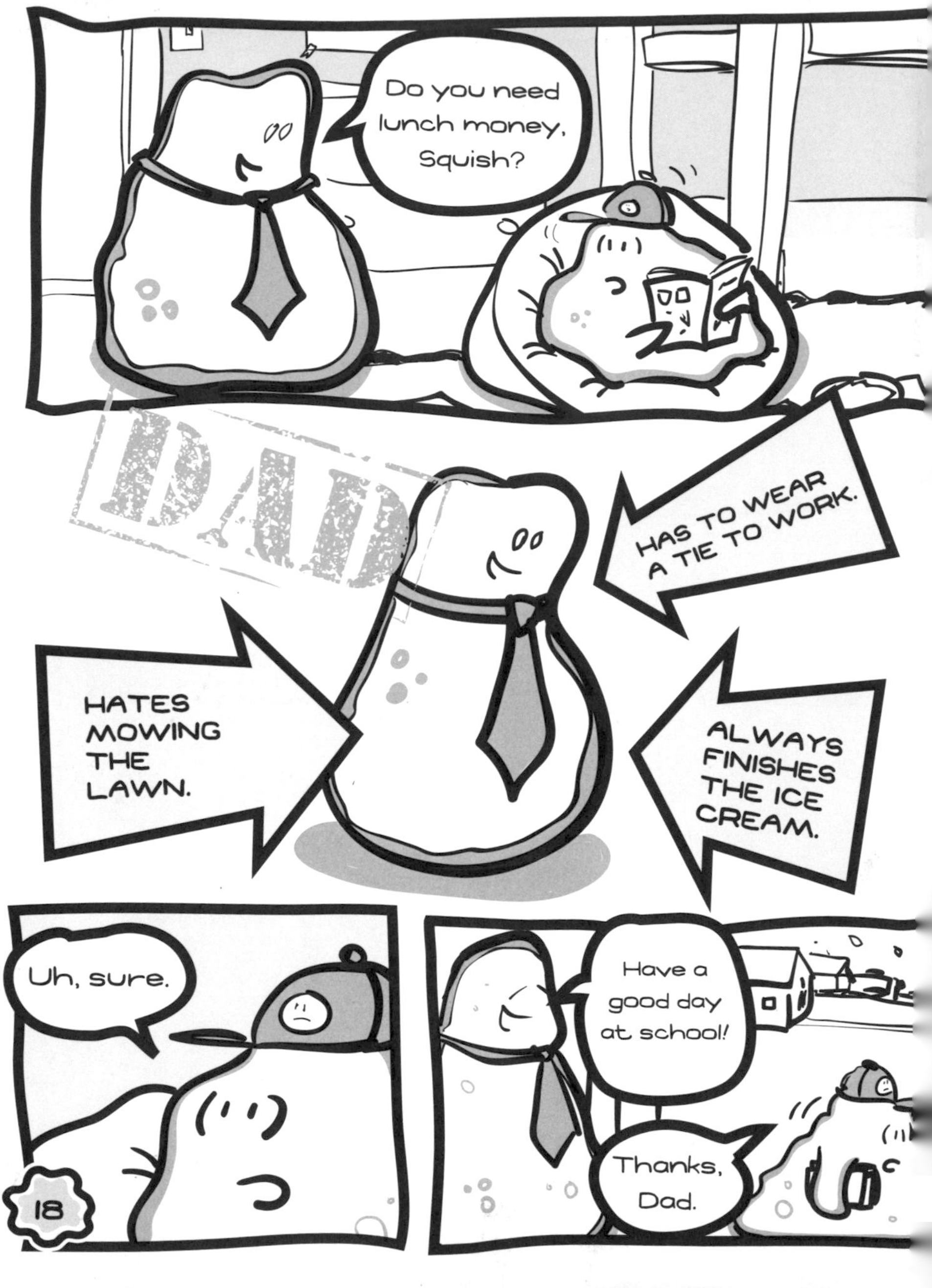
Do you need lunch money, Squish?
DAD
HAS TO WEAR A TIE TO WORK.
HATES MOWING THE LAWN.
ALWAYS FINISHES THE ICE CREAM.
Uh, sure.
Have a good day at school!
Thanks, Dad.

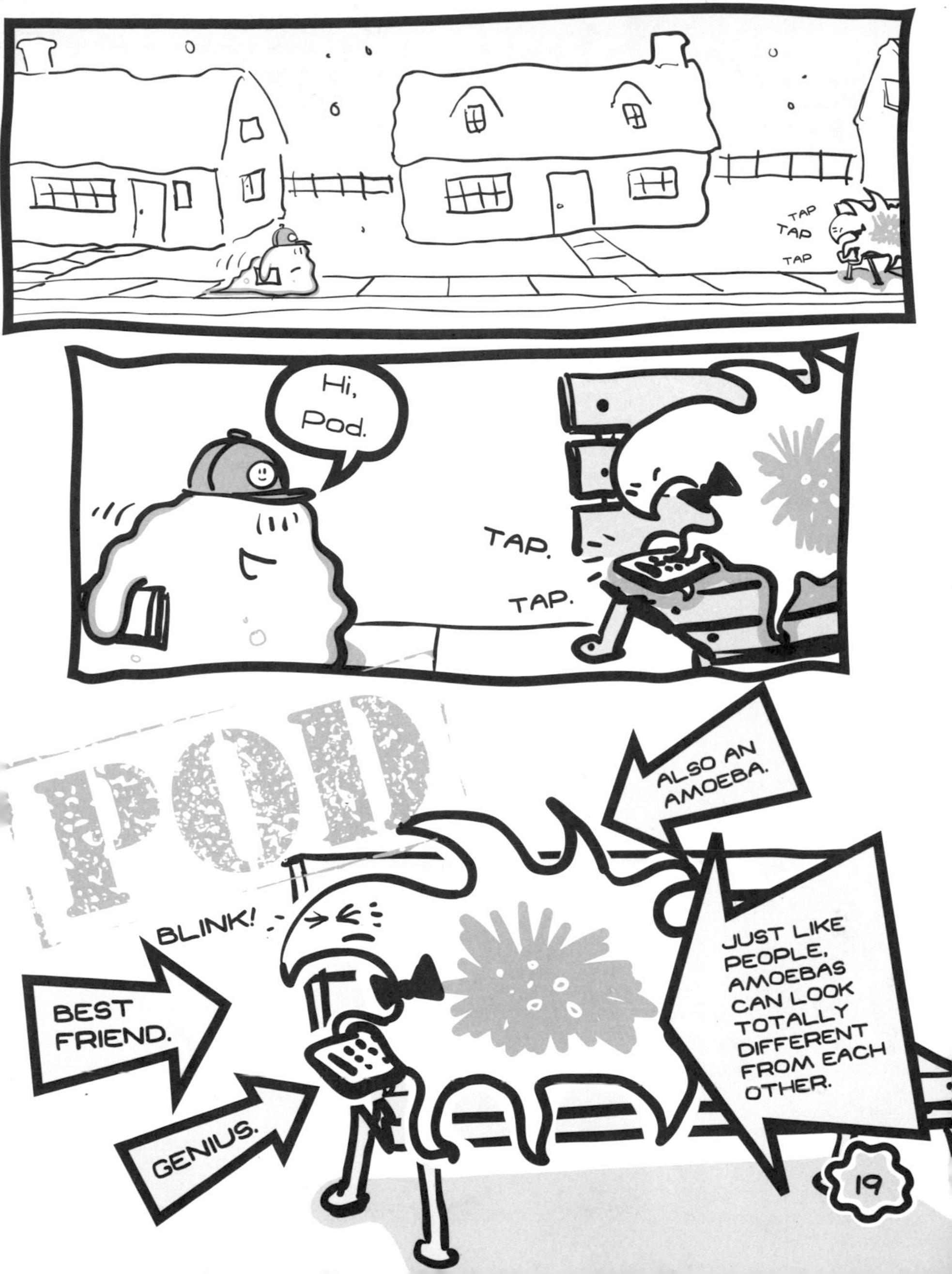
TAP
TAP
TAP
Hi, Pod.
TAP.
TAP.
POD
ALSO AN AMOEBA.
BLINK!
JUST LIKE PEOPLE, AMOEBAS CAN LOOK TOTALLY DIFFERENT FROM EACH OTHER.
BEST FRIEND.
GENIUS.

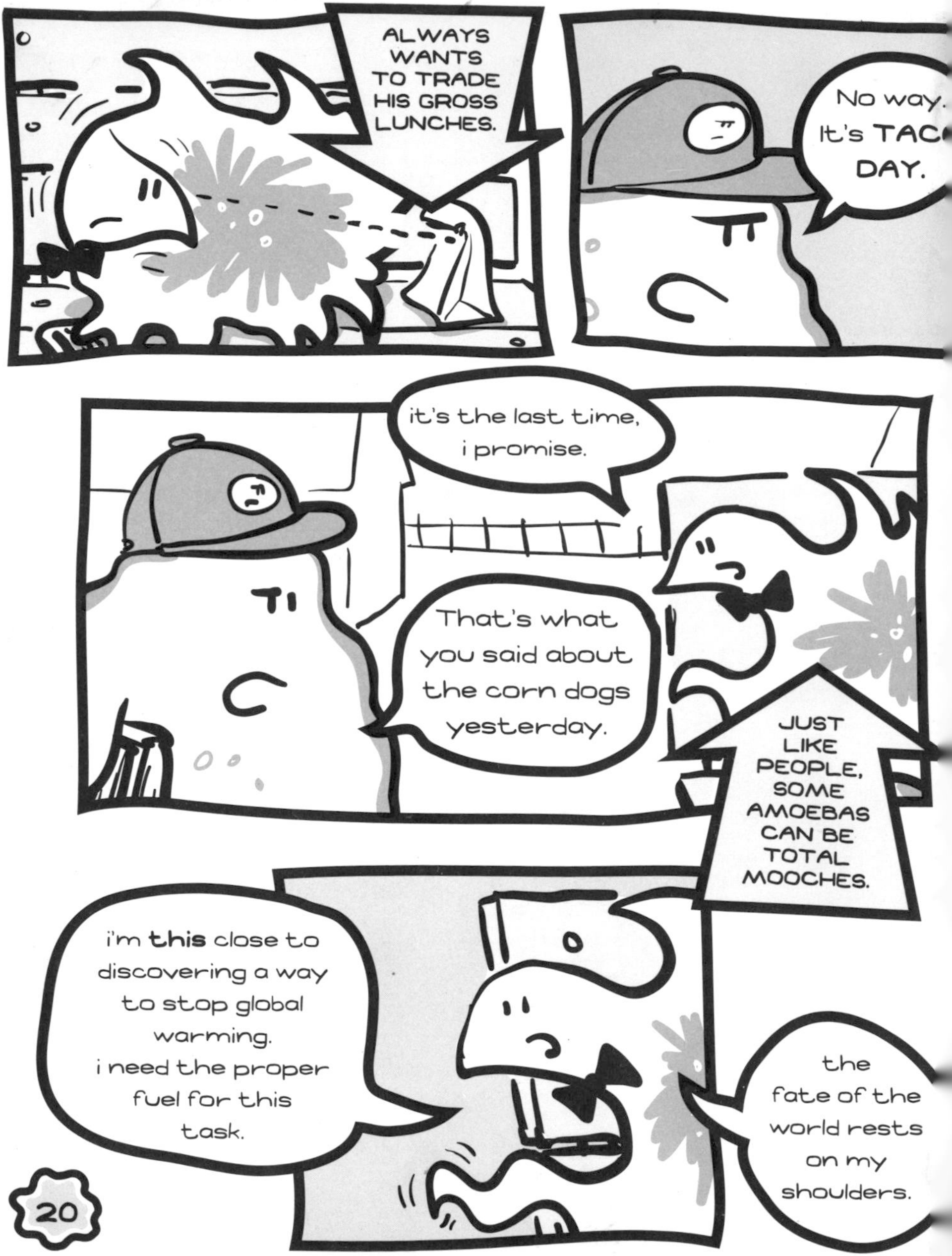
ALWAYS WANTS TO TRADE HIS GROSS LUNCHES.
No way. It's TACO DAY.
it's the last time, i promise.
That's what you said about the corn dogs yesterday.
JUST LIKE PEOPLE, SOME AMOEBAS CAN BE TOTAL MOOCHES.
i'm **this** close to discovering a way to stop global warming. i need the proper fuel for this task.
the fate of the world rests on my shoulders.

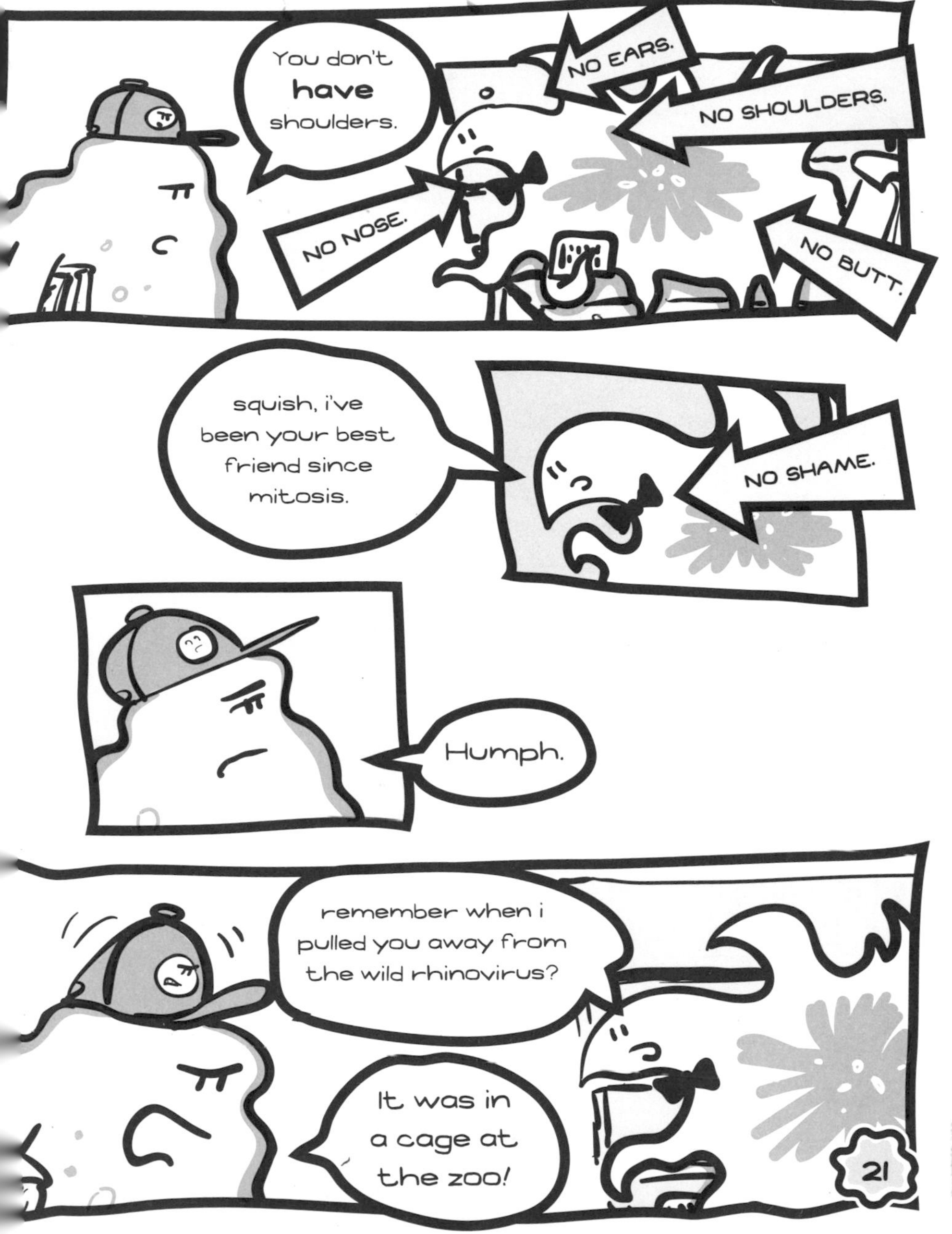
You don't **have** shoulders.
NO EARS.
NO SHOULDERS.
NO NOSE.
NO BUTT.
squish, i've been your best friend since mitosis.
NO SHAME.
Humph.
remember when i pulled you away from the wild rhinovirus?
It was in a cage at the zoo!

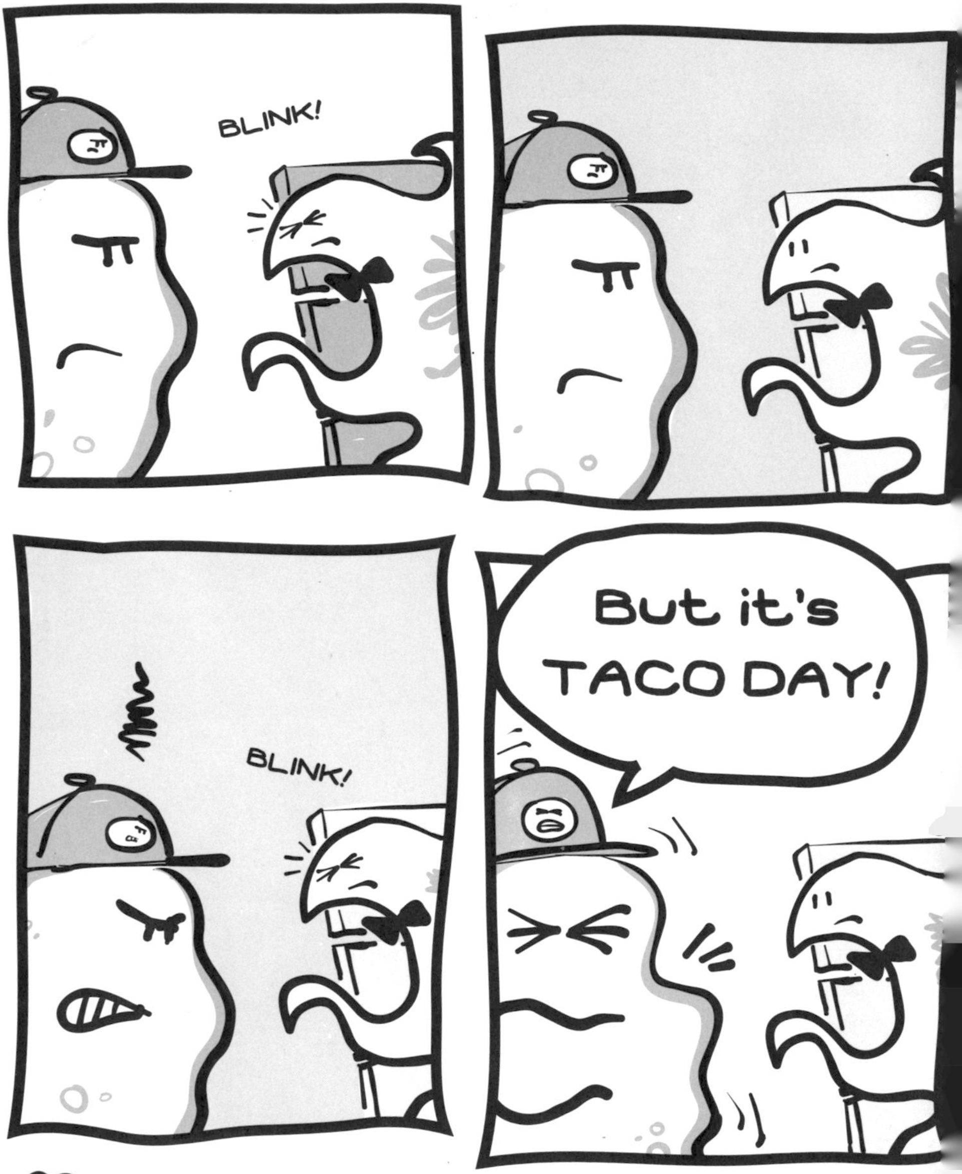
BLINK!
BLINK!
But it's TACO DAY!

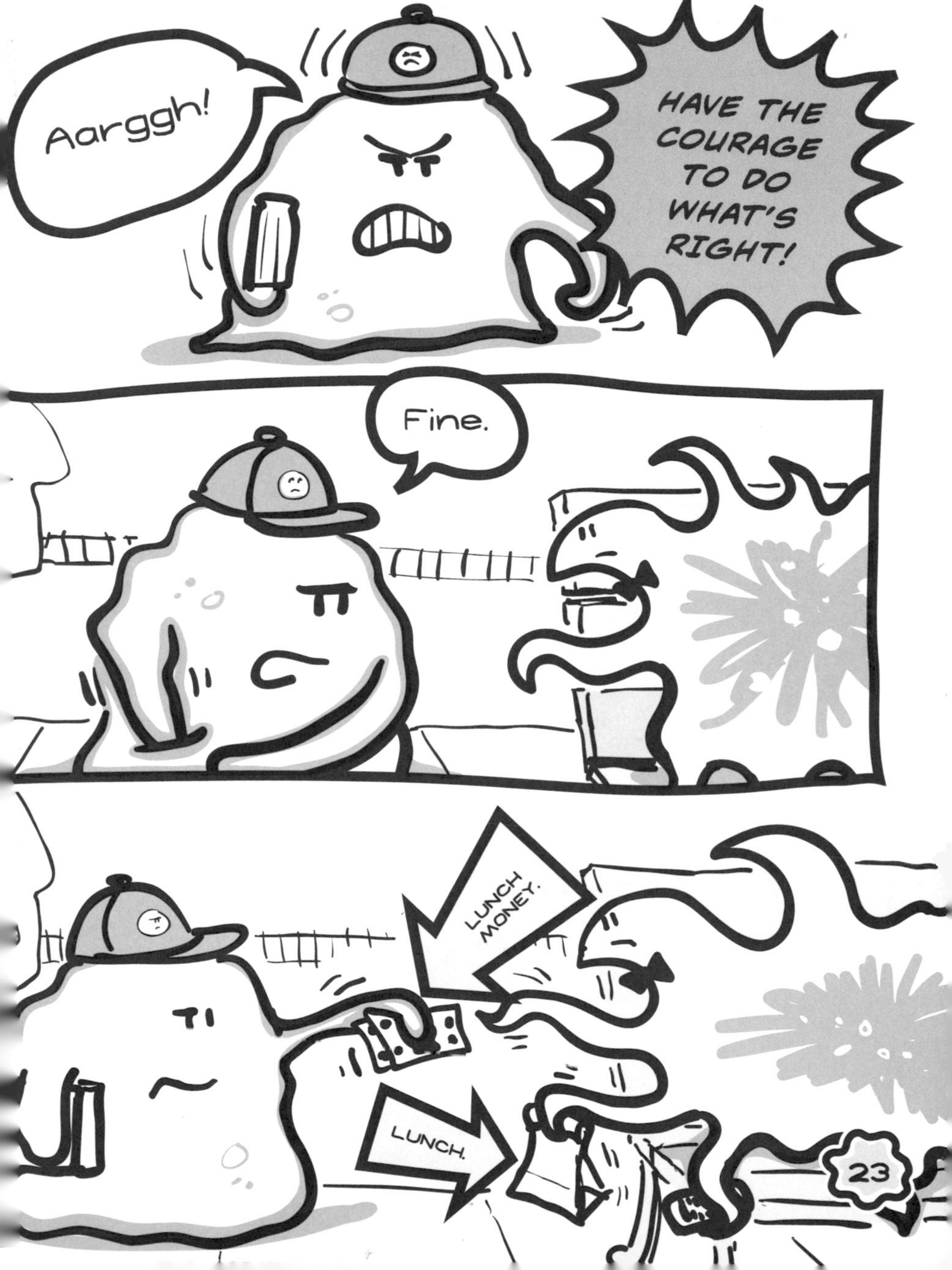
Aarggh!
HAVE THE COURAGE TO DO WHAT'S RIGHT!
Fine.
LUNCH MONEY.
LUNCH.

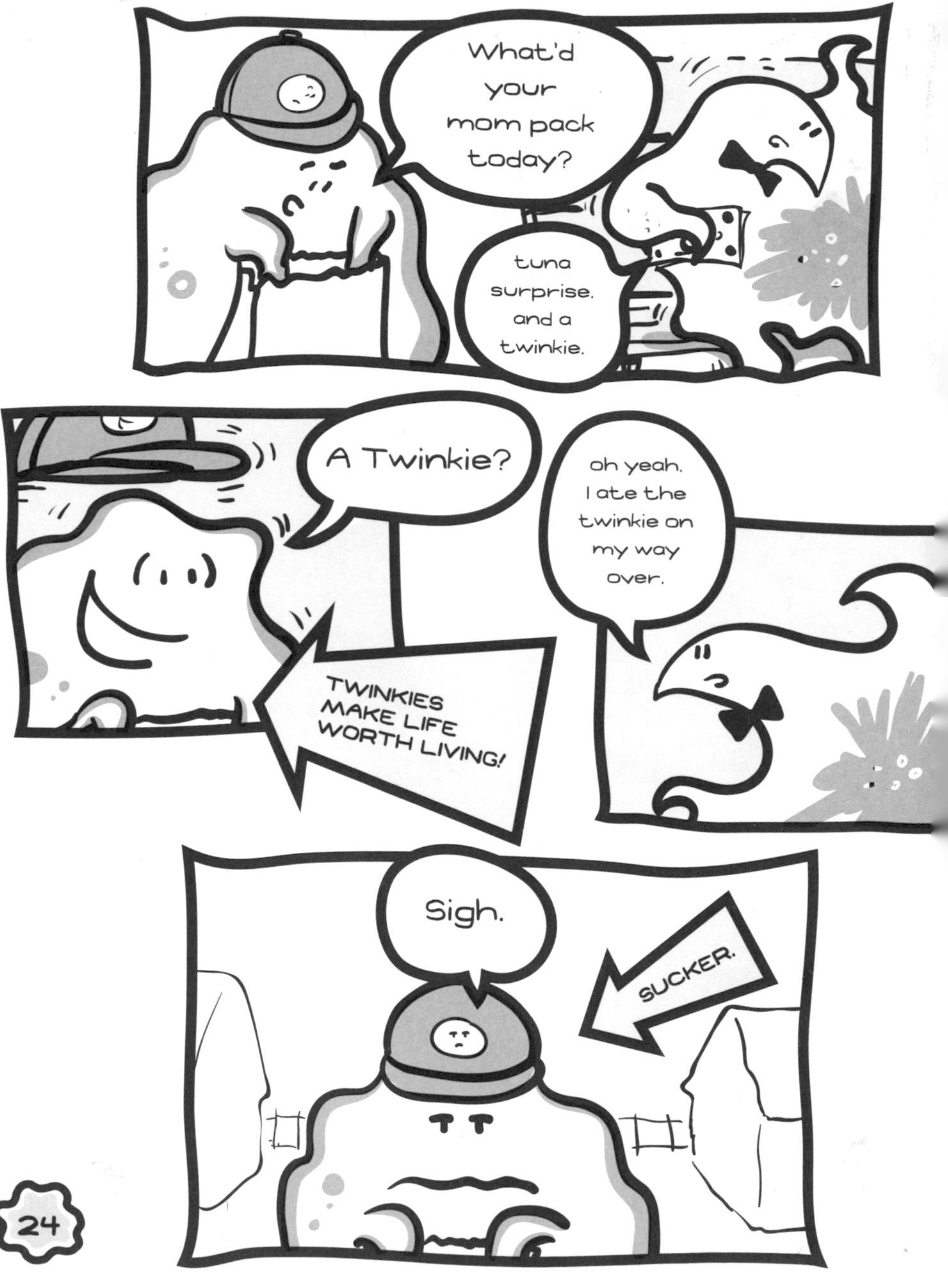
What'd your mom pack today?
tuna surprise. and a twinkie.
A Twinkie?
TWINKIES MAKE LIFE WORTH LIVING!
oh yeah. I ate the twinkie on my way over.
Sigh.
SUCKER.

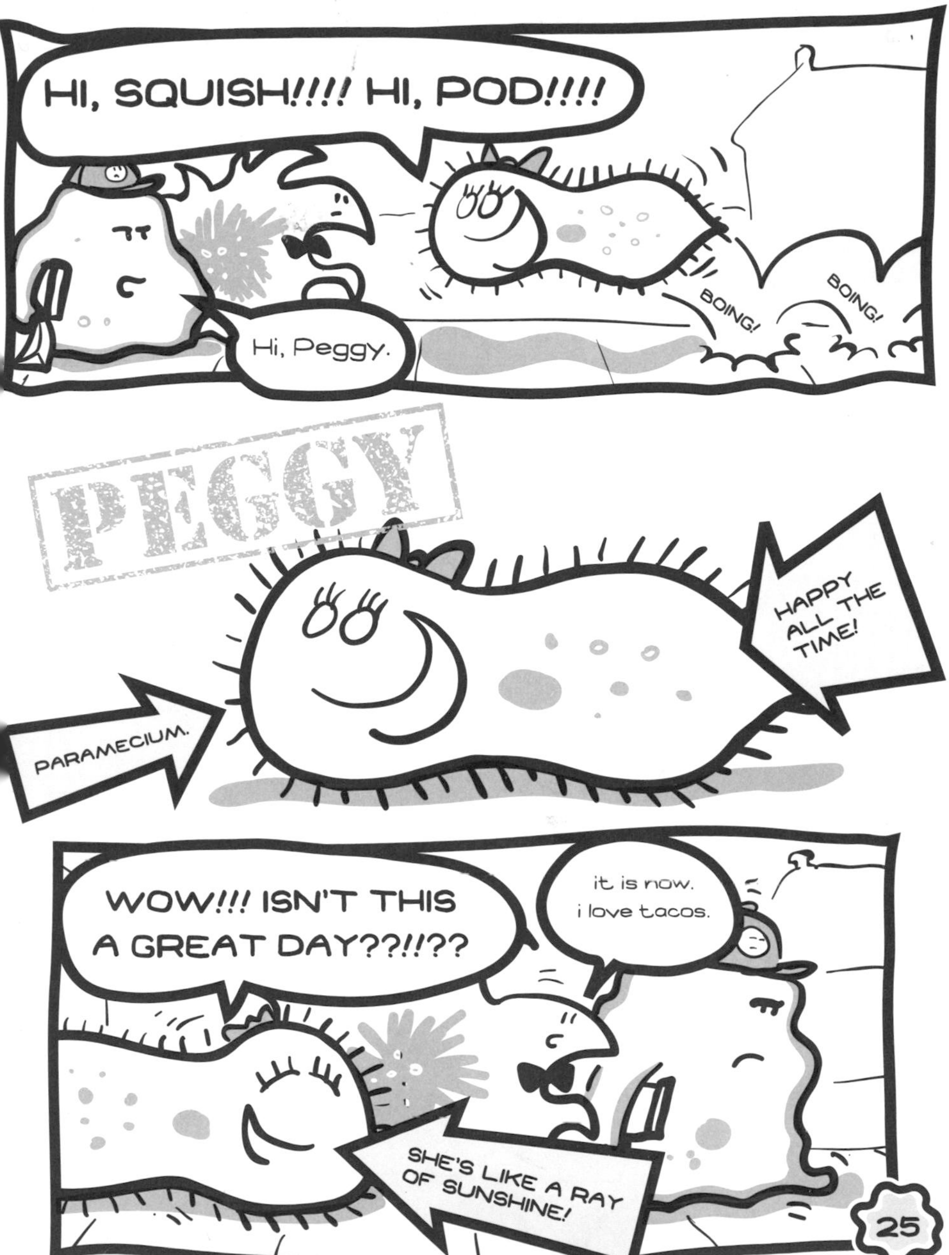
HI, SQUISH!!!! HI, POD!!!!
Hi, Peggy.
BOING!
BOING!
PEGGY
PARAMECIUM.
HAPPY ALL THE TIME!
WOW!!! ISN'T THIS A GREAT DAY??!!??
it is now. i love tacos.
SHE'S LIKE A RAY OF SUNSHINE!

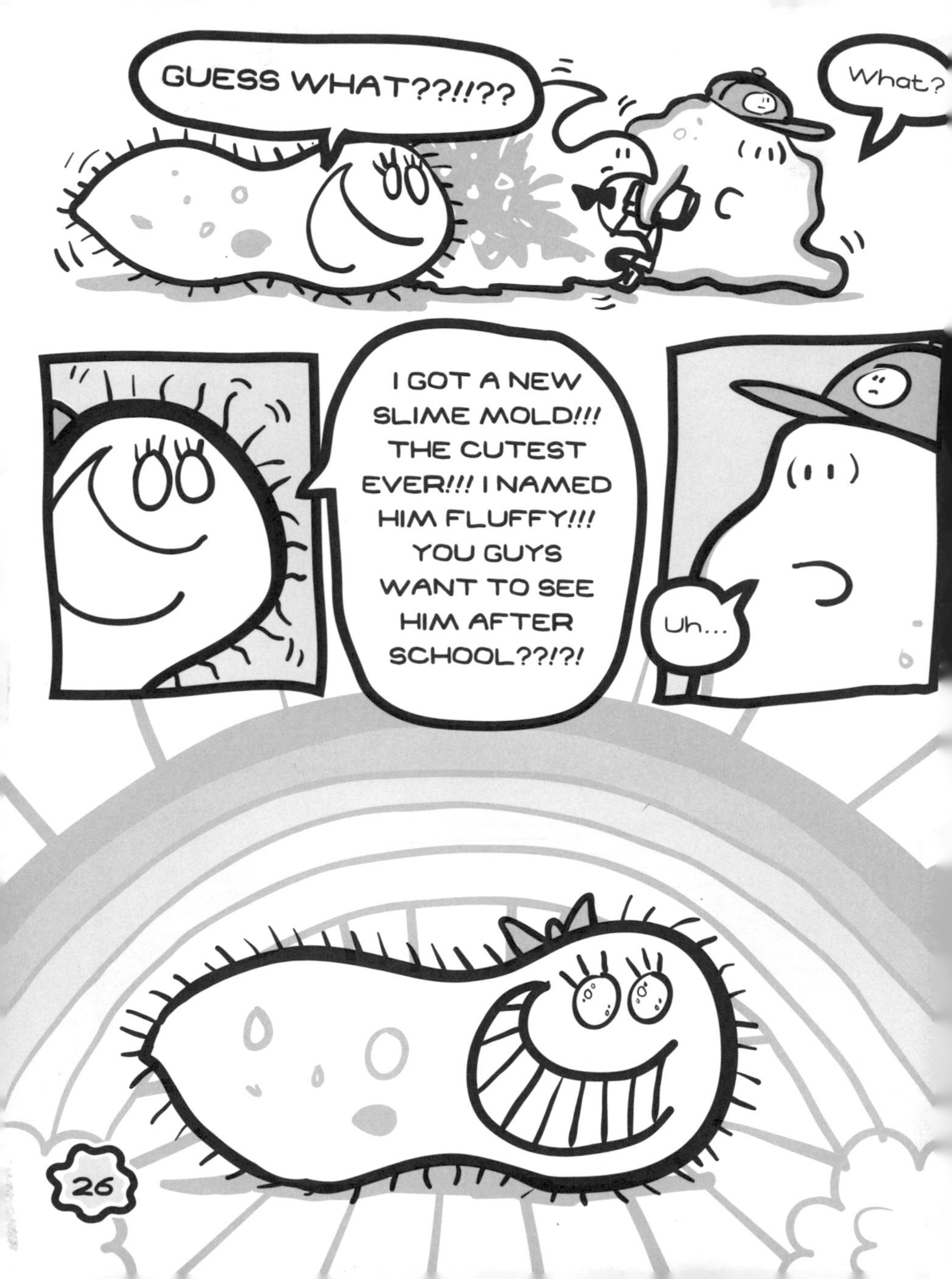
GUESS WHAT??!!??
What?
I GOT A NEW SLIME MOLD!!! THE CUTEST EVER!!! I NAMED HIM FLUFFY!!! YOU GUYS WANT TO SEE HIM AFTER SCHOOL??!?!
Uh...

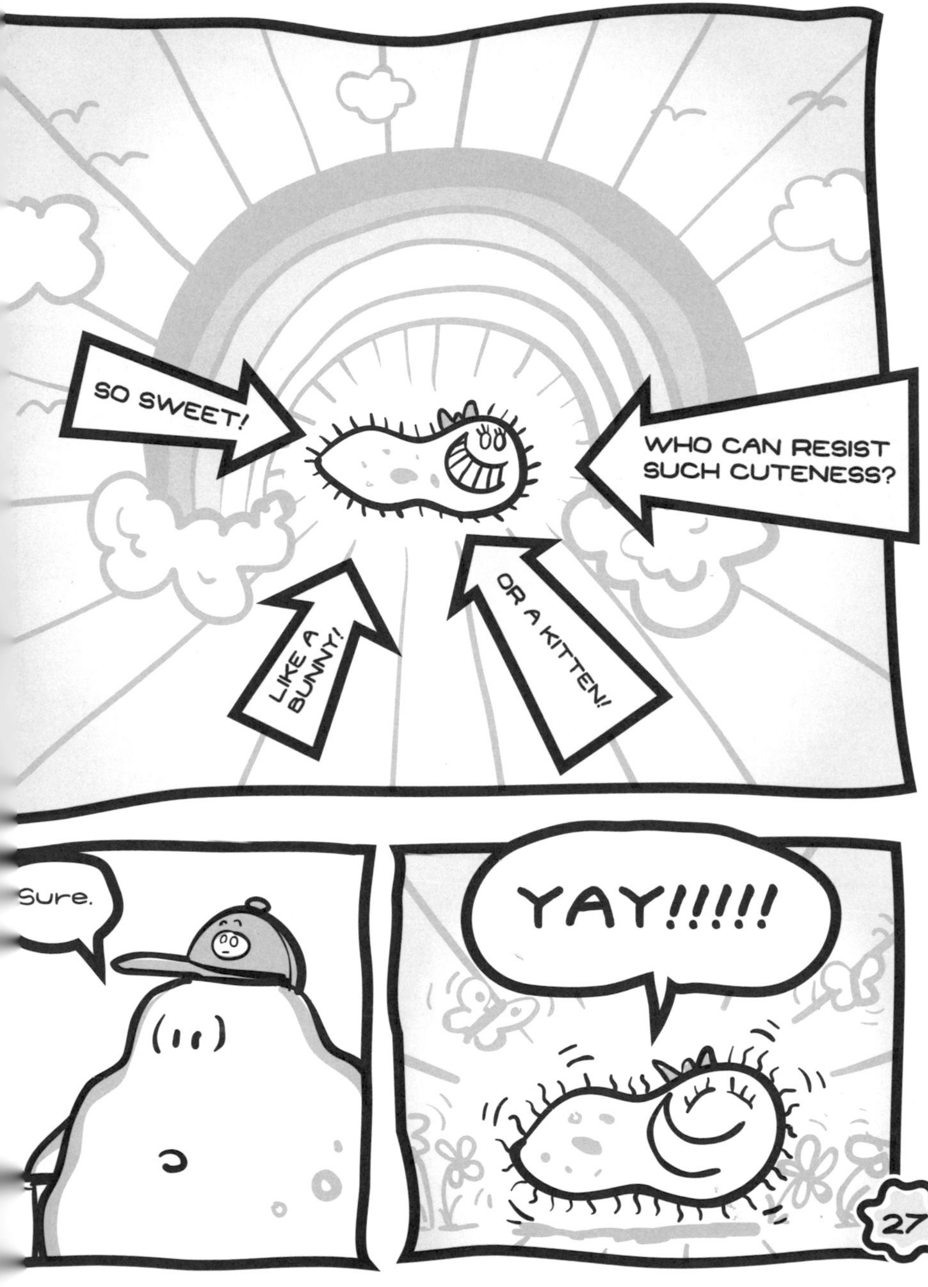
SO SWEET!
WHO CAN RESIST SUCH CUTENESS?
LIKE A BUNNY!
OR A KITTEN!
Sure.
YAY!!!!!!

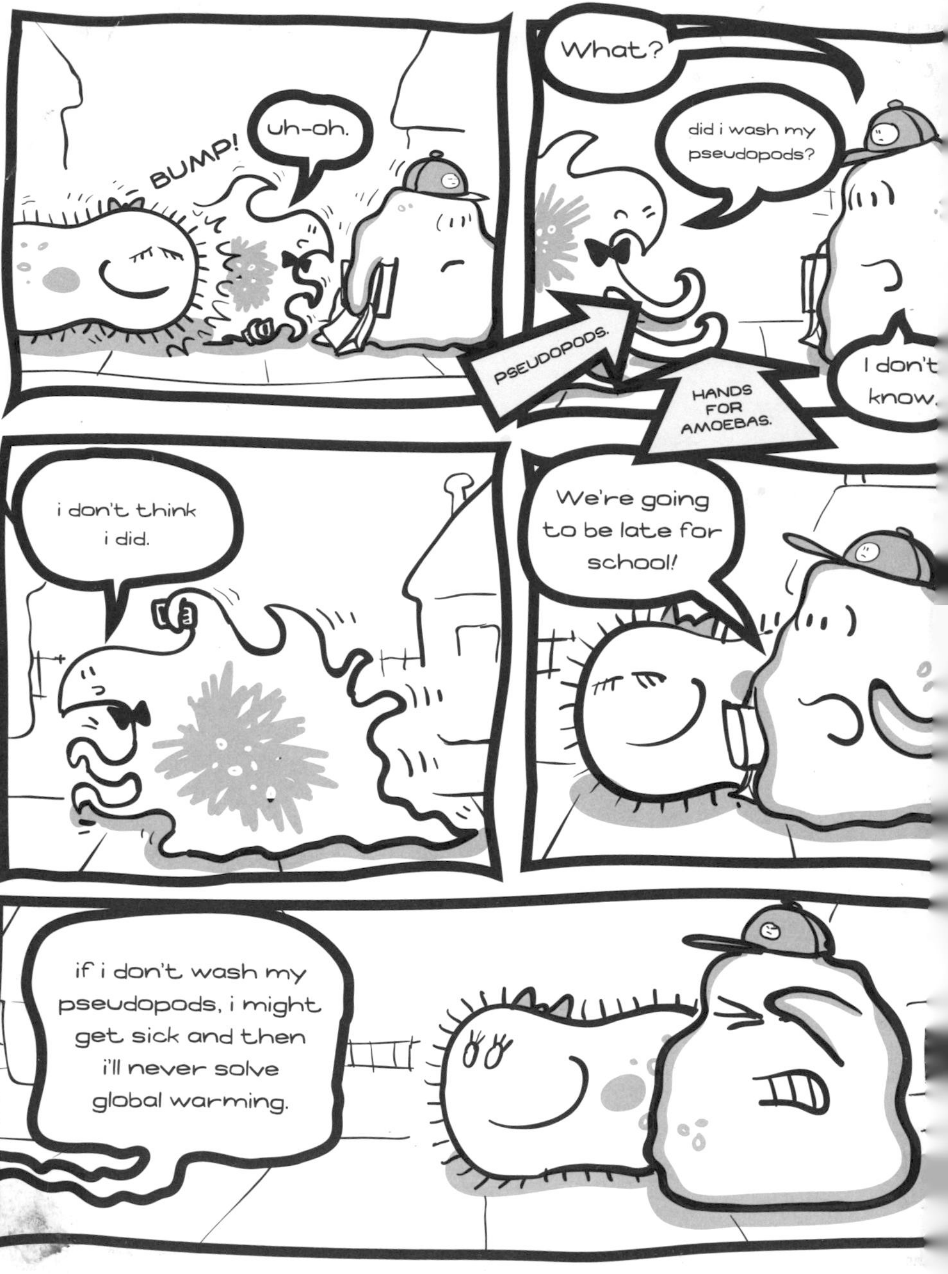
BUMP!
uh-oh.
What?
did i wash my pseudopods?
PSEUDOPODS.
HANDS FOR AMOEBAS.
I don't know.
i don't think i did.
We're going to be late for school!
if i don't wash my pseudopods, i might get sick and then i'll never solve global warming.

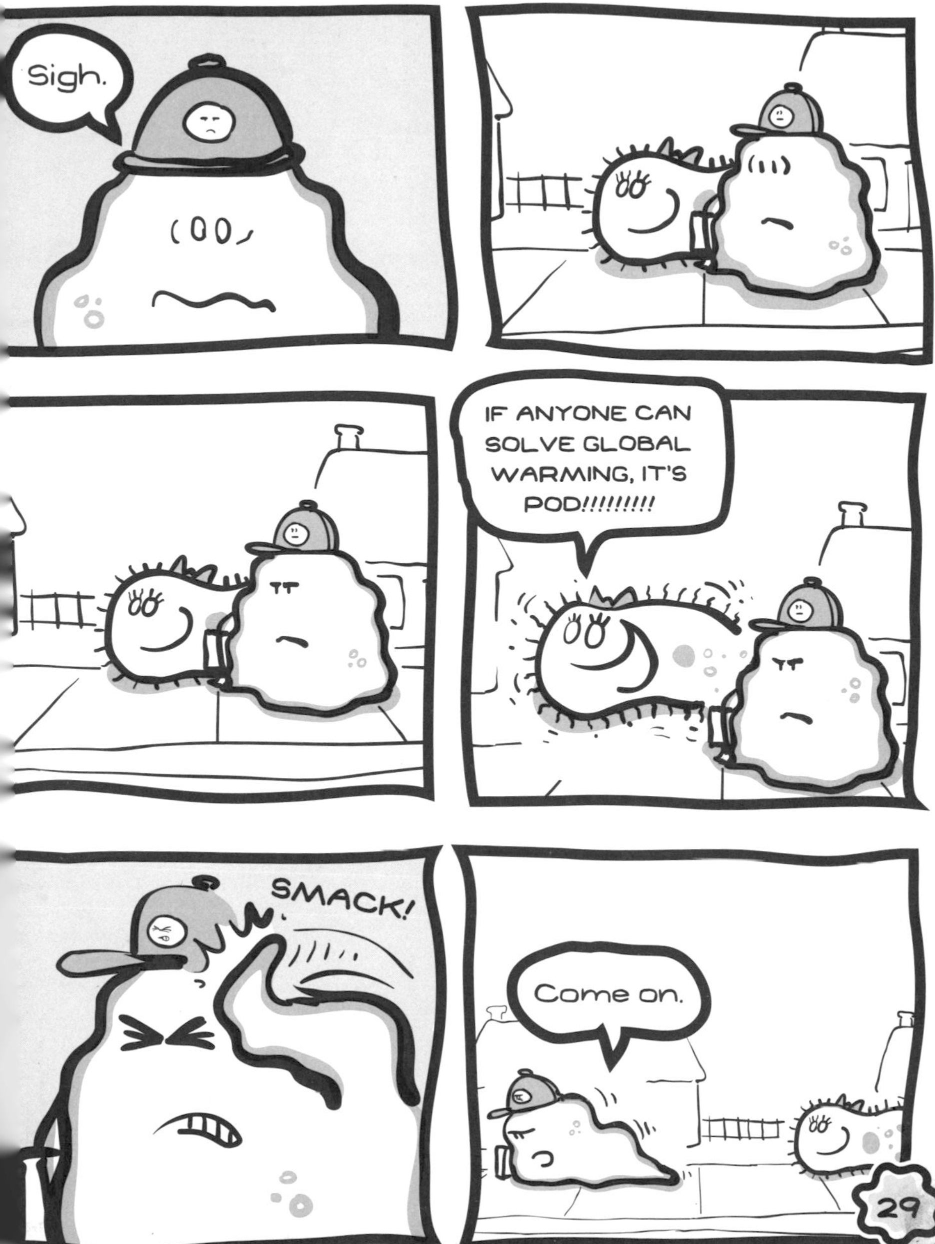
Sigh.
IF ANYONE CAN SOLVE GLOBAL WARMING, IT'S POD!!!!!!!!!!
SMACK!
Come on.

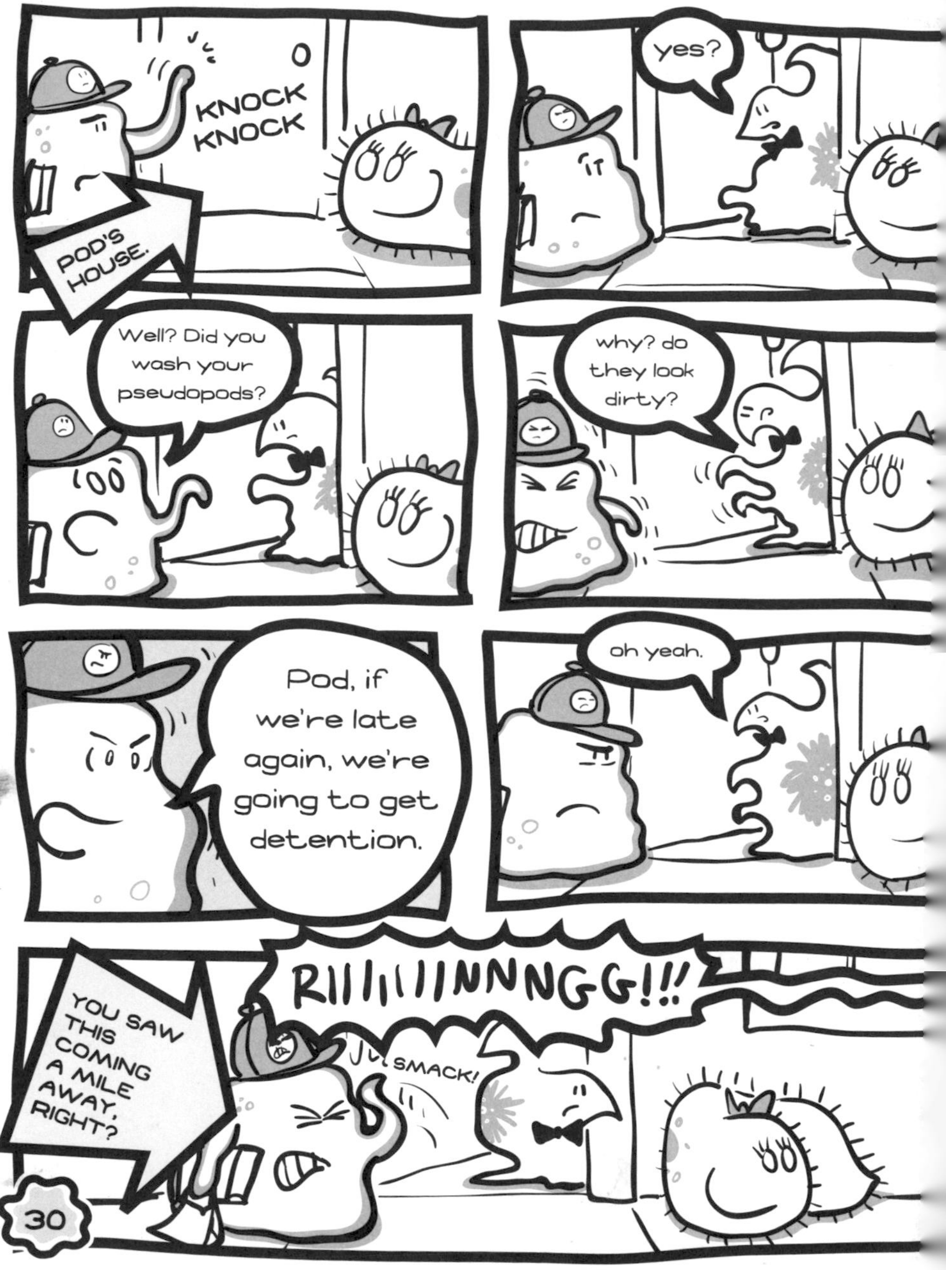
KNOCK KNOCK
POD'S HOUSE.
yes?
Well? Did you wash your pseudopods?
why? do they look dirty?
Pod, if we're late again, we're going to get detention.
oh yeah.
RIIIIIIINNNGG!!!
YOU SAW THIS COMING A MILE AWAY, RIGHT?
SMACK!

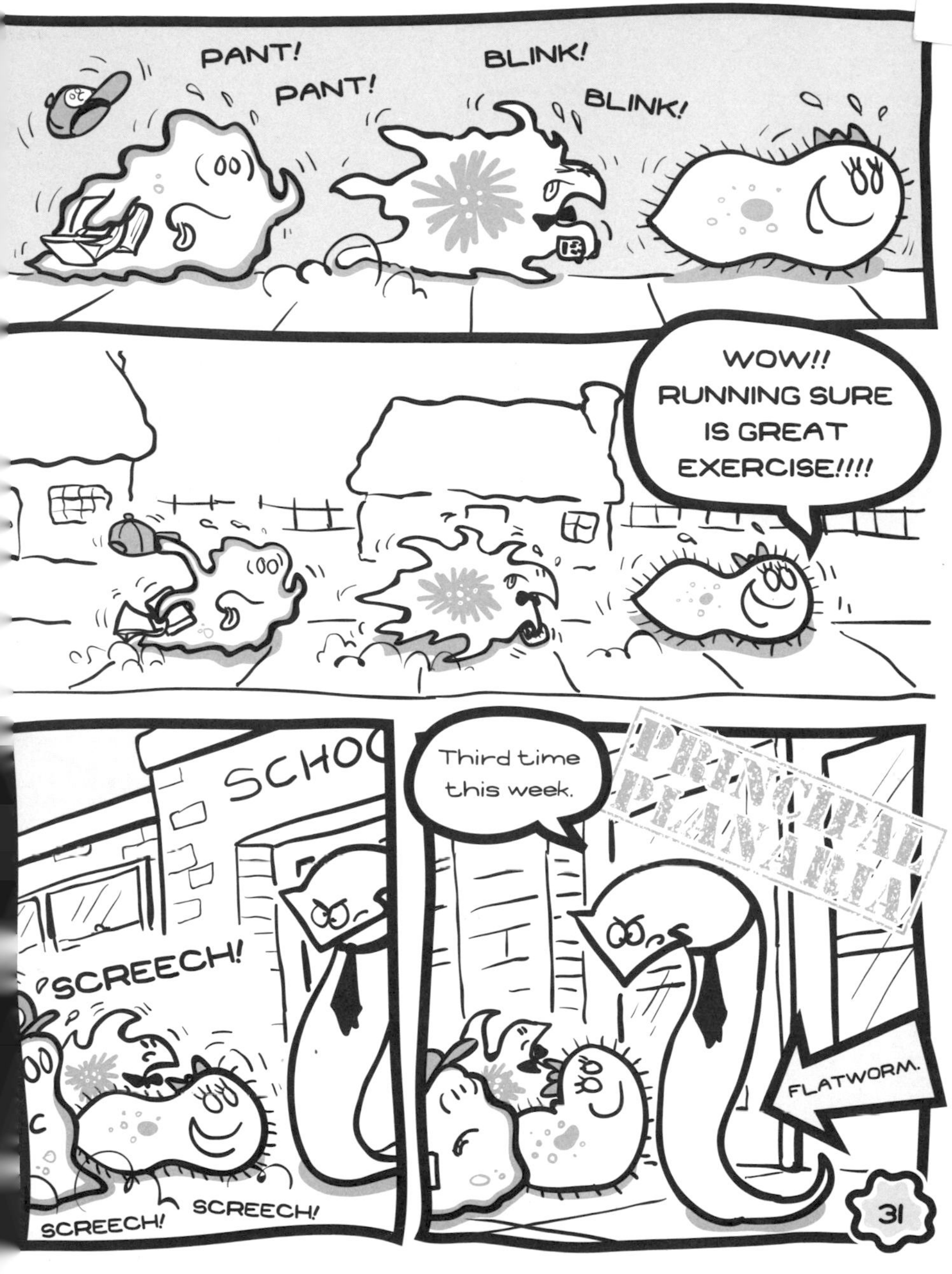

PANT!
PANT!
BLINK!
BLINK!
WOW!! RUNNING SURE IS GREAT EXERCISE!!!!
SCHO
SCREECH!
SCREECH!
SCREECH!
Third time this week.
PRINCIPAL PLANARIA
FLATWORM.

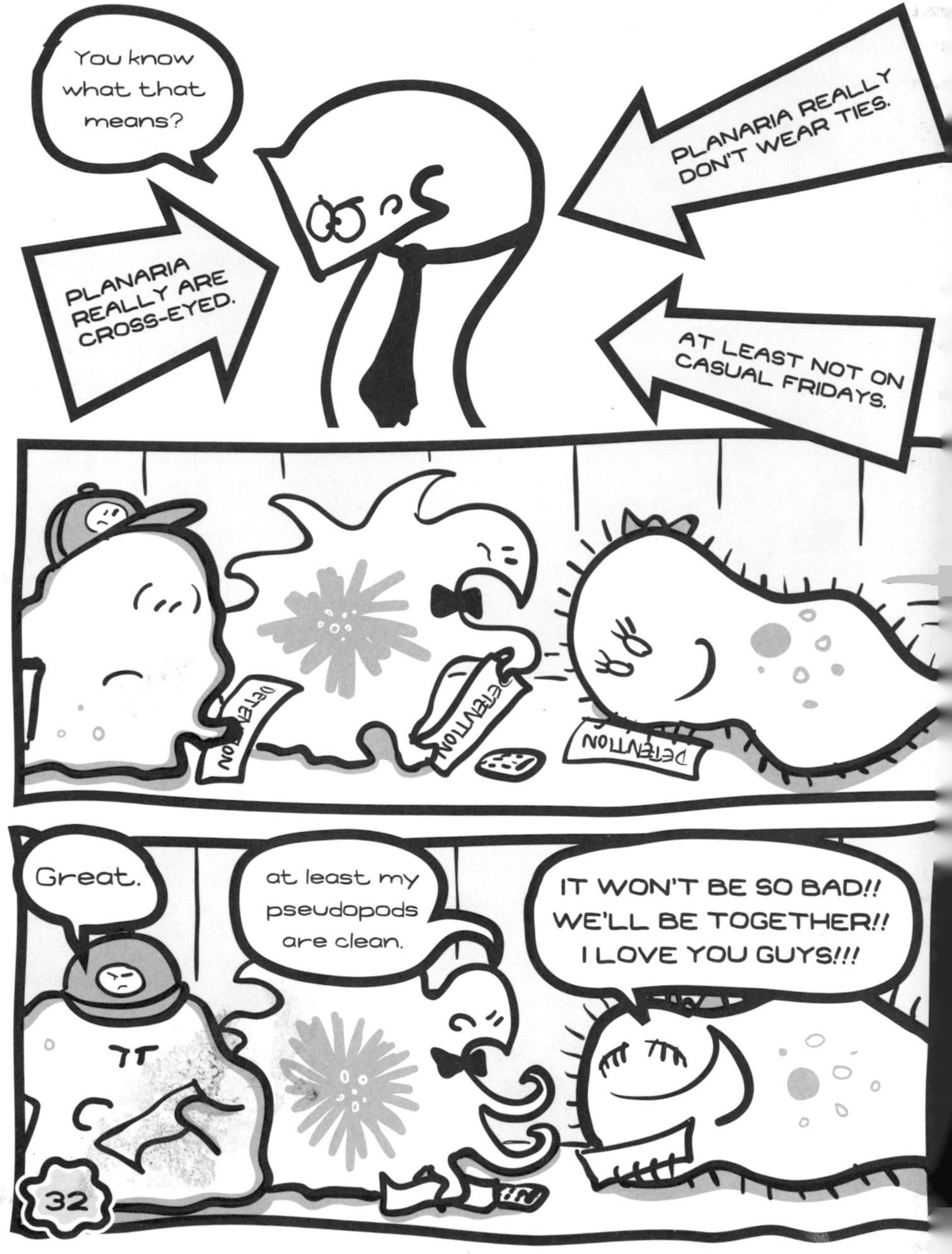
You know what that means?
PLANARIA REALLY ARE CROSS-EYED.
PLANARIA REALLY DON'T WEAR TIES.
AT LEAST NOT ON CASUAL FRIDAYS.
DETENTION
DETENTION
DETENTION
Great.
at least my pseudopods are clean.
IT WON'T BE SO BAD!! WE'LL BE TOGETHER!! I LOVE YOU GUYS!!!

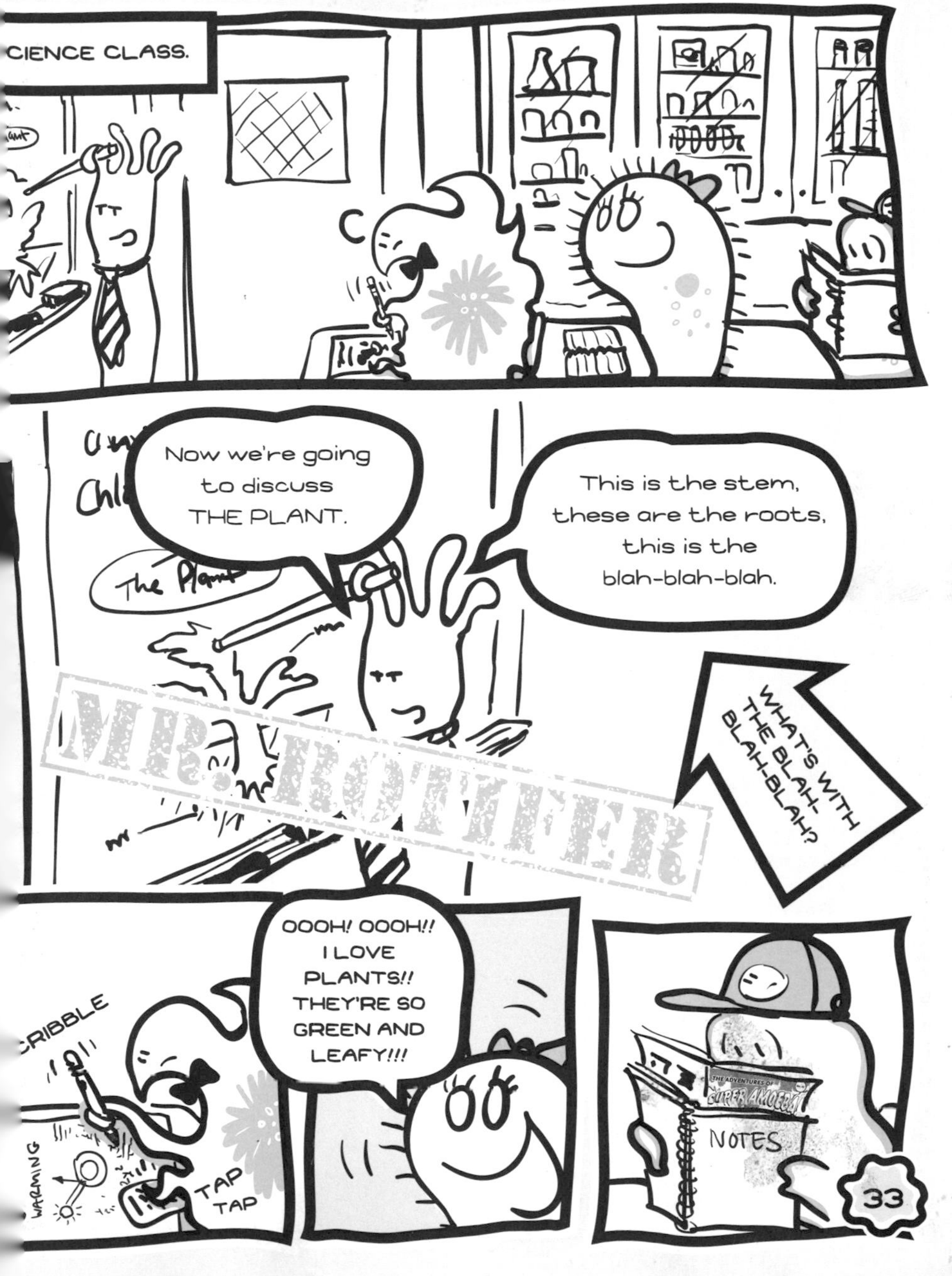

CIENCE CLASS.
Now we're going to discuss THE PLANT.
This is the stem, these are the roots, this is the blah-blah-blah.
The Plant
MR. ROTIFER
WHAT'S WITH THE BLAH-BLAH-BLAH?
CRIBBLE
WARMING
TAP TAP
OOOH! OOOH!! I LOVE PLANTS!! THEY'RE SO GREEN AND LEAFY!!!
THE ADVENTURES OF SUPER AMOEBA
NOTES

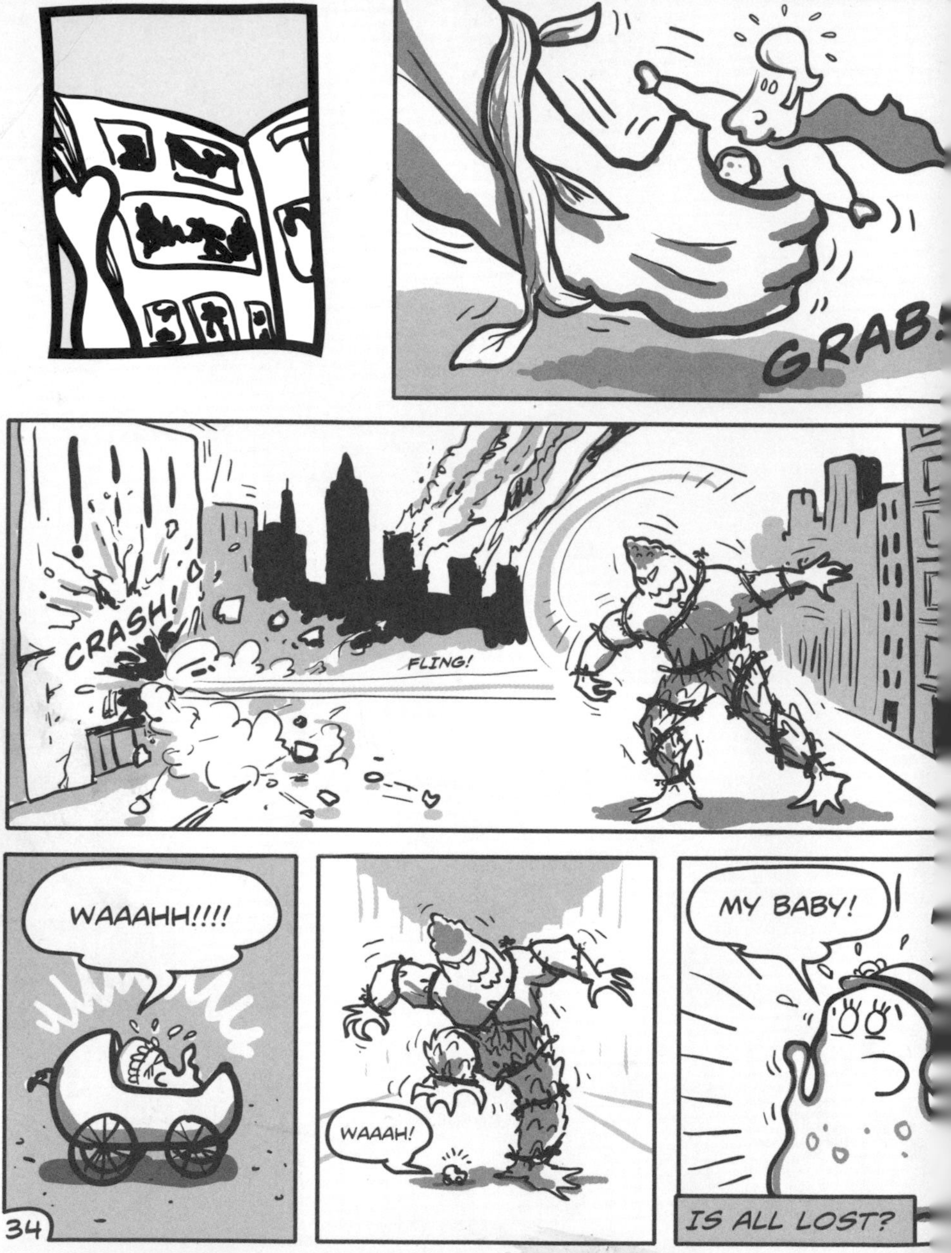
GRAB!
CRASH!
FLING!
WAAAHH!!!!
WAAAH!
MY BABY!
IS ALL LOST?

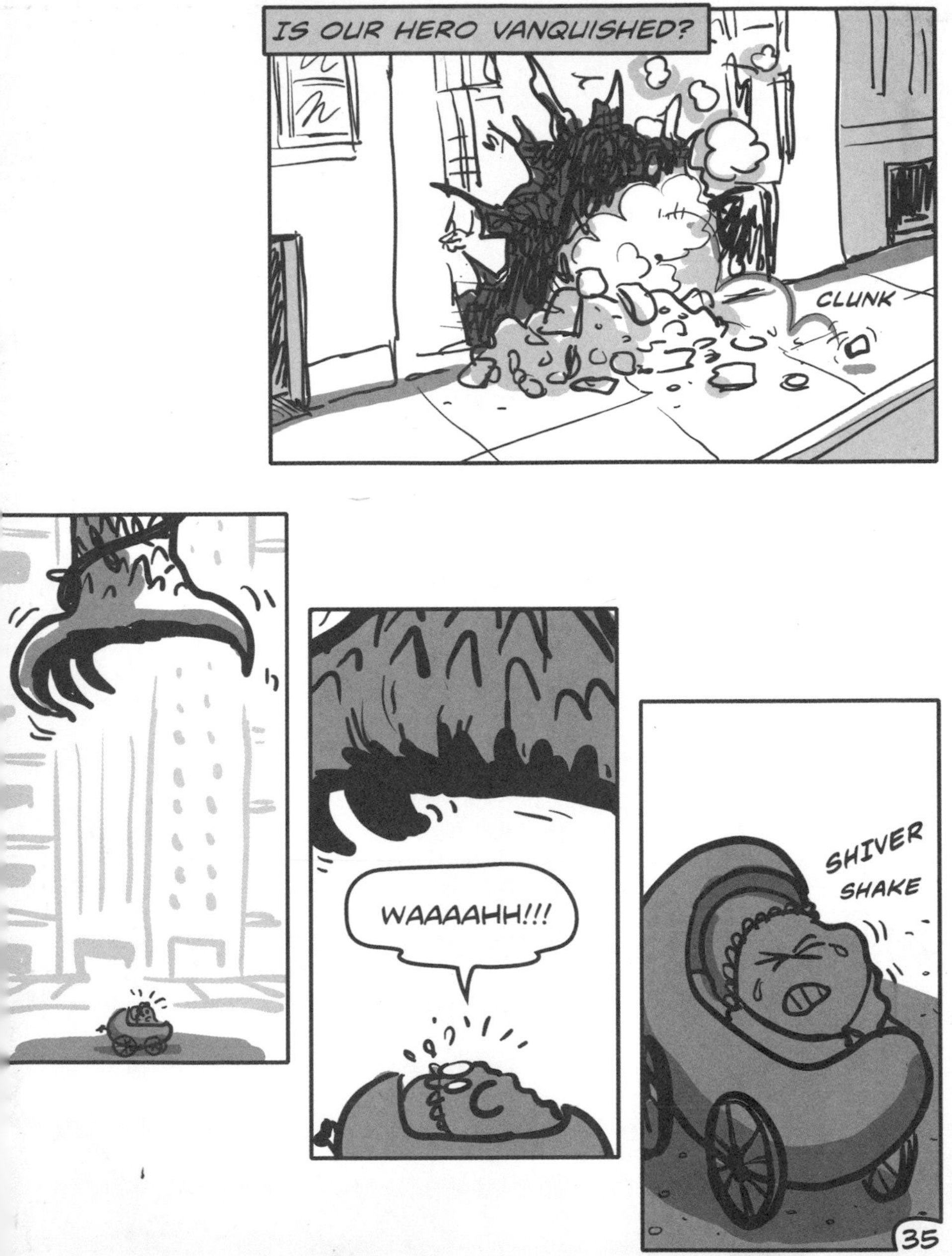
IS OUR HERO VANQUISHED?
CLUNK
WAAAAHH!!!
SHIVER
SHAKE

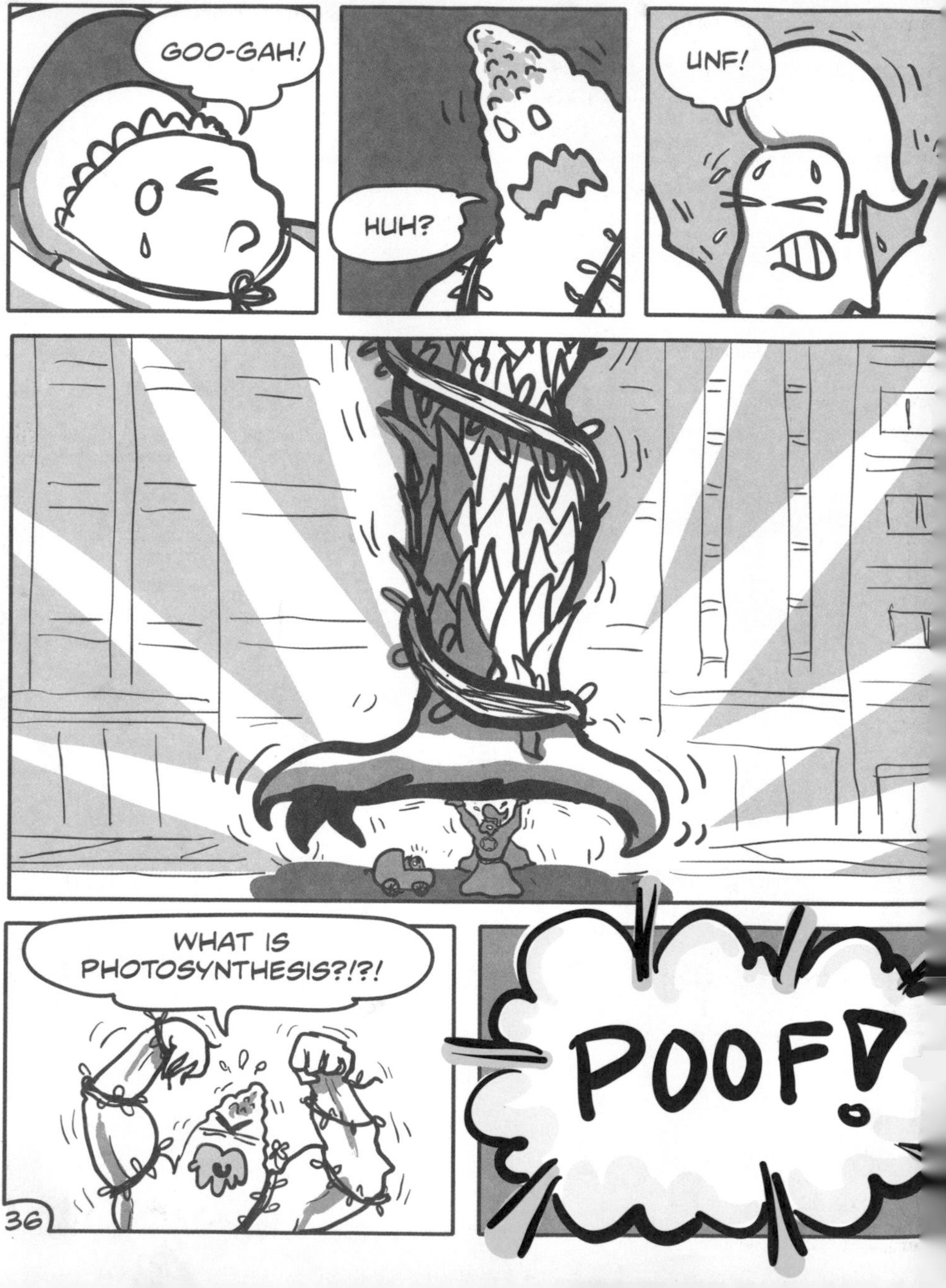
GOO-GAH!
HUH?
UNF!
WHAT IS PHOTOSYNTHESIS?!?!
POOF!

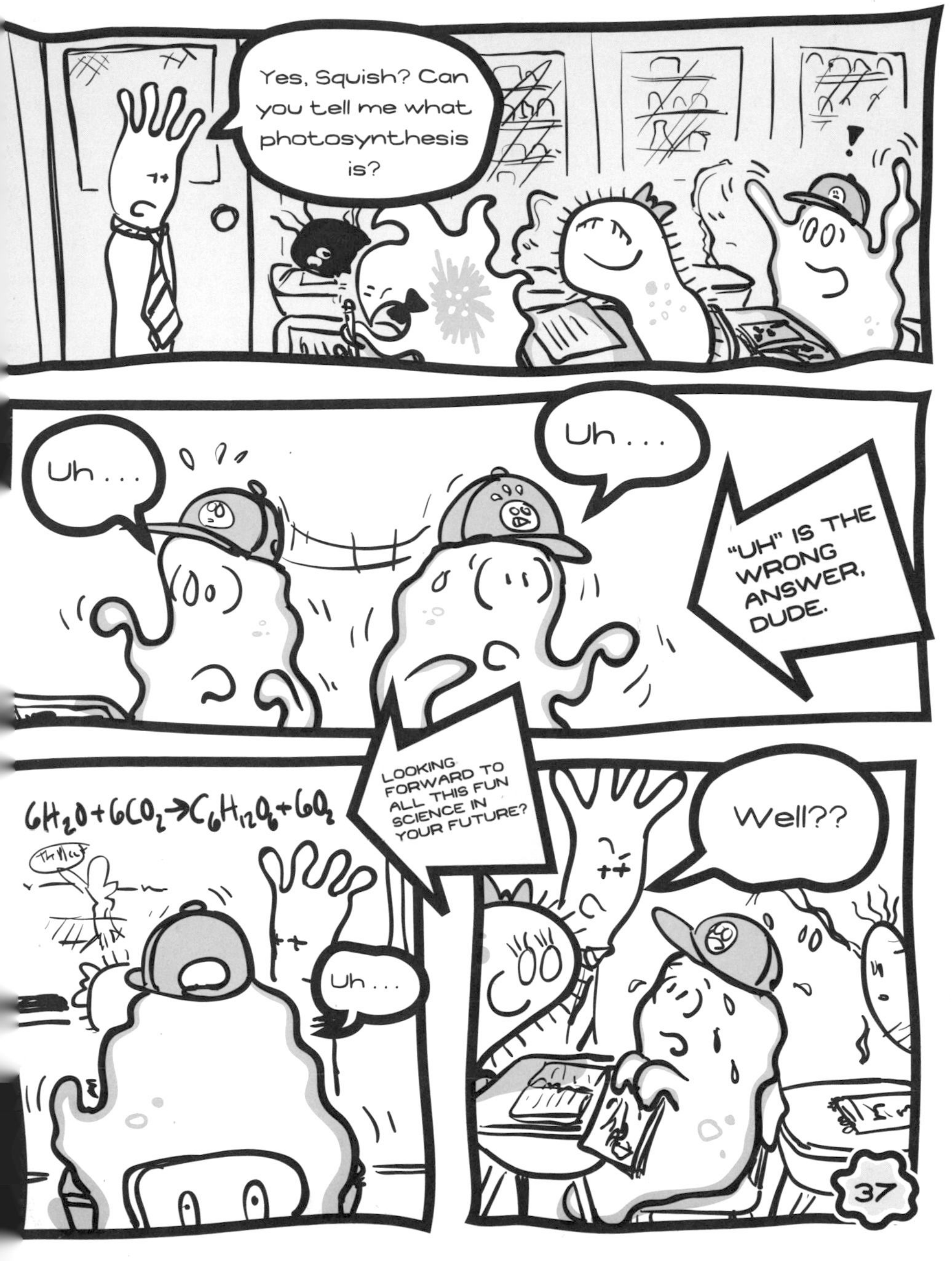
Yes, Squish? Can you tell me what photosynthesis is?
Uh . . .
Uh . . .
"UH" IS THE WRONG ANSWER, DUDE.
LOOKING FORWARD TO ALL THIS FUN SCIENCE IN YOUR FUTURE?
$6H_2O + 6CO_2 \rightarrow C_6H_{12}O_6 + 6O_2$
Uh . . .
Well??

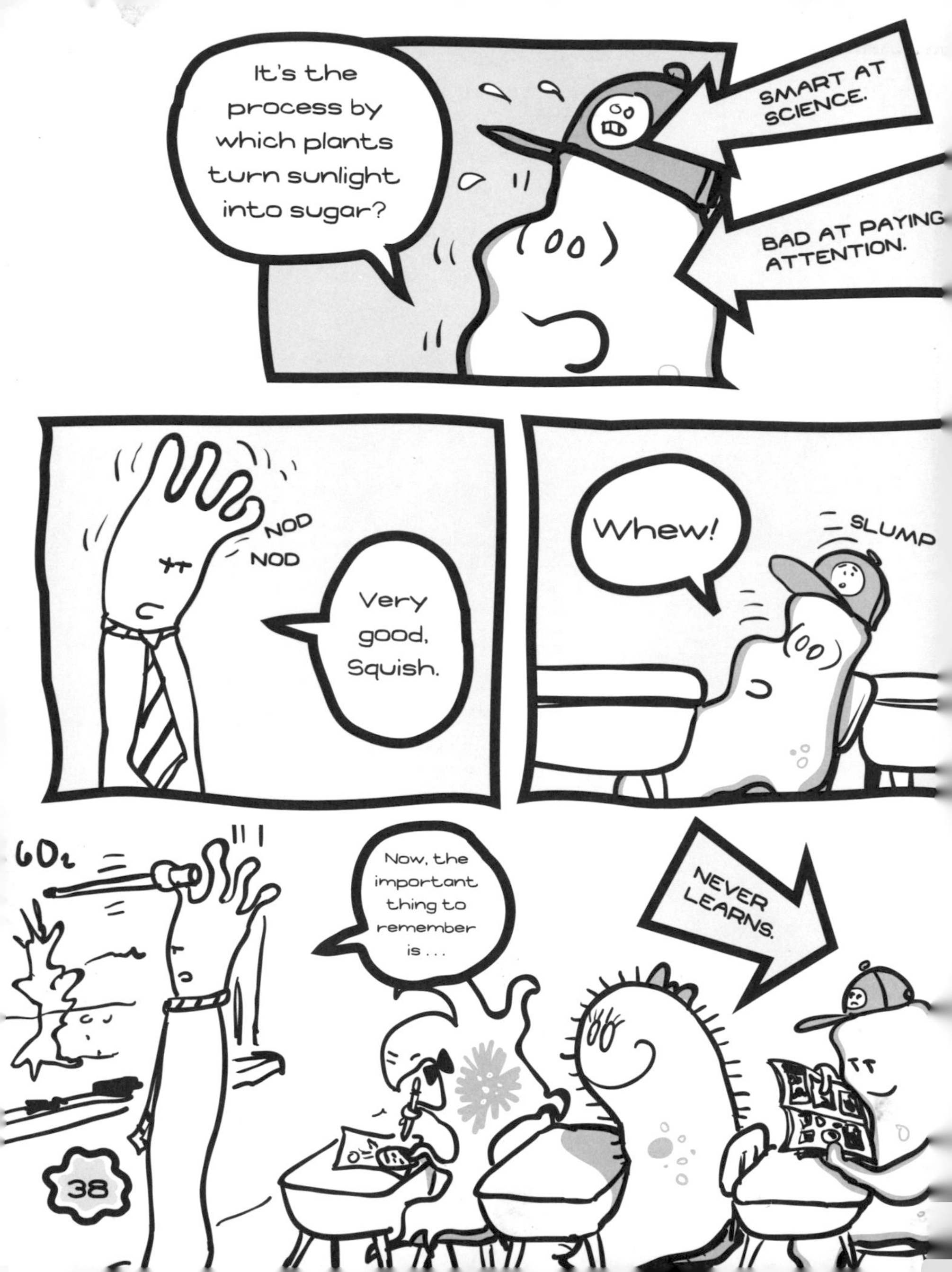
It's the process by which plants turn sunlight into sugar?
SMART AT SCIENCE.
BAD AT PAYING ATTENTION.
NOD NOD
Very good, Squish.
Whew!
SLUMP
Now, the important thing to remember is . . .
NEVER LEARNS.

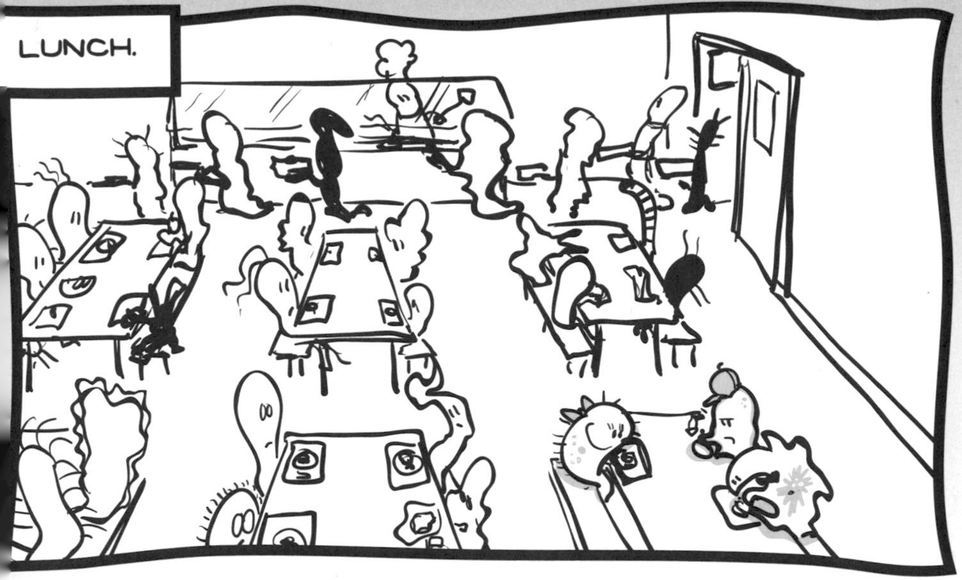
LUNCH.

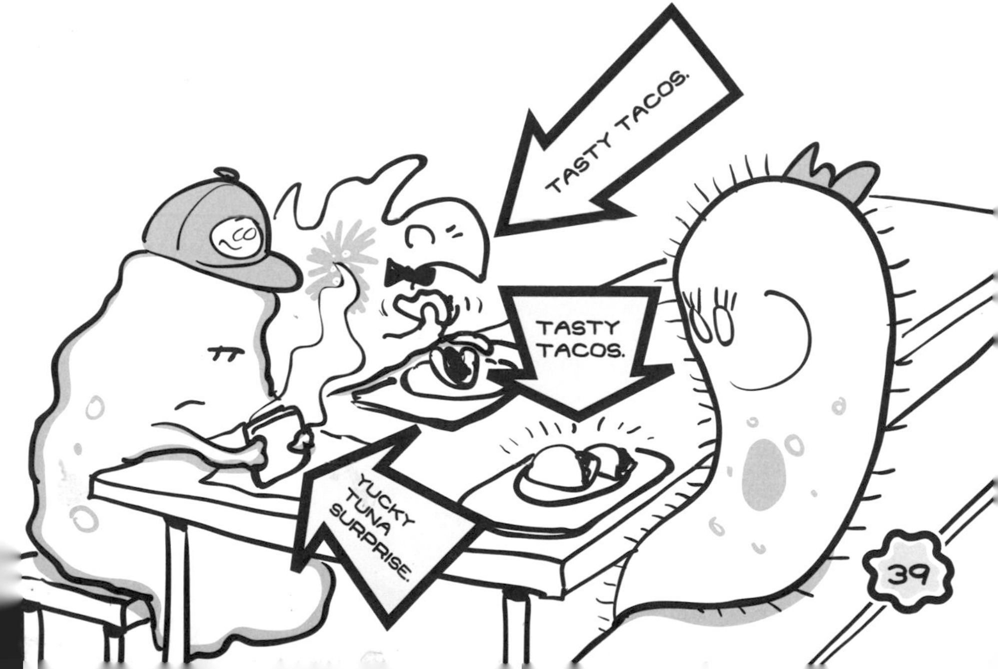
TASTY TACOS.
TASTY TACOS.
YUCKY TUNA SURPRISE.

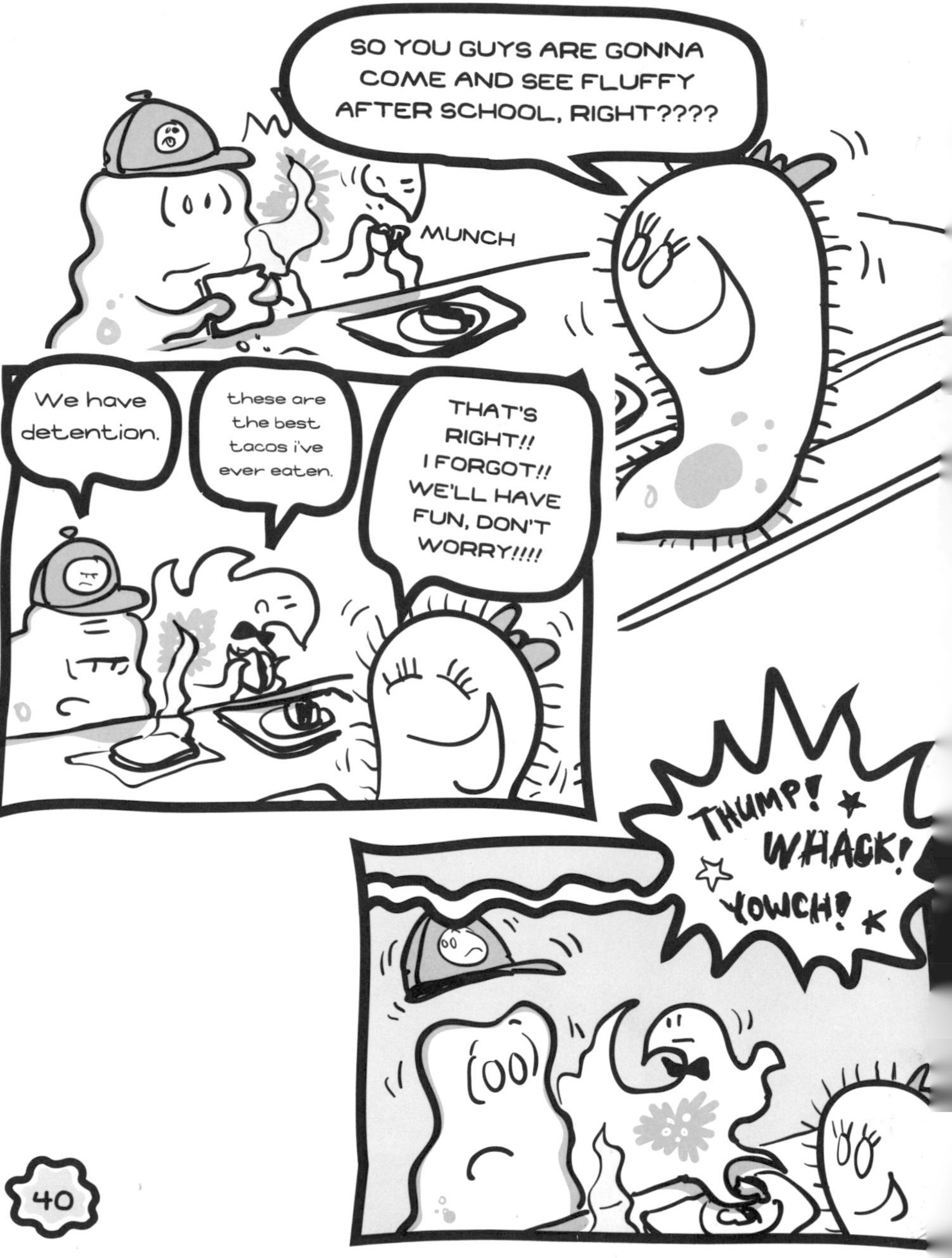

SO YOU GUYS ARE GONNA COME AND SEE FLUFFY AFTER SCHOOL, RIGHT????
MUNCH
We have detention.
these are the best tacos i've ever eaten.
THAT'S RIGHT!! I FORGOT!! WE'LL HAVE FUN, DON'T WORRY!!!!
THUMP!
WHACK!
YOWCH!

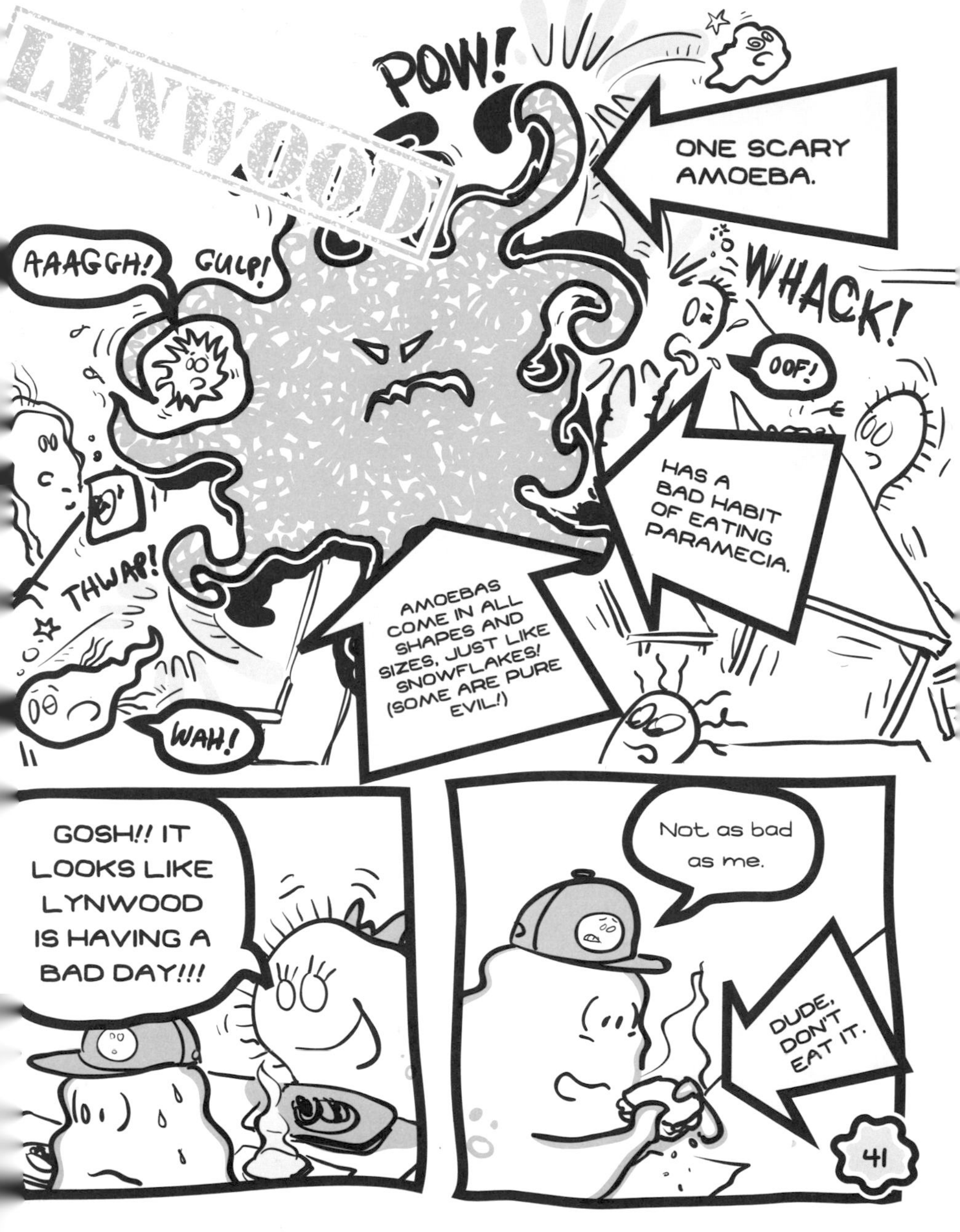
LYNWOOD
POW!
ONE SCARY AMOEBA.
AAAGGH!
GULP!
WHACK!
OOF!
HAS A BAD HABIT OF EATING PARAMECIA.
THWAP!
AMOEBAS COME IN ALL SHAPES AND SIZES, JUST LIKE SNOWFLAKES! (SOME ARE PURE EVIL!)
WAH!
GOSH!! IT LOOKS LIKE LYNWOOD IS HAVING A BAD DAY!!!
Not as bad as me.
DUDE, DON'T EAT IT.

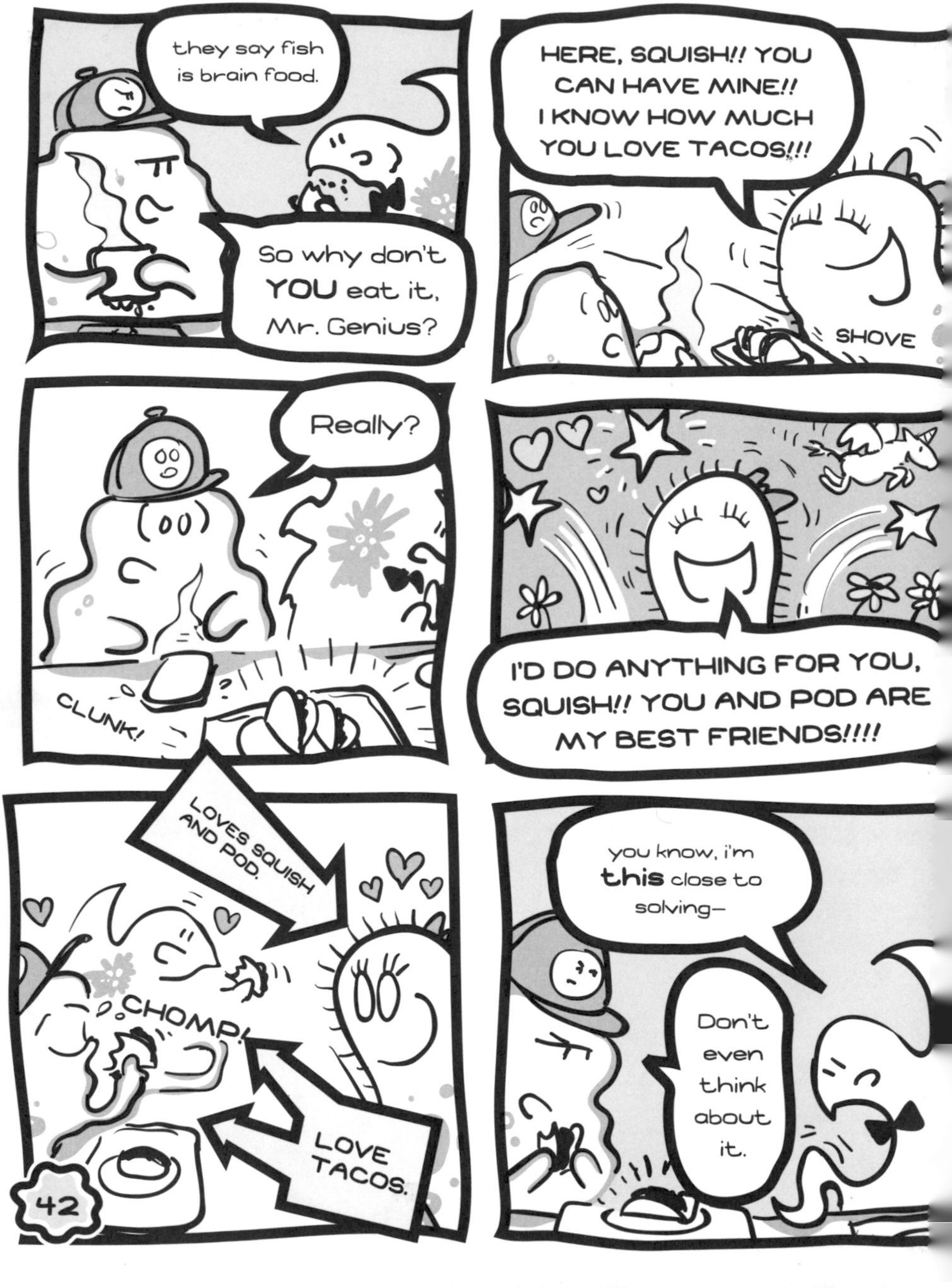
they say fish is brain food.
So why don't **YOU** eat it, Mr. Genius?
HERE, SQUISH!! YOU CAN HAVE MINE!! I KNOW HOW MUCH YOU LOVE TACOS!!!
SHOVE
Really?
CLUNK!
I'D DO ANYTHING FOR YOU, SQUISH!! YOU AND POD ARE MY BEST FRIENDS!!!!
LOVES SQUISH AND POD.
CHOMP!
LOVE TACOS.
you know, i'm **this** close to solving—
Don't even think about it.

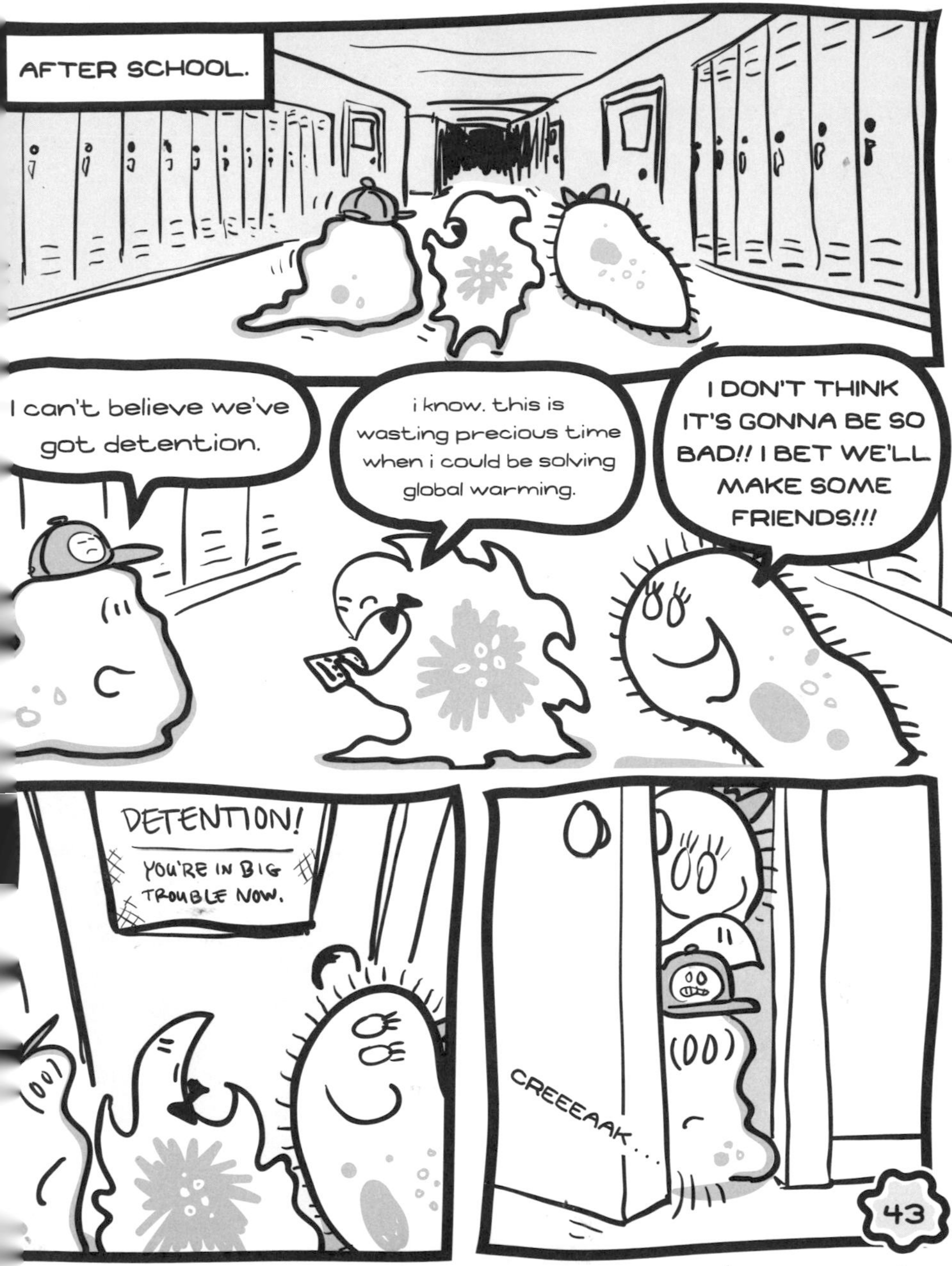
AFTER SCHOOL.
I can't believe we've got detention.
i know. this is wasting precious time when i could be solving global warming.
I DON'T THINK IT'S GONNA BE SO BAD!! I BET WE'LL MAKE SOME FRIENDS!!!
DETENTION!
YOU'RE IN BIG TROUBLE NOW.
CREEEAAK...

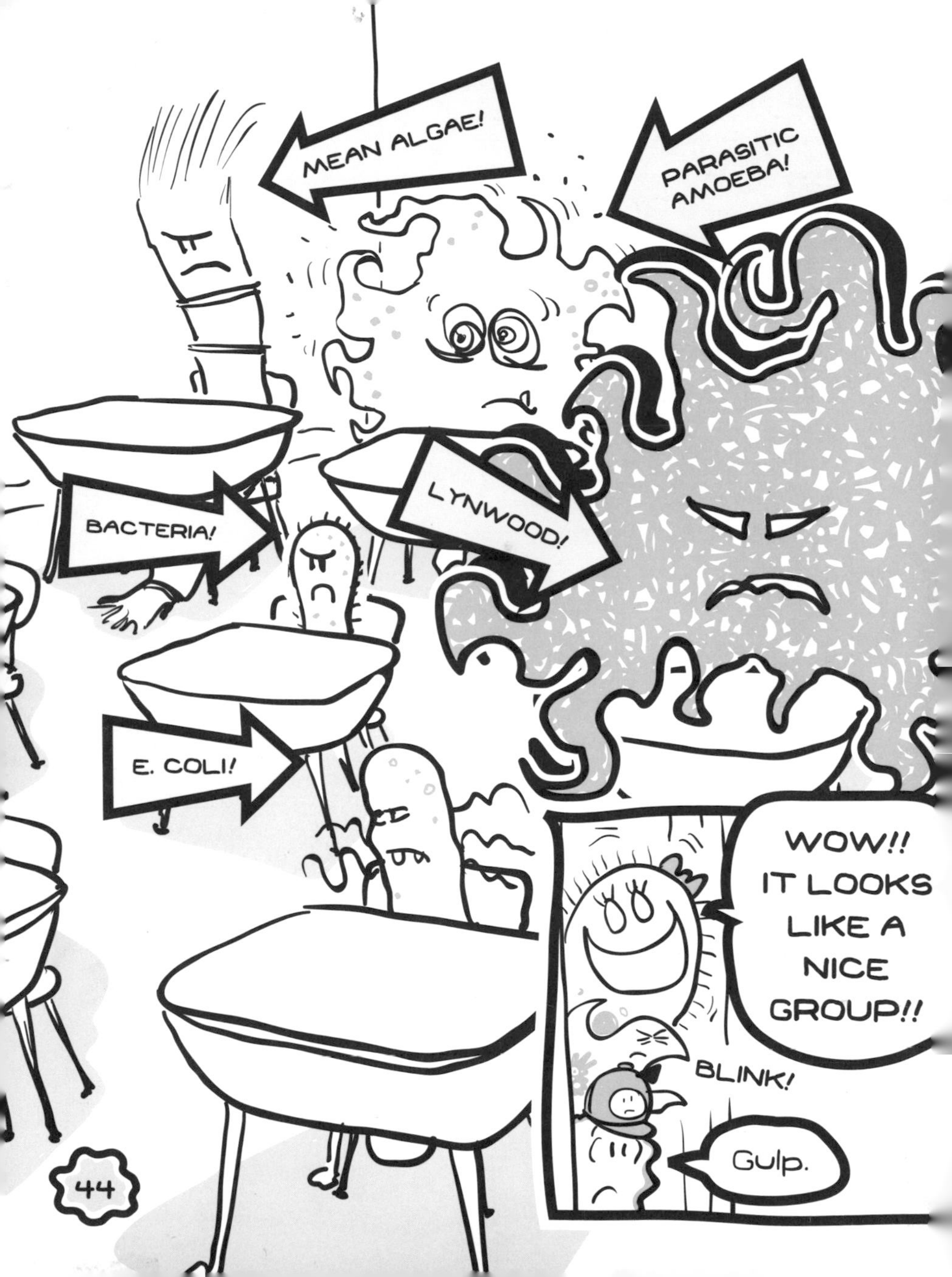
MEAN ALGAE!
PARASITIC AMOEBA!
BACTERIA!
LYNWOOD!
E. COLI!
WOW!! IT LOOKS LIKE A NICE GROUP!!
BLINK!
Gulp.

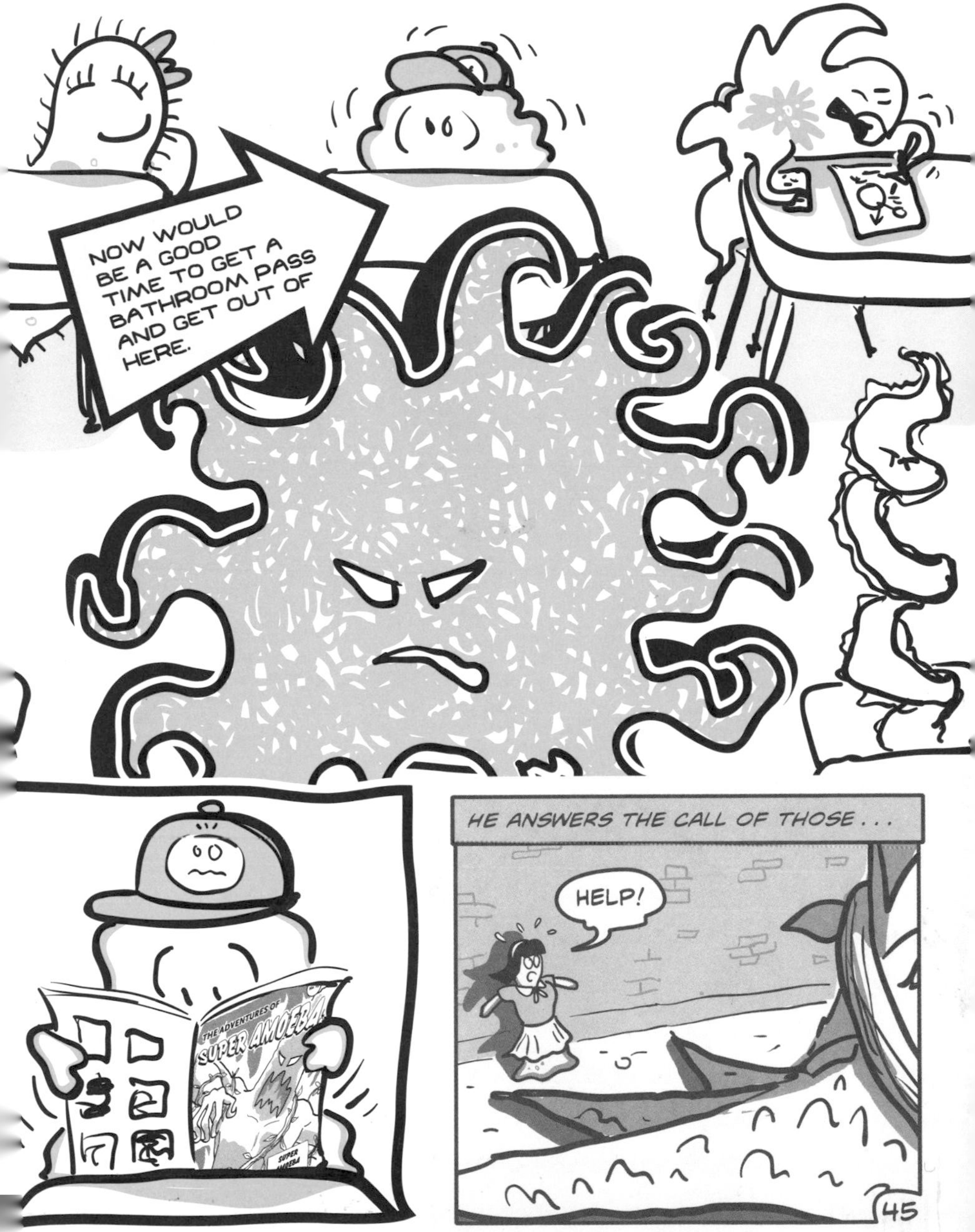
NOW WOULD BE A GOOD TIME TO GET A BATHROOM PASS AND GET OUT OF HERE.
THE ADVENTURES OF SUPER AMOEBA
SUPER AMOEBA
HE ANSWERS THE CALL OF THOSE . . .
HELP!

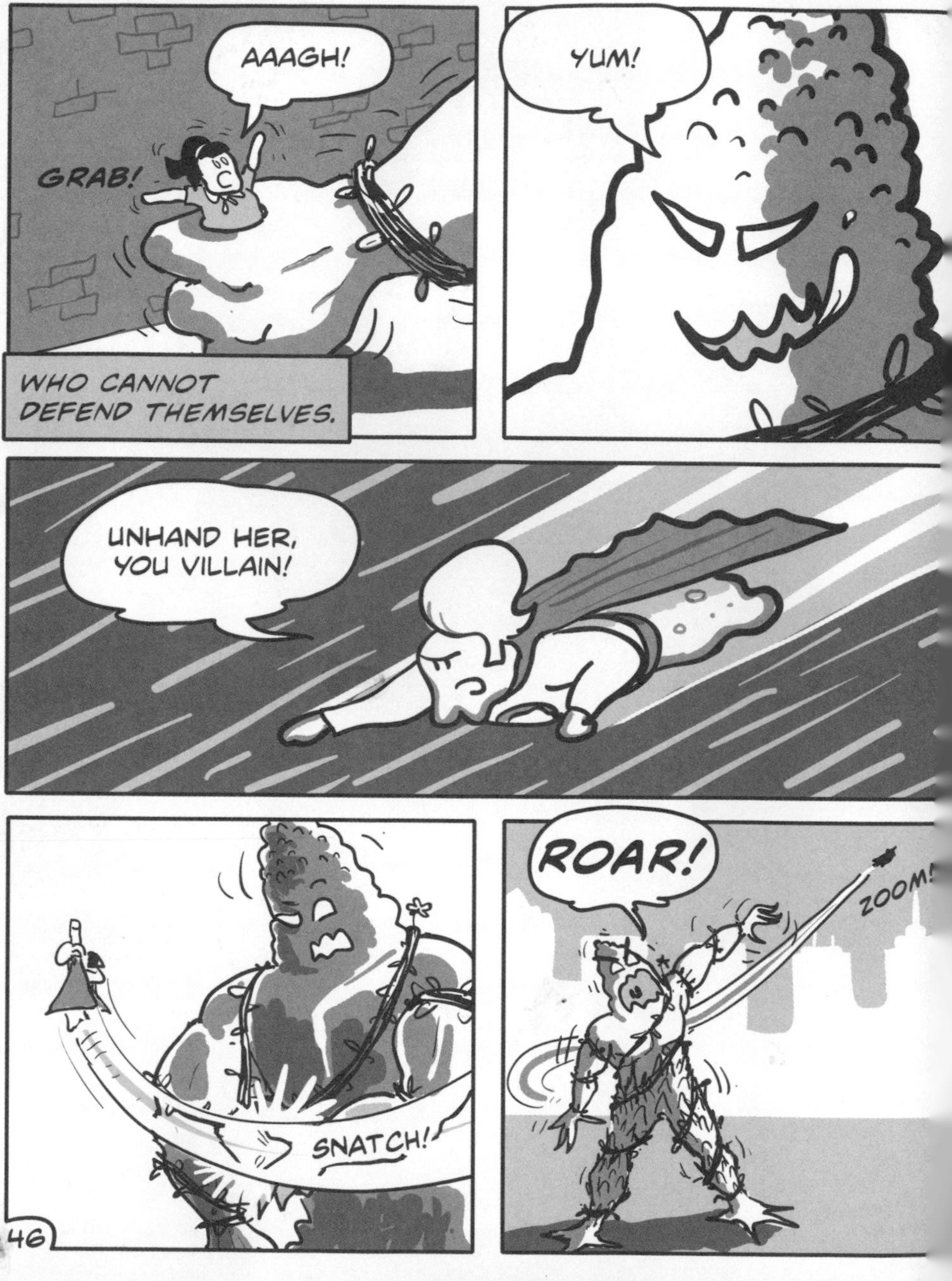
AAAGH!
GRAB!
WHO CANNOT DEFEND THEMSELVES.
YUM!
UNHAND HER, YOU VILLAIN!
SNATCH!
ROAR!
ZOOM!

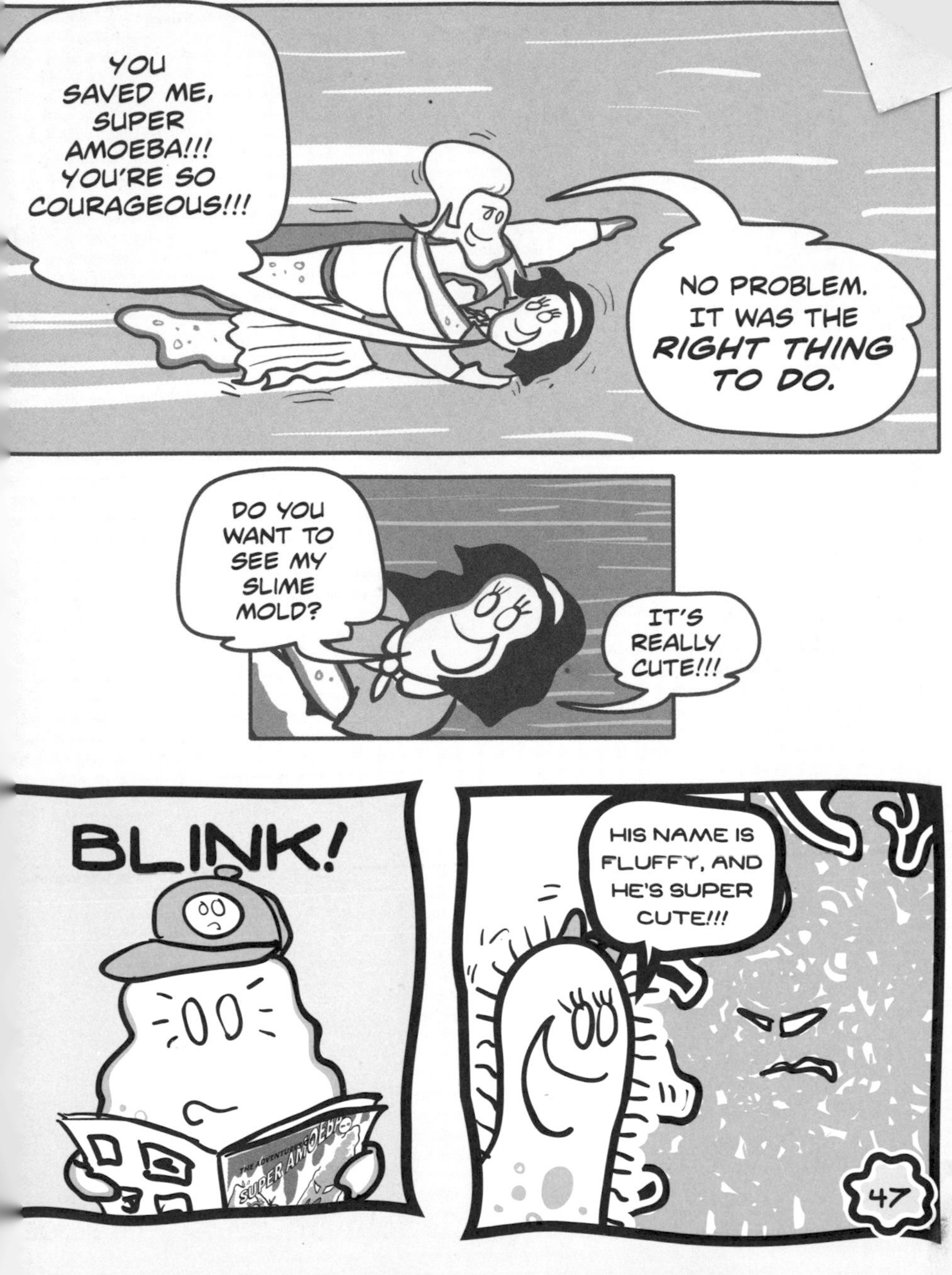
YOU SAVED ME, SUPER AMOEBA!!! YOU'RE SO COURAGEOUS!!!
NO PROBLEM. IT WAS THE RIGHT THING TO DO.
DO YOU WANT TO SEE MY SLIME MOLD?
IT'S REALLY CUTE!!!
BLINK!
THE ADVENTURES OF SUPER AMOEBA
HIS NAME IS FLUFFY, AND HE'S SUPER CUTE!!!

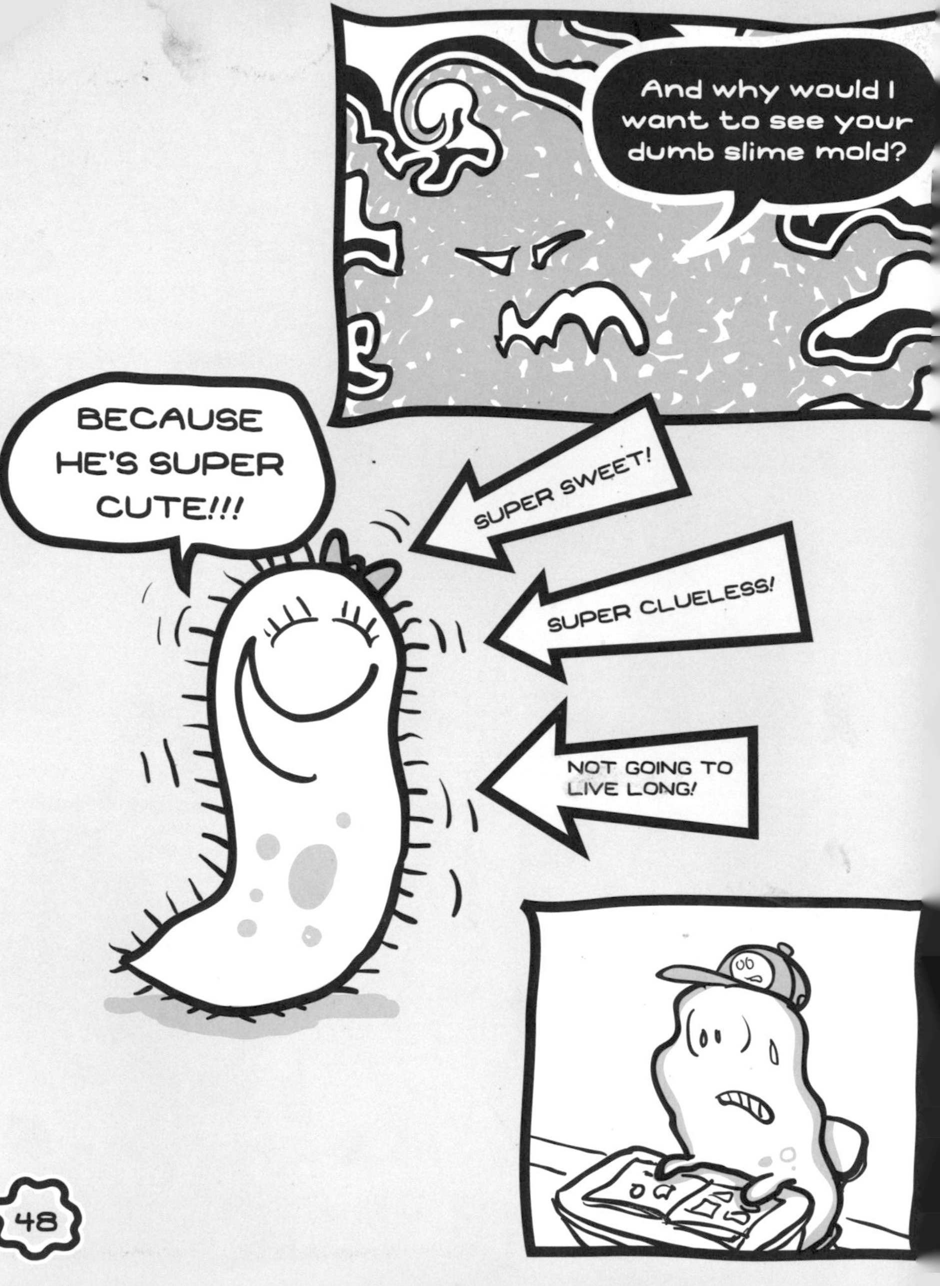

And why would I want to see your dumb slime mold?
BECAUSE HE'S SUPER CUTE!!!
SUPER SWEET!
SUPER CLUELESS!
NOT GOING TO LIVE LONG!

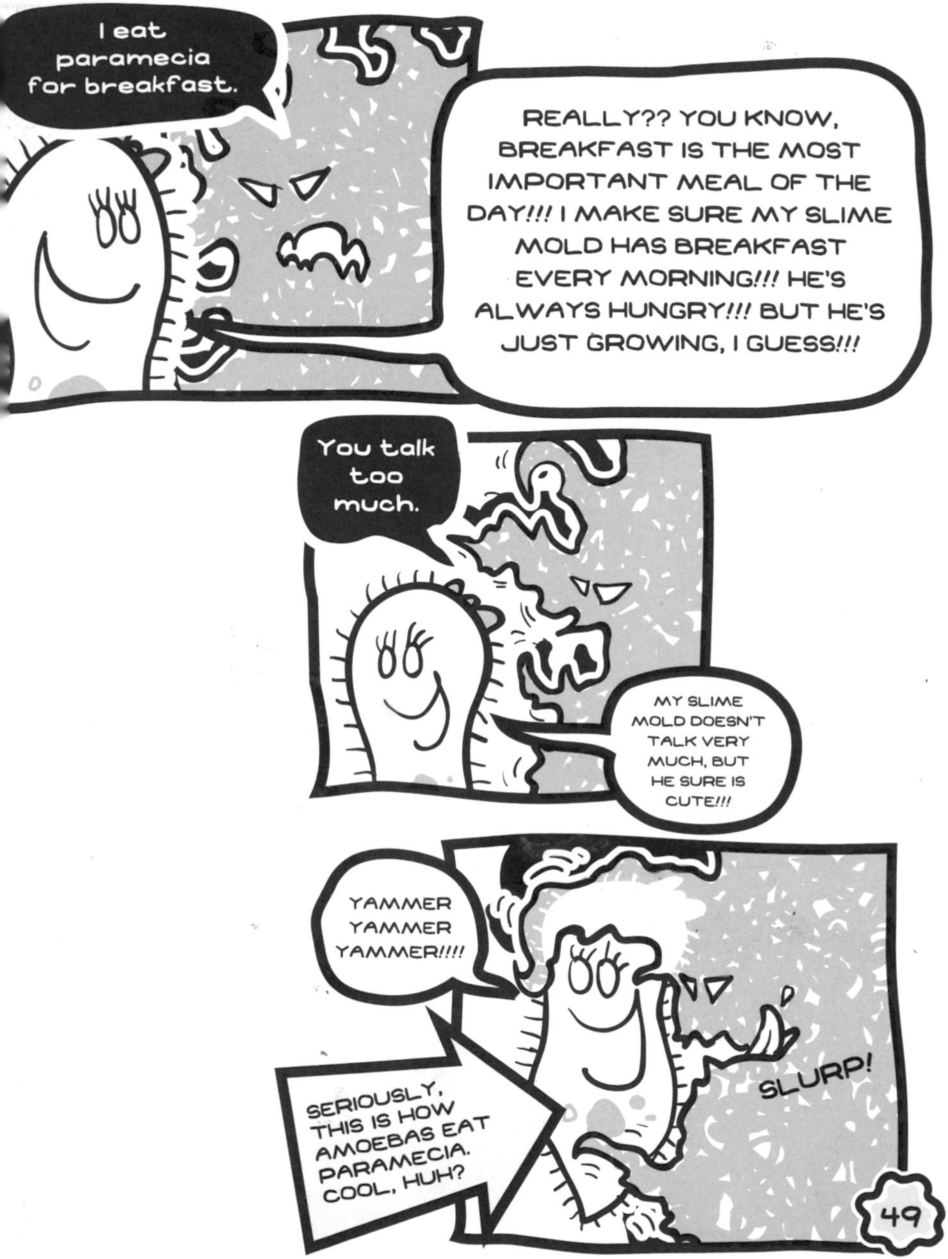
I eat paramecia for breakfast.
REALLY?? YOU KNOW, BREAKFAST IS THE MOST IMPORTANT MEAL OF THE DAY!!! I MAKE SURE MY SLIME MOLD HAS BREAKFAST EVERY MORNING!!! HE'S ALWAYS HUNGRY!!! BUT HE'S JUST GROWING, I GUESS!!!
You talk too much.
MY SLIME MOLD DOESN'T TALK VERY MUCH, BUT HE SURE IS CUTE!!!
YAMMER YAMMER YAMMER!!!!
SLURP!
SERIOUSLY, THIS IS HOW AMOEBAS EAT PARAMECIA. COOL, HUH?

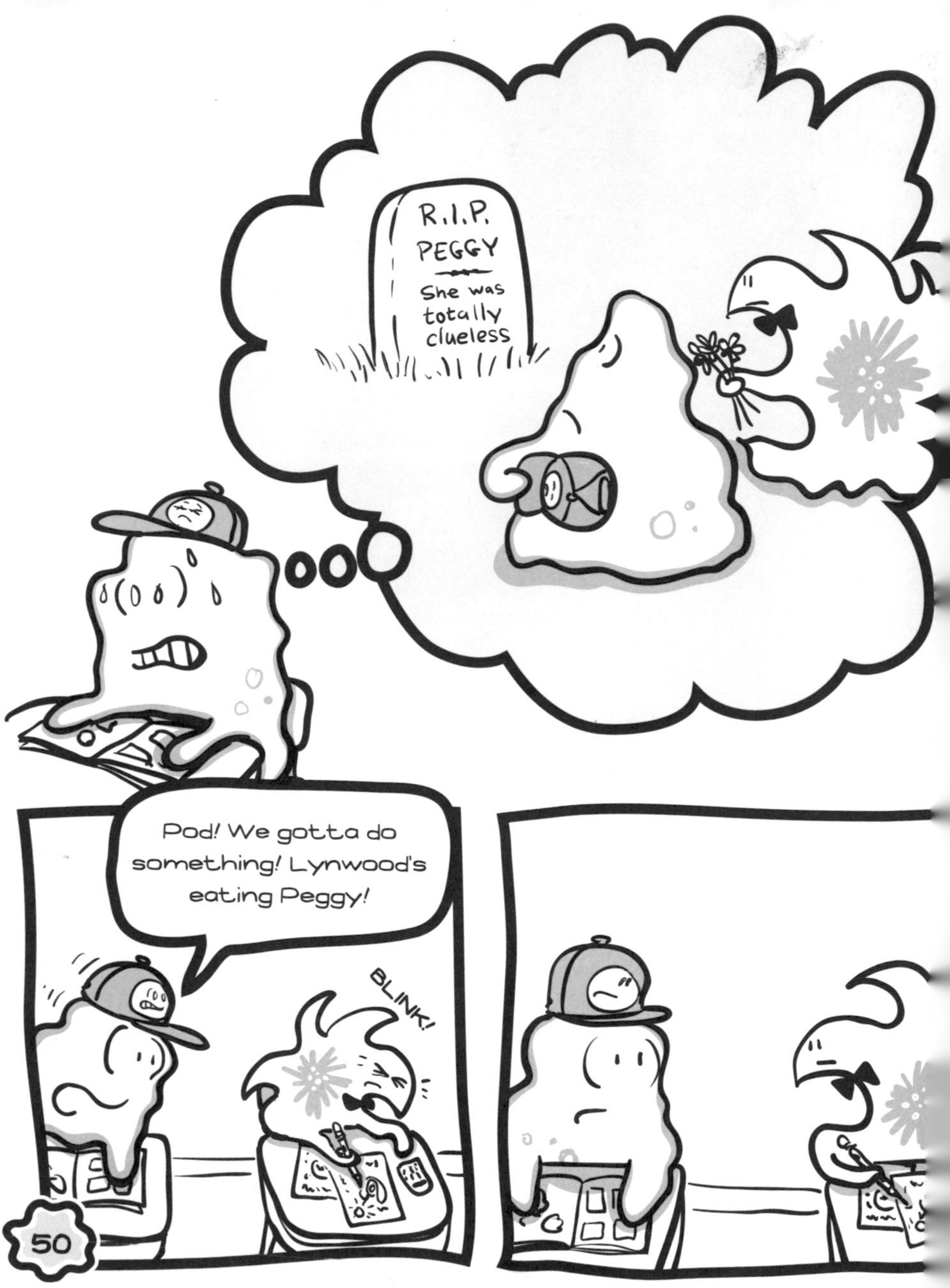
R.I.P.
PEGGY
She was totally clueless
Pod! We gotta do something! Lynwood's eating Peggy!
BLINK!

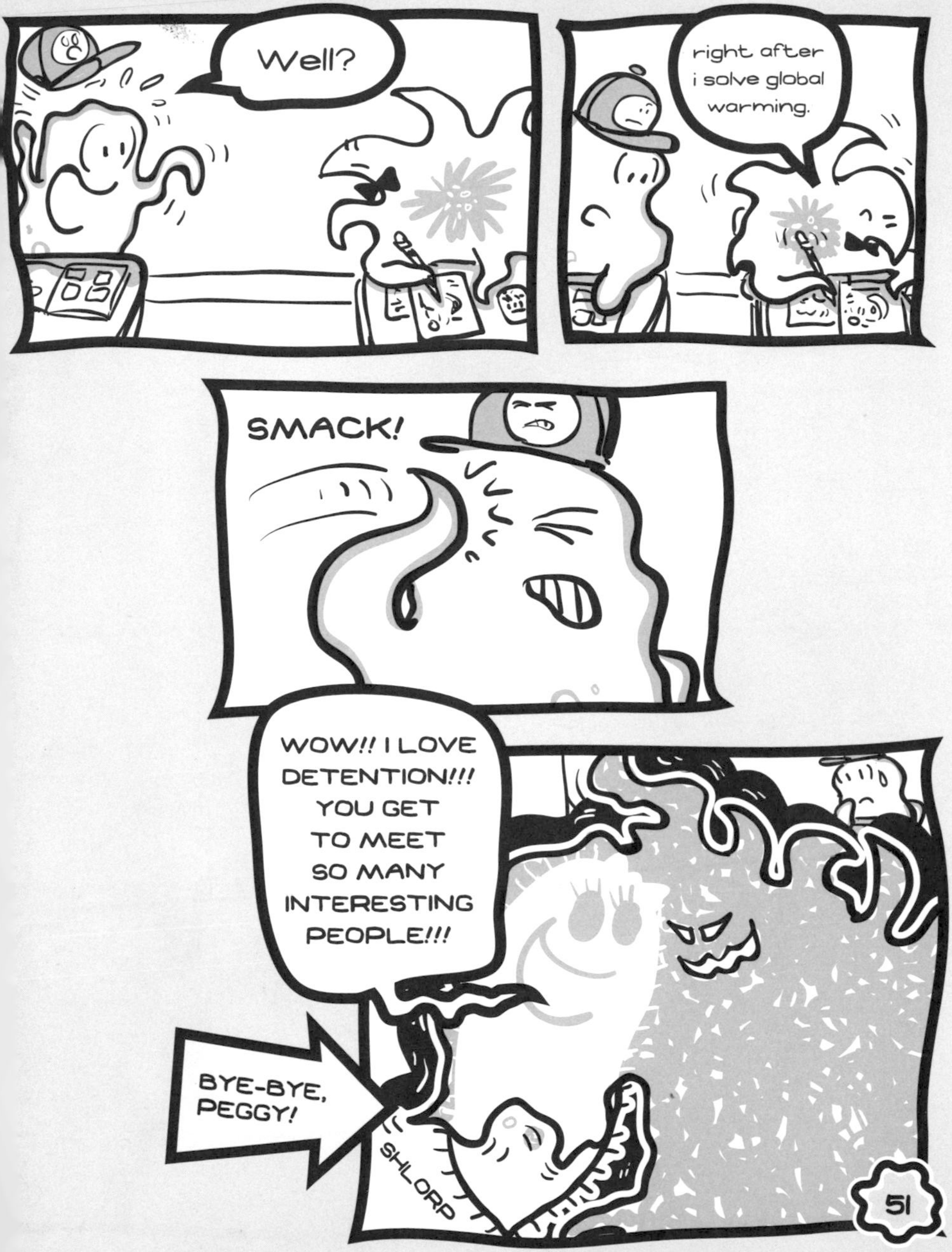

Well?
right after i solve global warming.
SMACK!
WOW!! I LOVE DETENTION!!! YOU GET TO MEET SO MANY INTERESTING PEOPLE!!!
BYE-BYE, PEGGY!
SHLORP

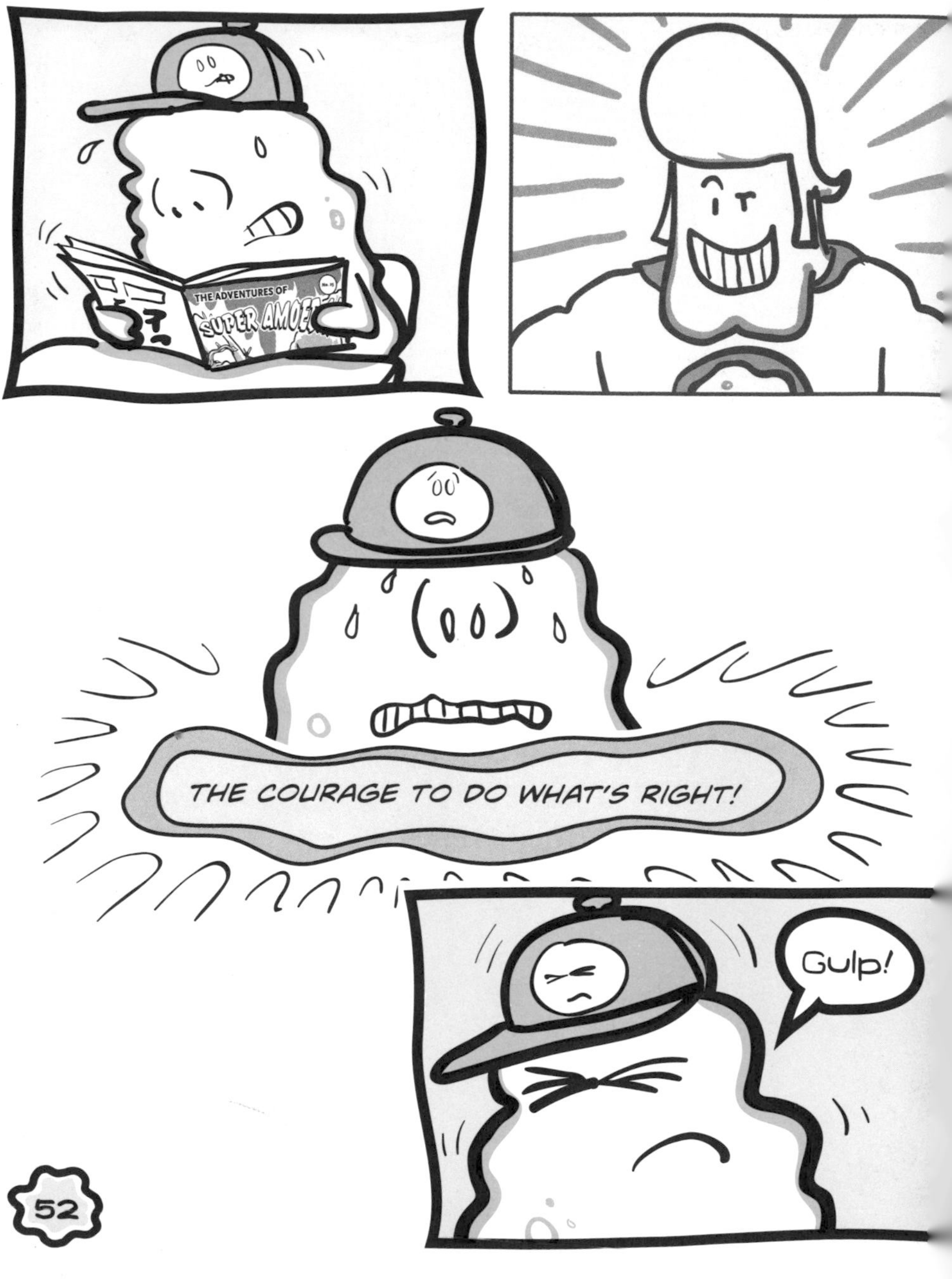
THE ADVENTURES OF
SUPER AMOEBA
THE COURAGE TO DO WHAT'S RIGHT!
Gulp!

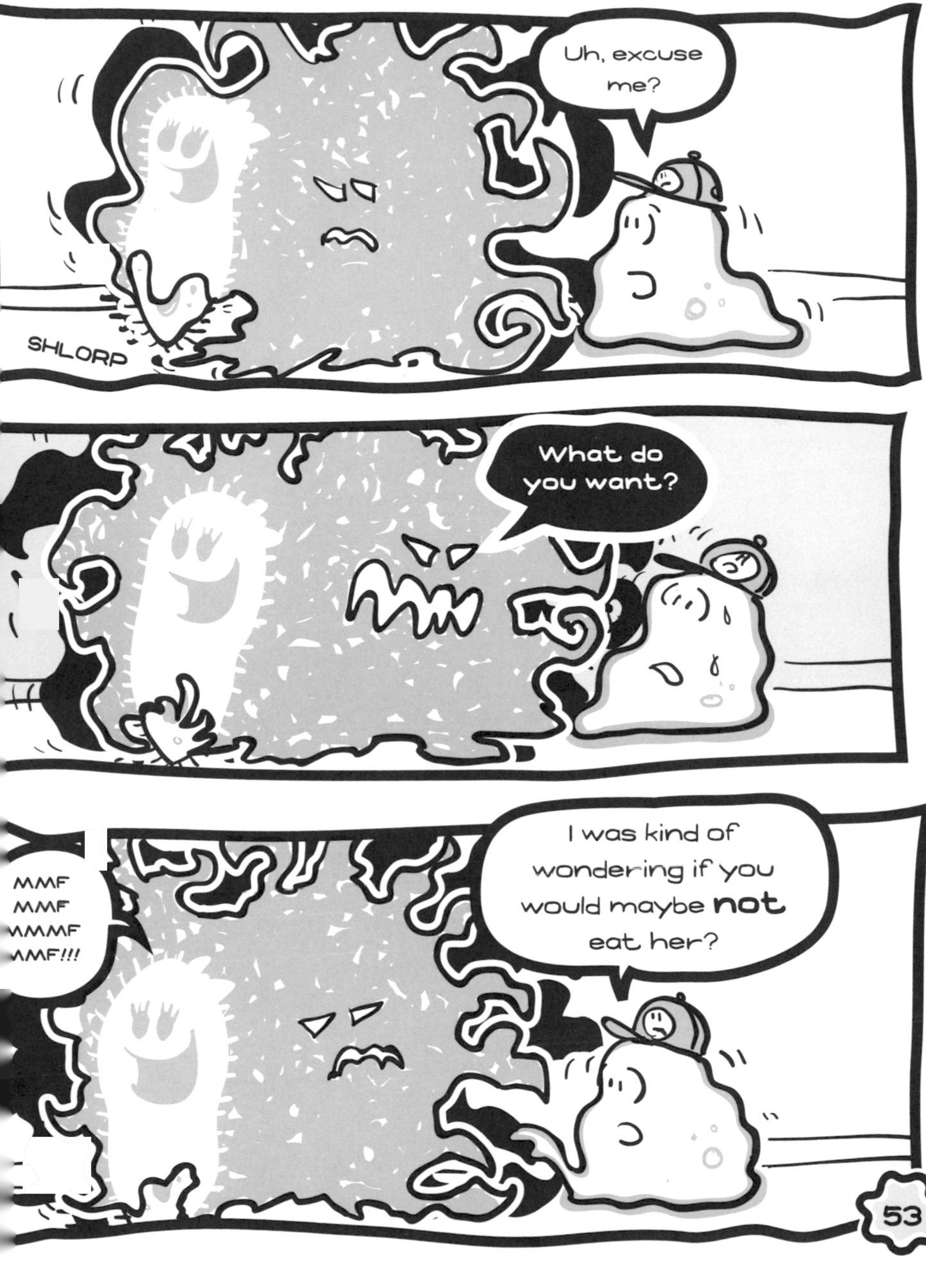
Uh, excuse me?
SHLORP
What do you want?
MMF MMF MMMF MMF!!!
I was kind of wondering if you would maybe **not** eat her?

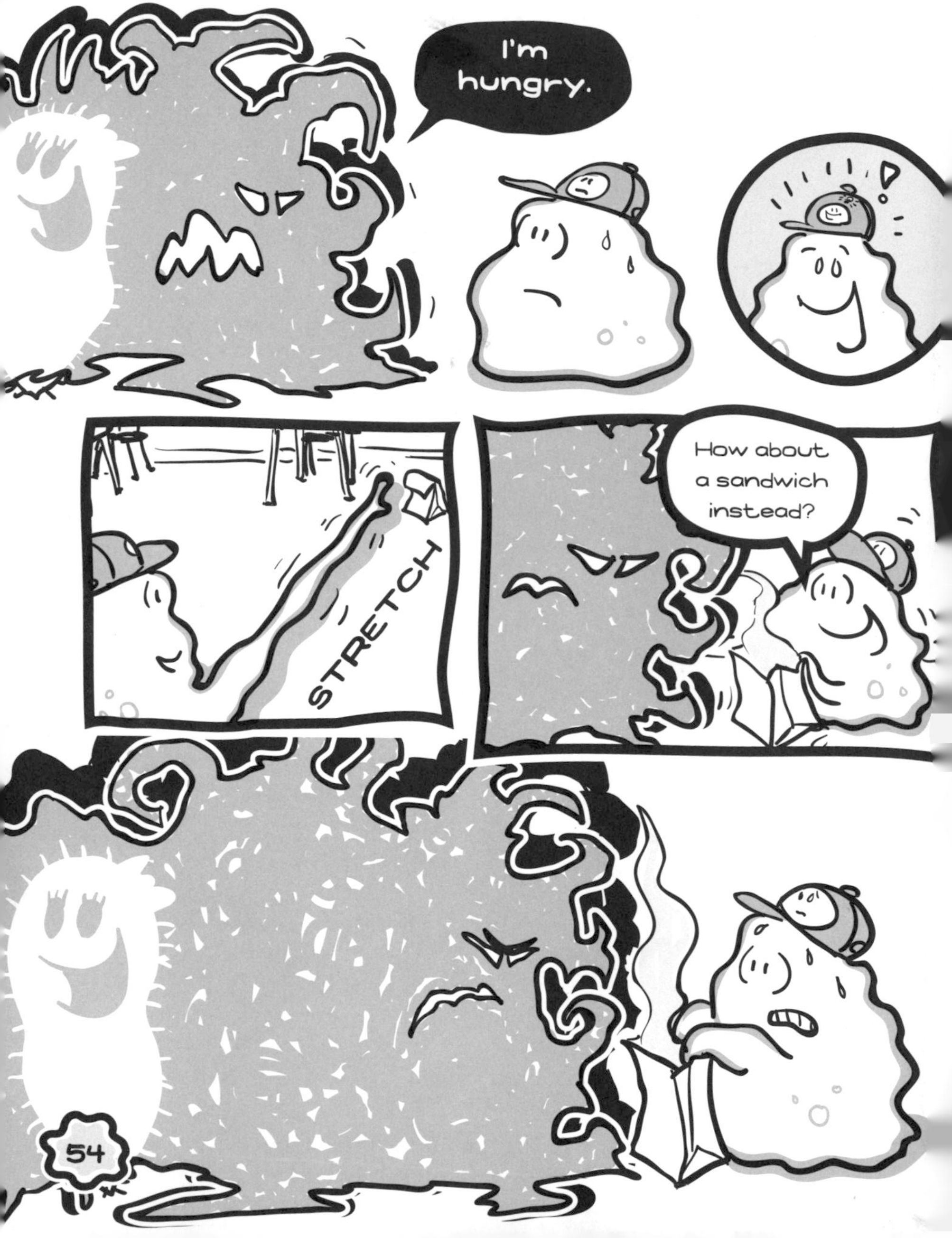
I'm hungry.
STRETCH
How about a sandwich instead?

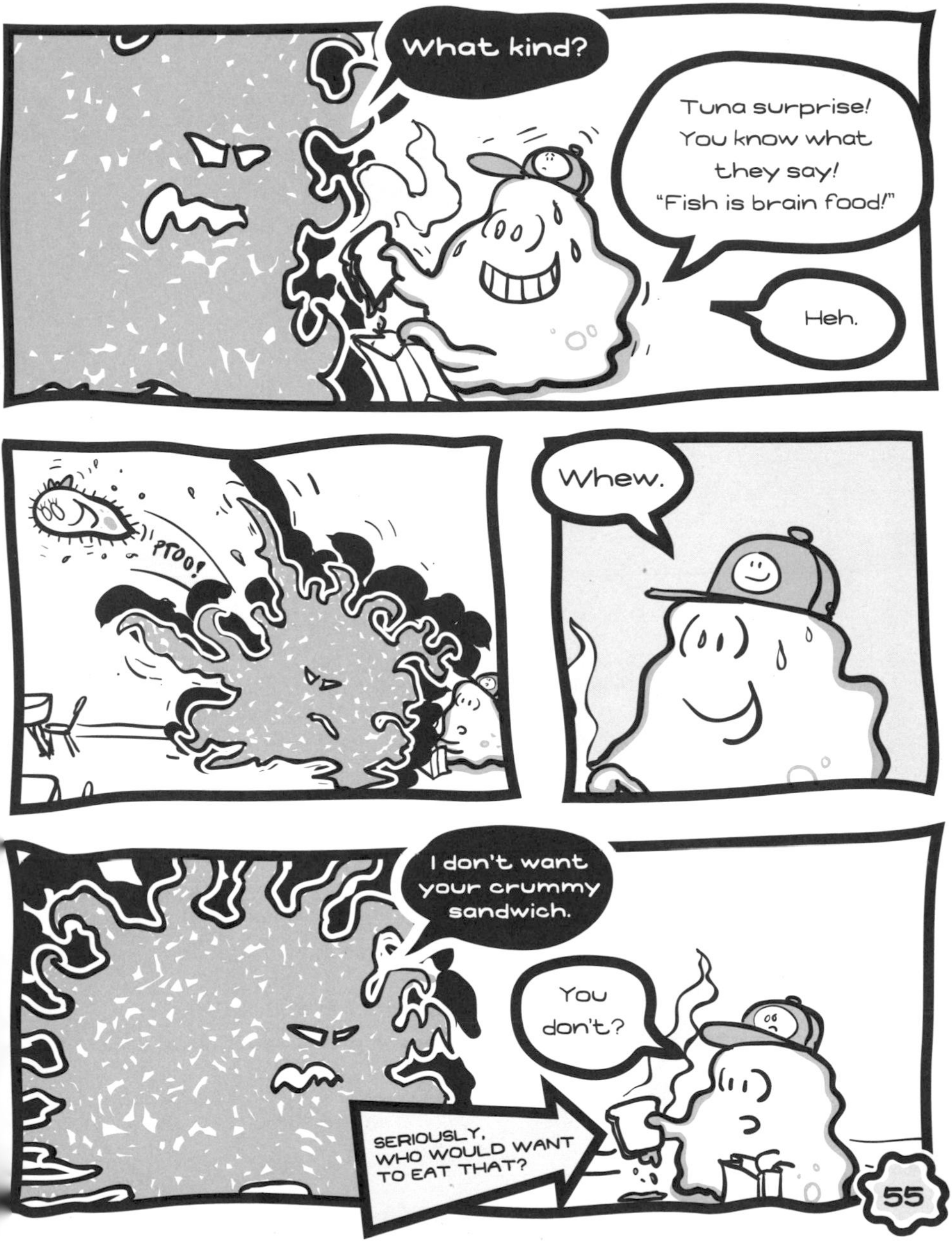
What kind?
Tuna surprise! You know what they say! "Fish is brain food!"
Heh.
PTOO!
Whew.
I don't want your crummy sandwich.
You don't?
SERIOUSLY, WHO WOULD WANT TO EAT THAT?

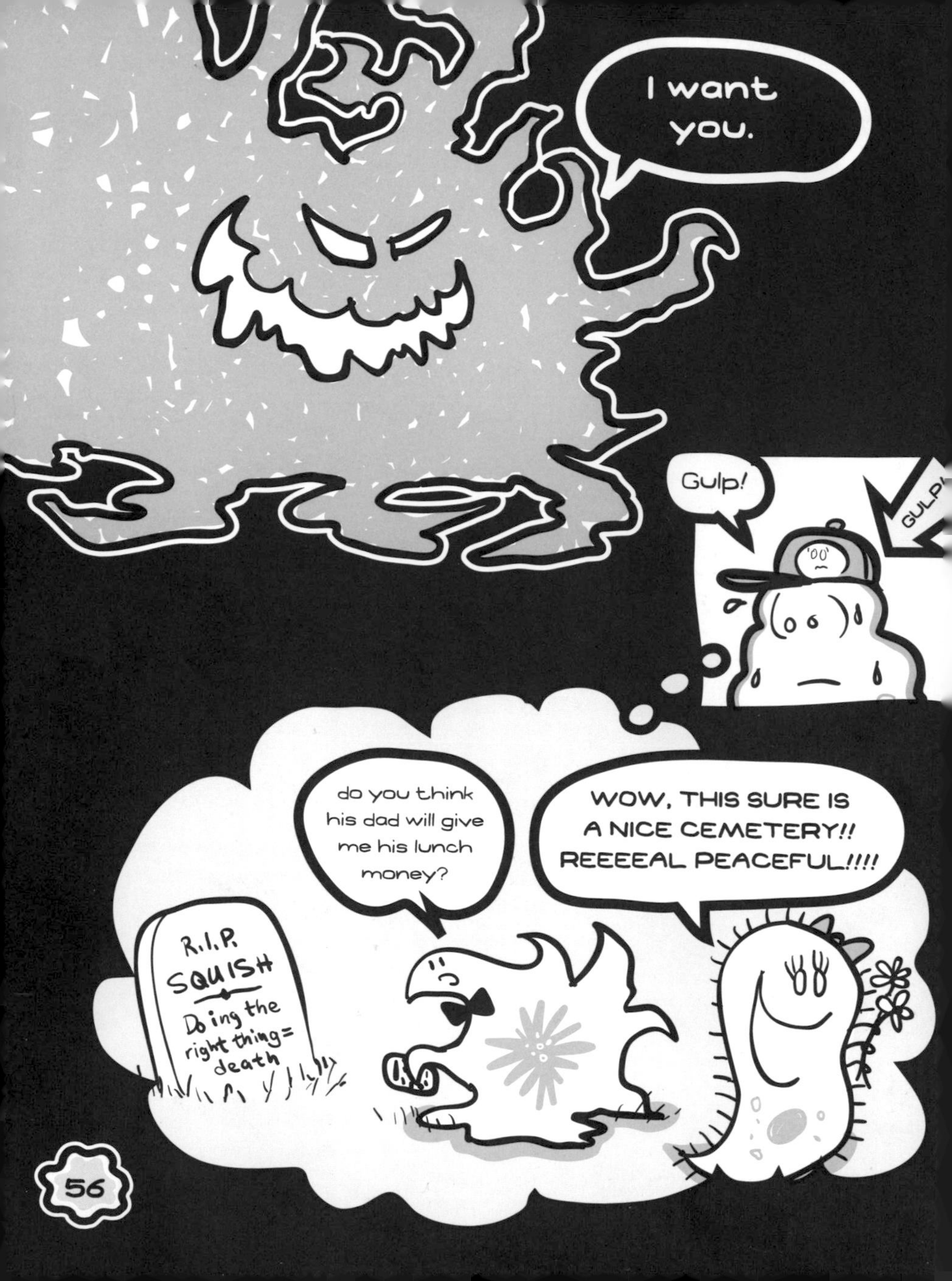
I want you.
Gulp!
GULP!
do you think his dad will give me his lunch money?
WOW, THIS SURE IS A NICE CEMETERY!! REEEEAL PEACEFUL!!!!
R.I.P.
SQUISH
Doing the right thing = death

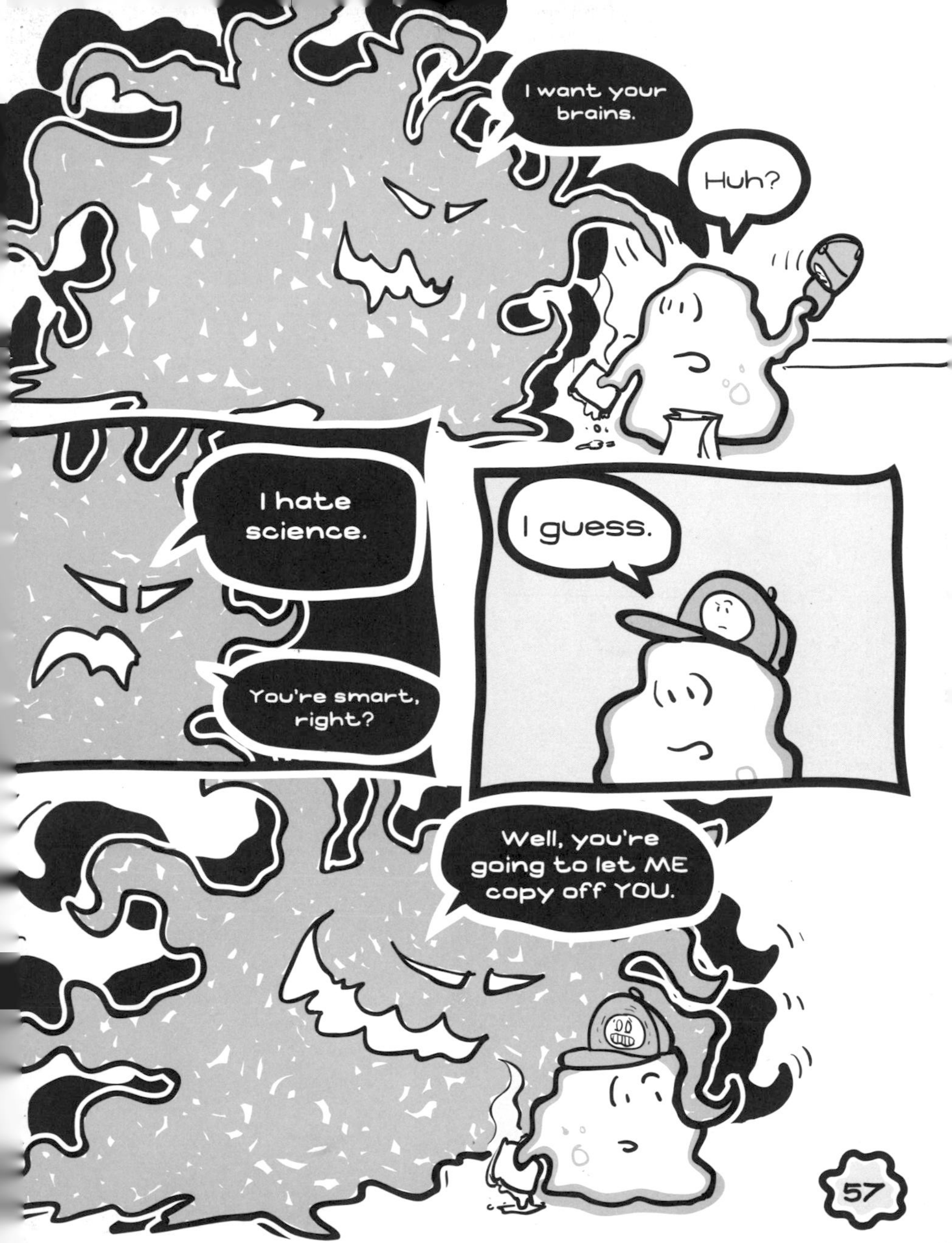
I want your brains.
Huh?
I hate science.
You're smart, right?
I guess.
Well, you're going to let ME copy off YOU.

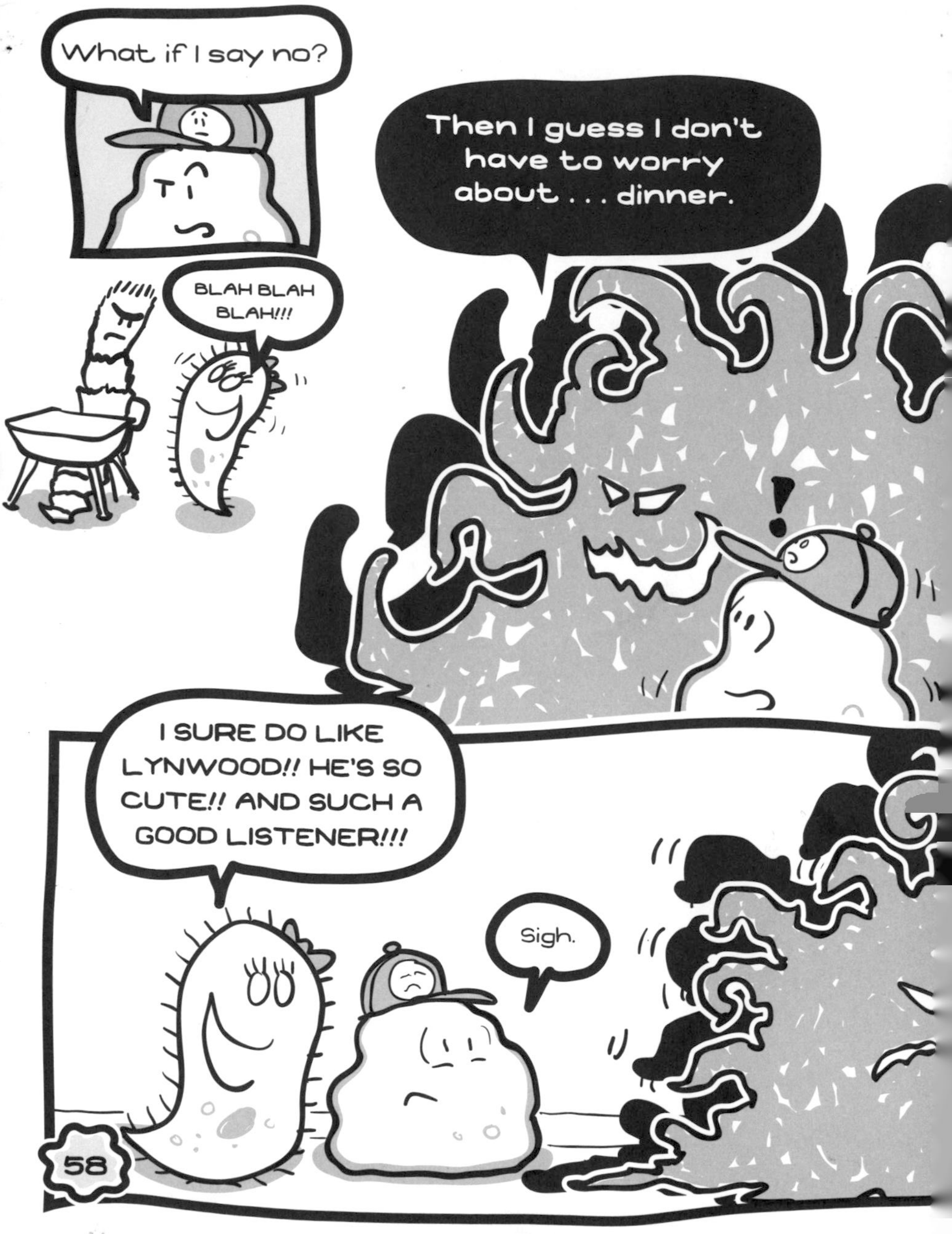
What if I say no?
Then I guess I don't have to worry about . . . dinner.
BLAH BLAH BLAH!!!
I SURE DO LIKE LYNWOOD!! HE'S SO CUTE!! AND SUCH A GOOD LISTENER!!!
Sigh.

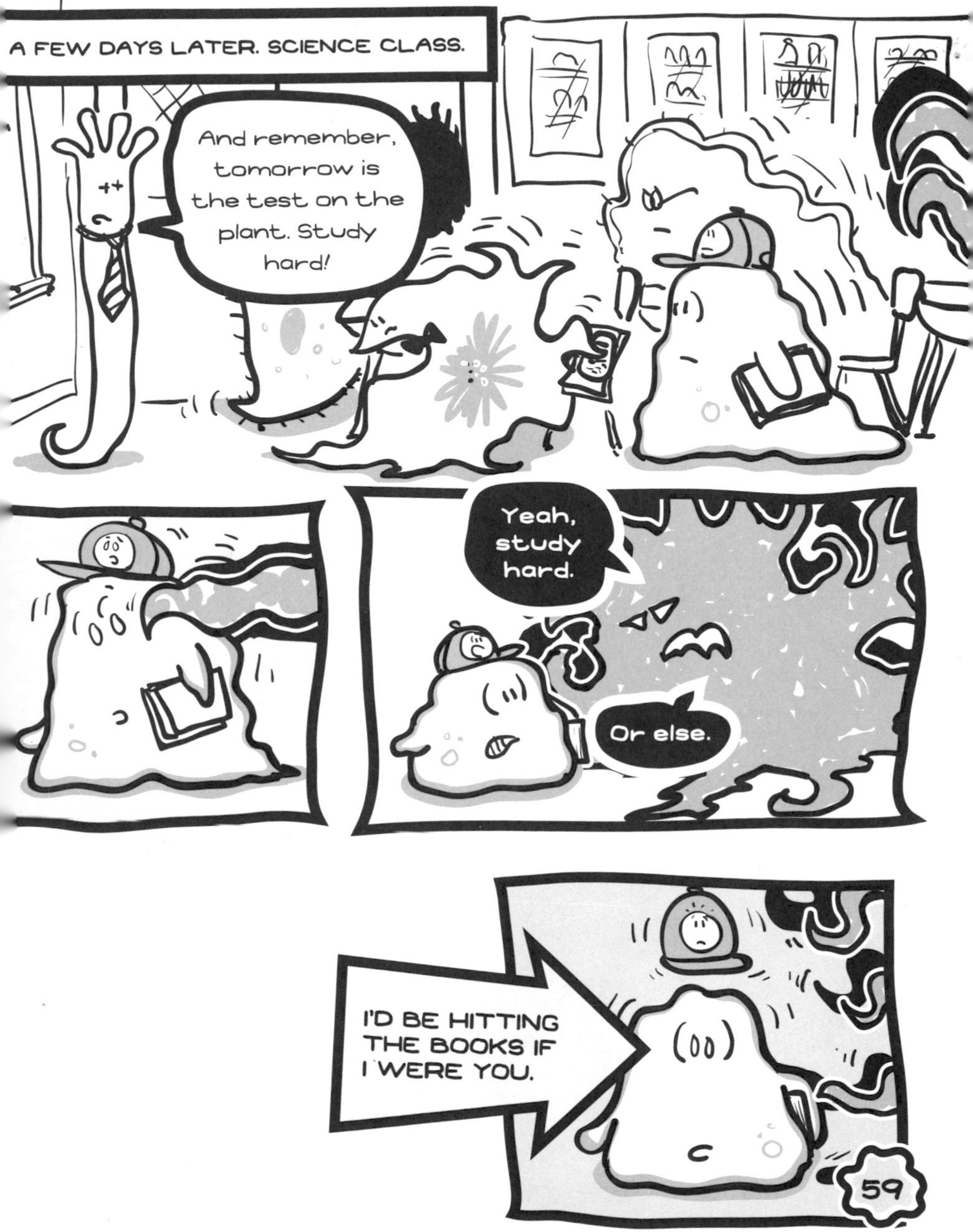
A FEW DAYS LATER. SCIENCE CLASS.
And remember, tomorrow is the test on the plant. Study hard!
Yeah, study hard.
Or else.
I'D BE HITTING THE BOOKS IF I WERE YOU.

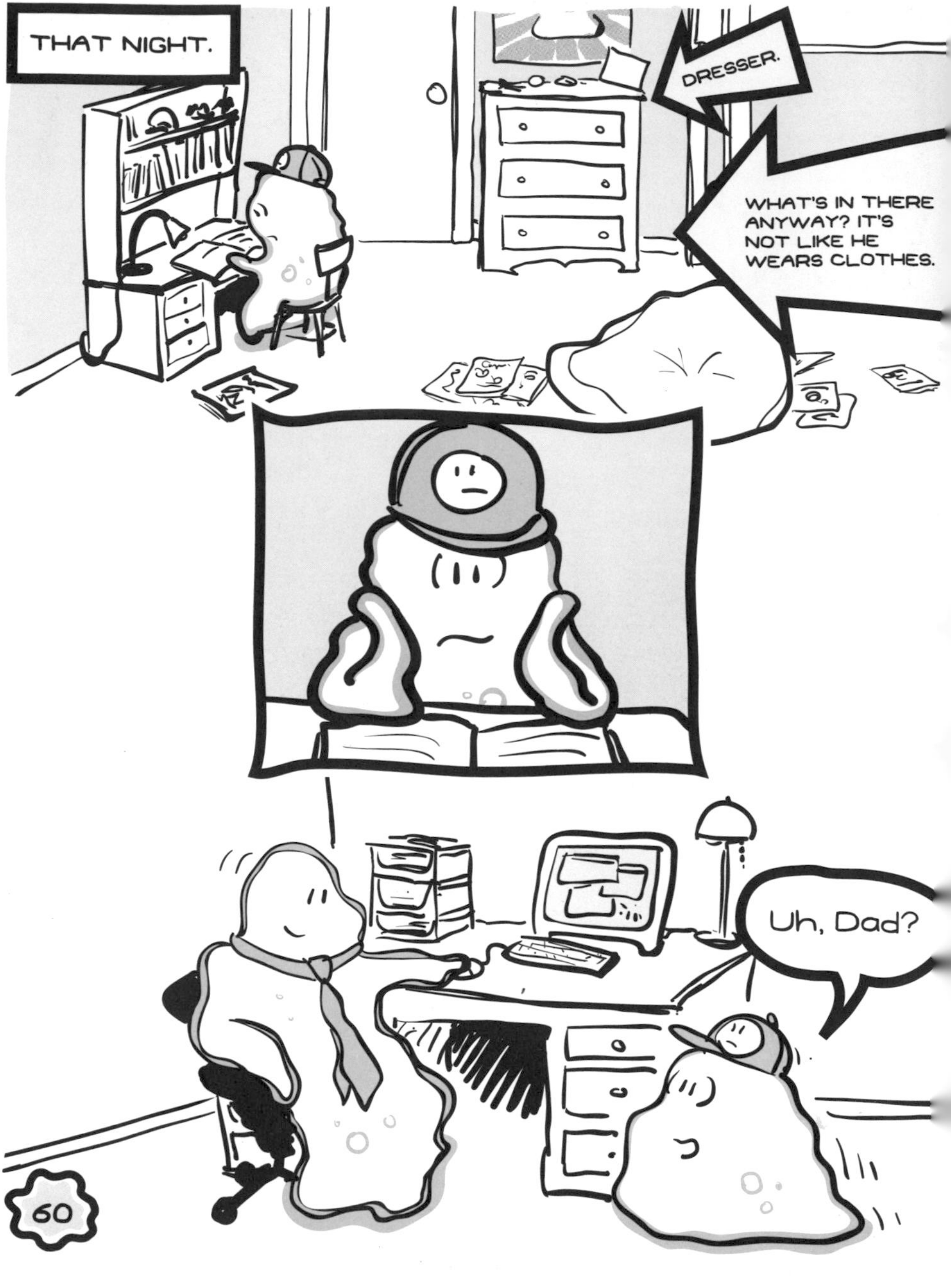
THAT NIGHT.
DRESSER.
WHAT'S IN THERE ANYWAY? IT'S NOT LIKE HE WEARS CLOTHES.
Uh, Dad?

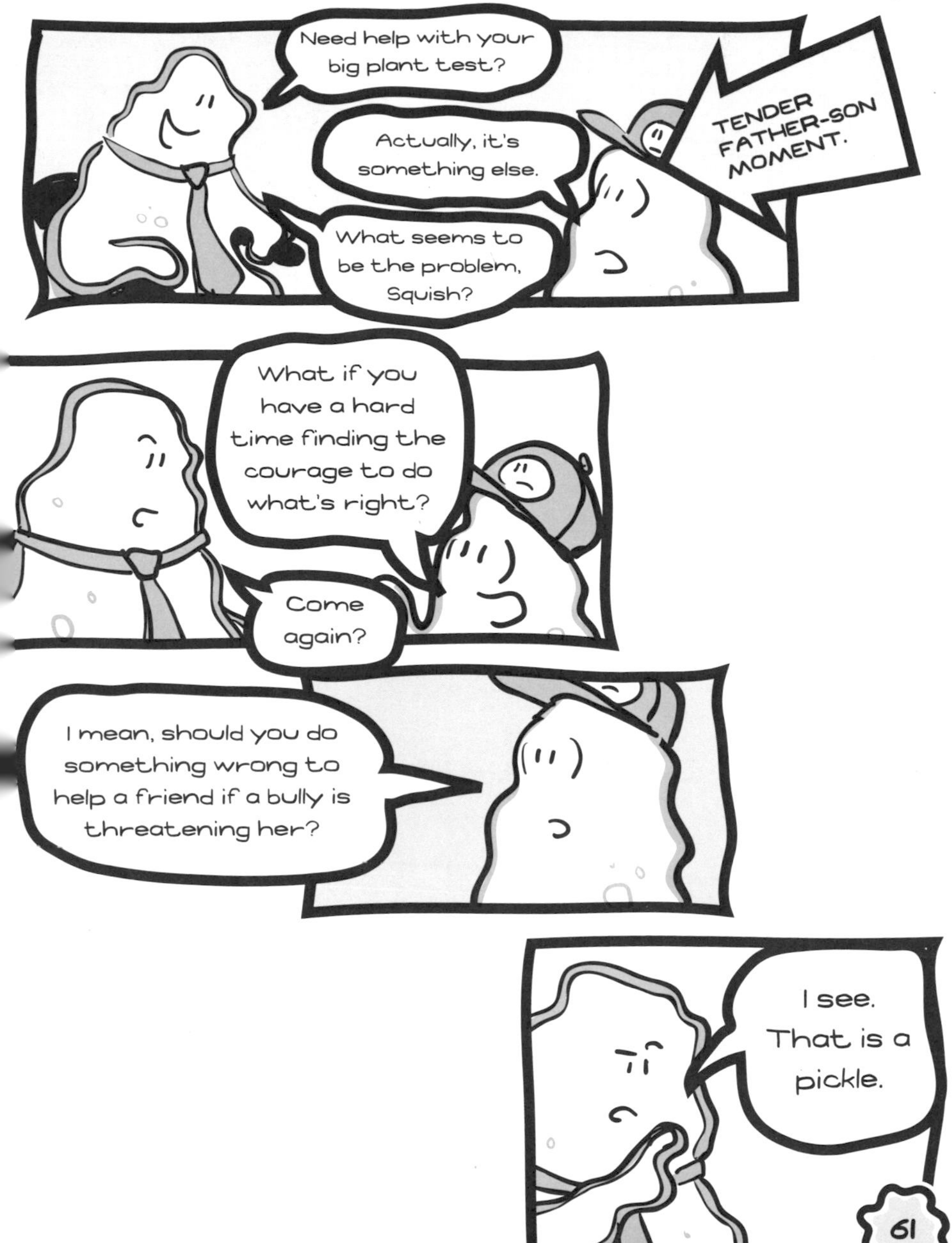
Need help with your big plant test?
Actually, it's something else.
TENDER FATHER-SON MOMENT.
What seems to be the problem, Squish?
What if you have a hard time finding the courage to do what's right?
Come again?
I mean, should you do something wrong to help a friend if a bully is threatening her?
I see. That is a pickle.

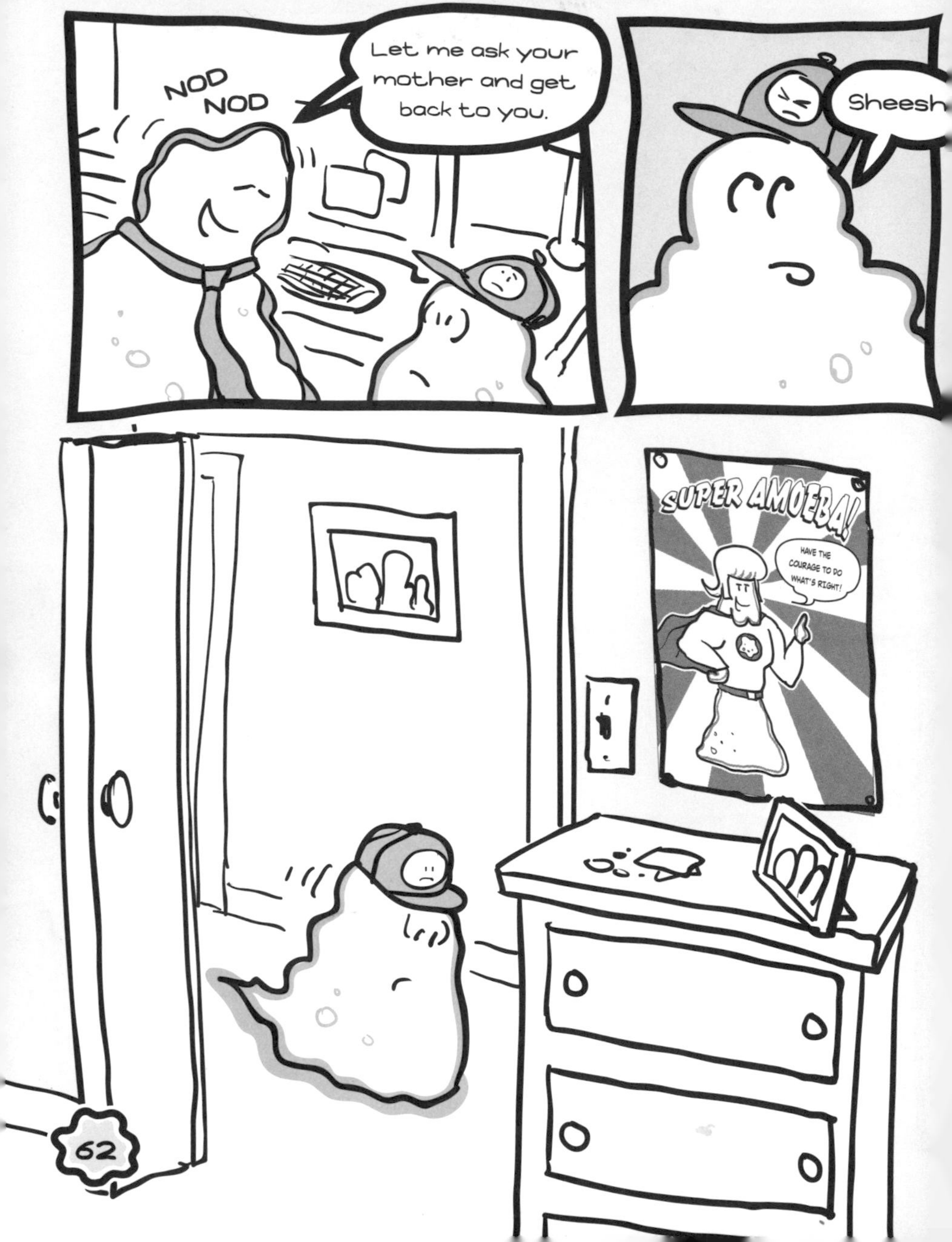
NOD
NOD
Let me ask your mother and get back to you.
Sheesh
SUPER AMOEBA!
HAVE THE COURAGE TO DO WHAT'S RIGHT!

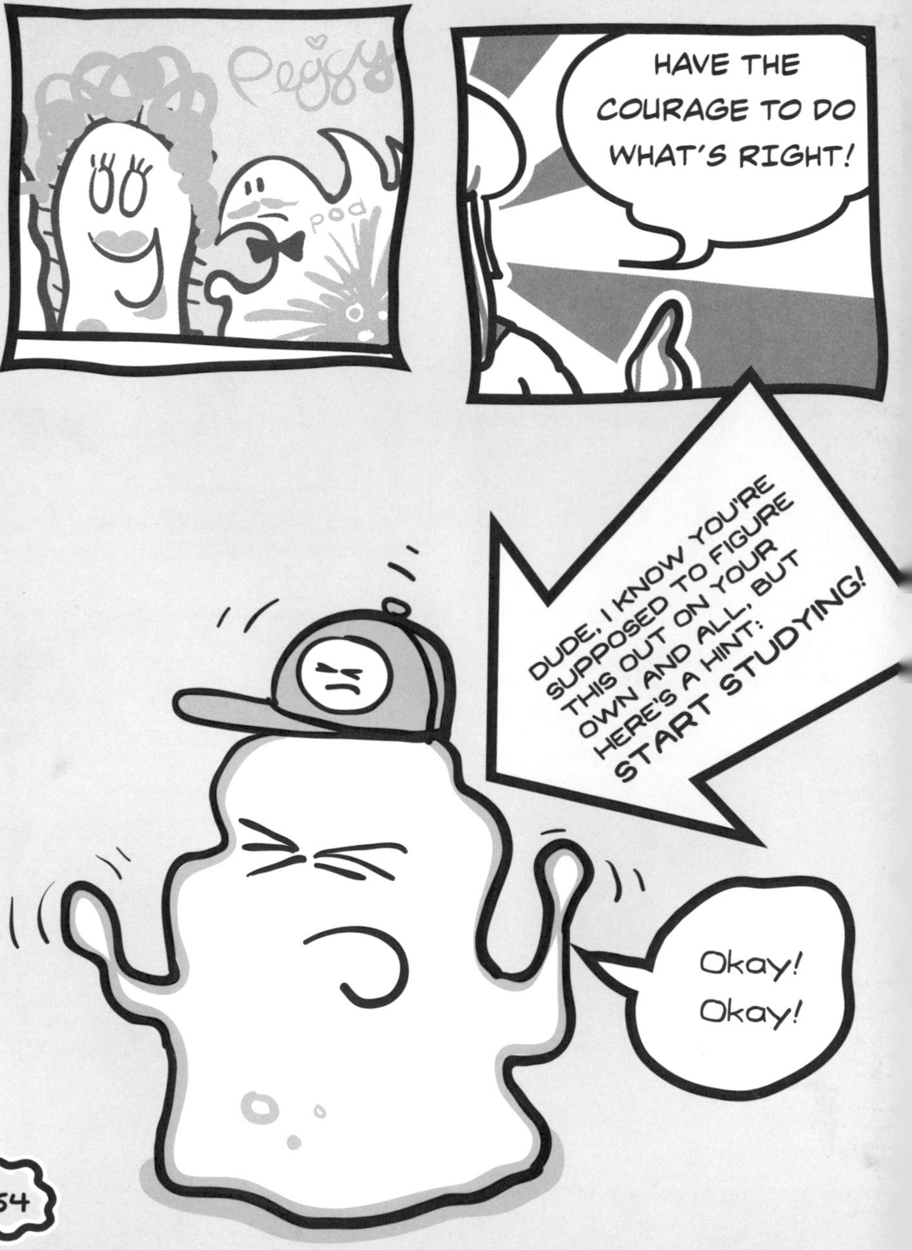

Peggy
pod
HAVE THE COURAGE TO DO WHAT'S RIGHT!
DUDE, I KNOW YOU'RE SUPPOSED TO FIGURE THIS OUT ON YOUR OWN AND ALL, BUT HERE'S A HINT: START STUDYING!
Okay! Okay!

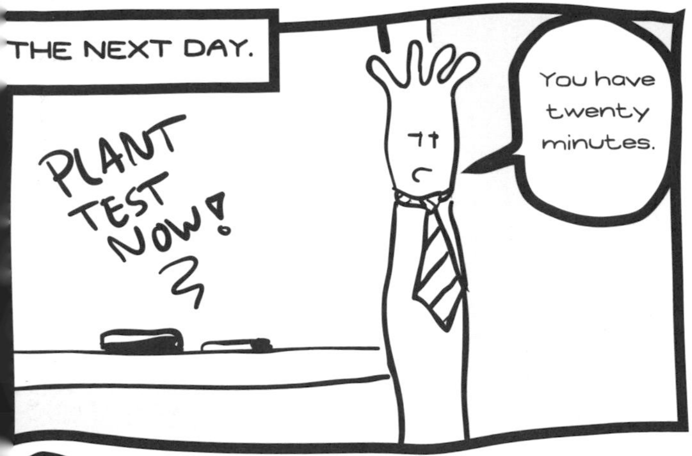
THE NEXT DAY.
PLANT TEST NOW!
You have twenty minutes.

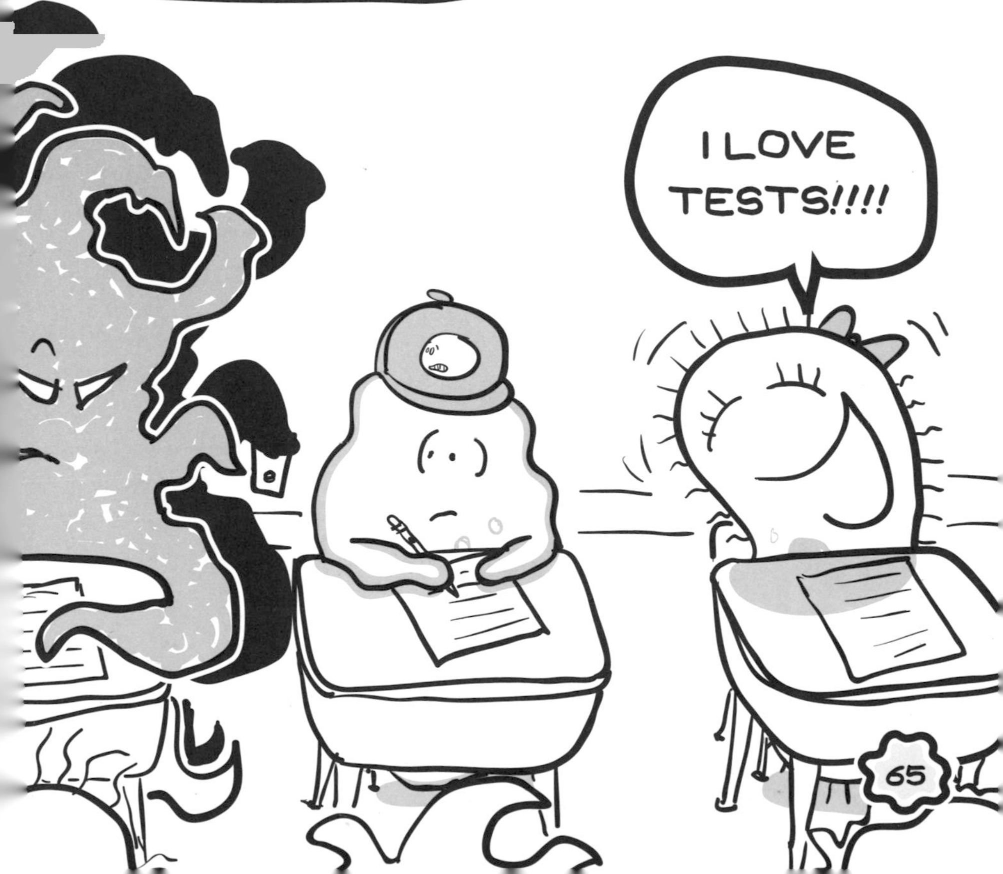
I LOVE TESTS!!!!

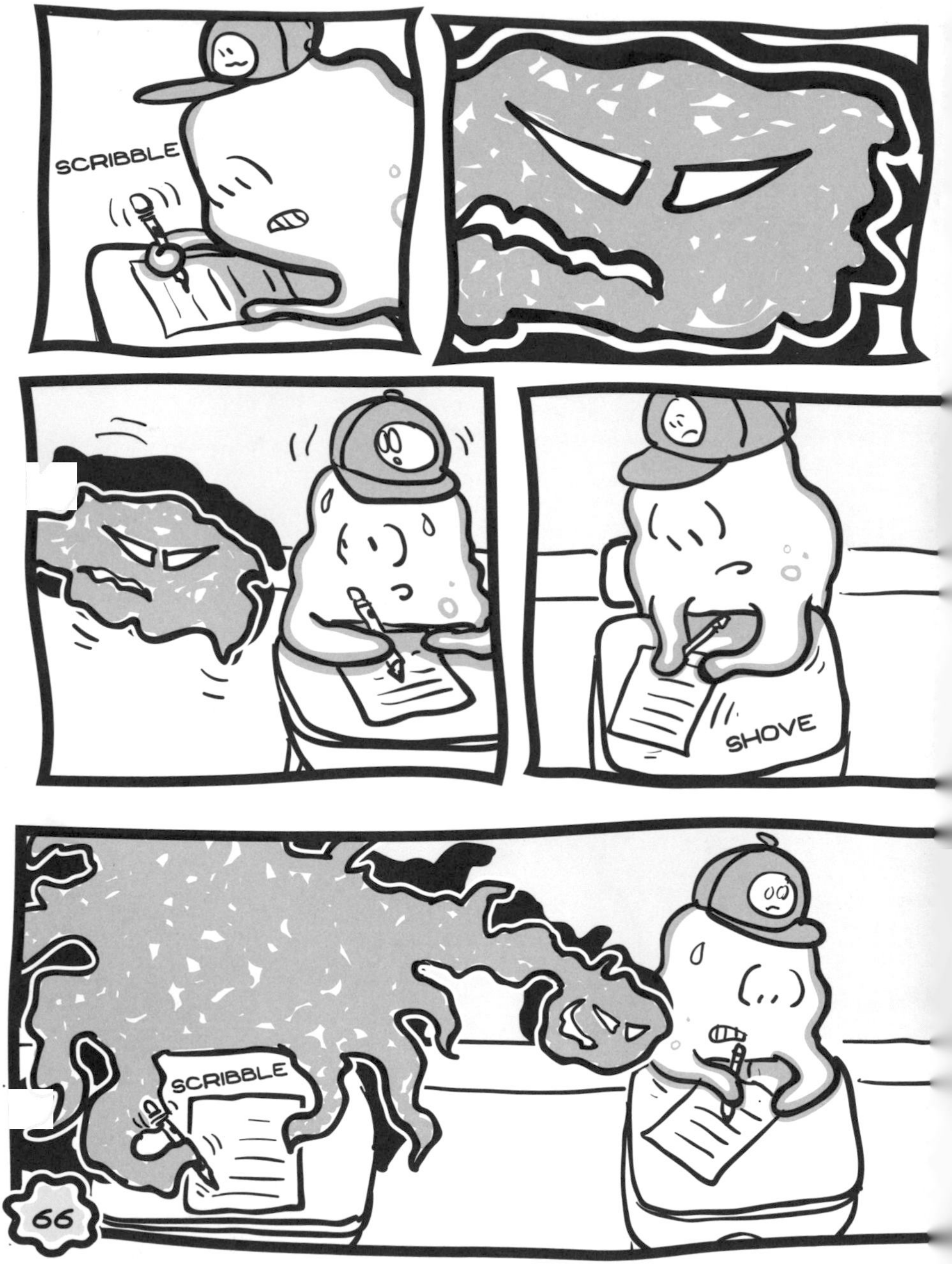
SCRIBBLE
SHOVE
SCRIBBLE

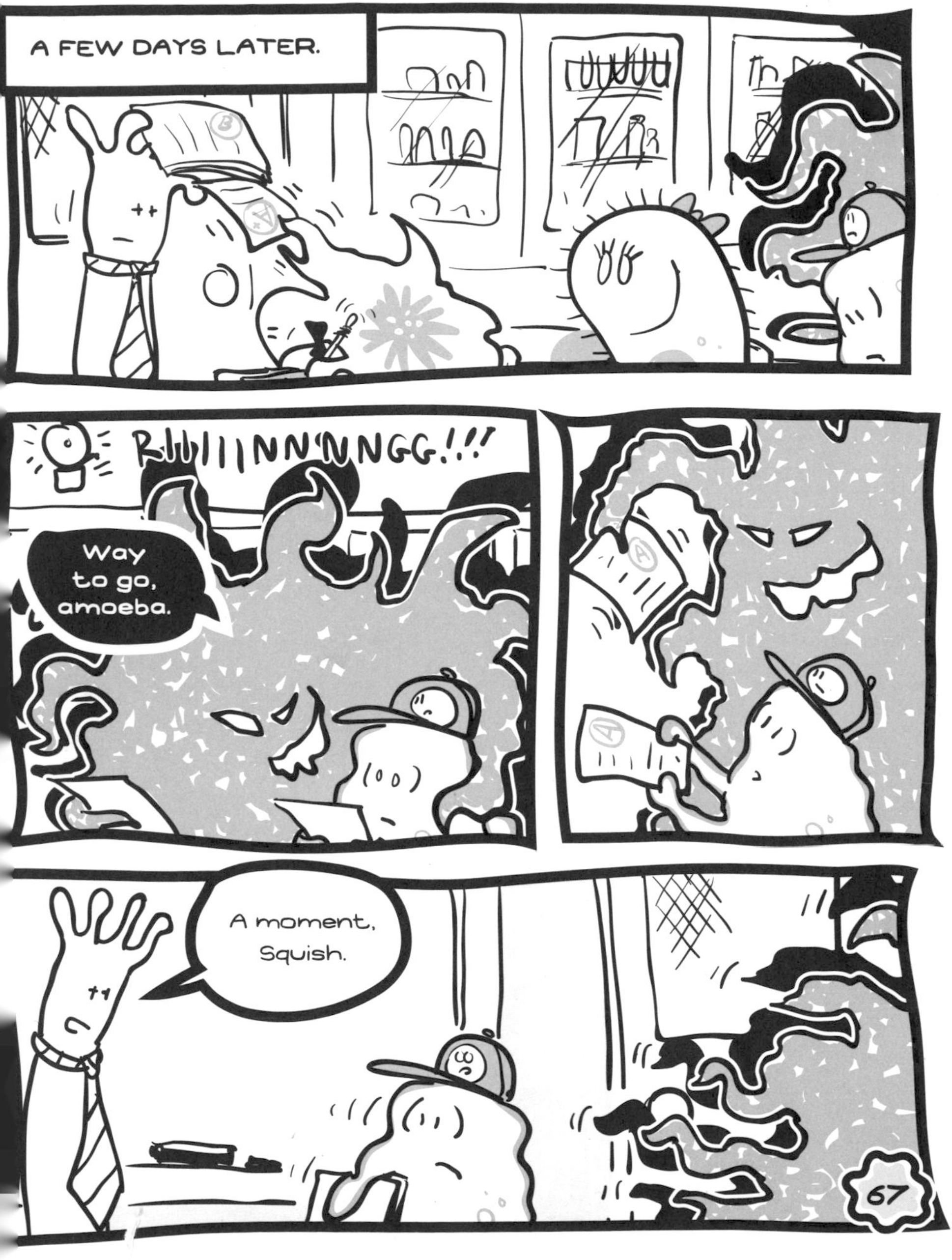
A FEW DAYS LATER.
RIIIIINNNNGG!!!
Way to go, amoeba.
A moment, Squish.

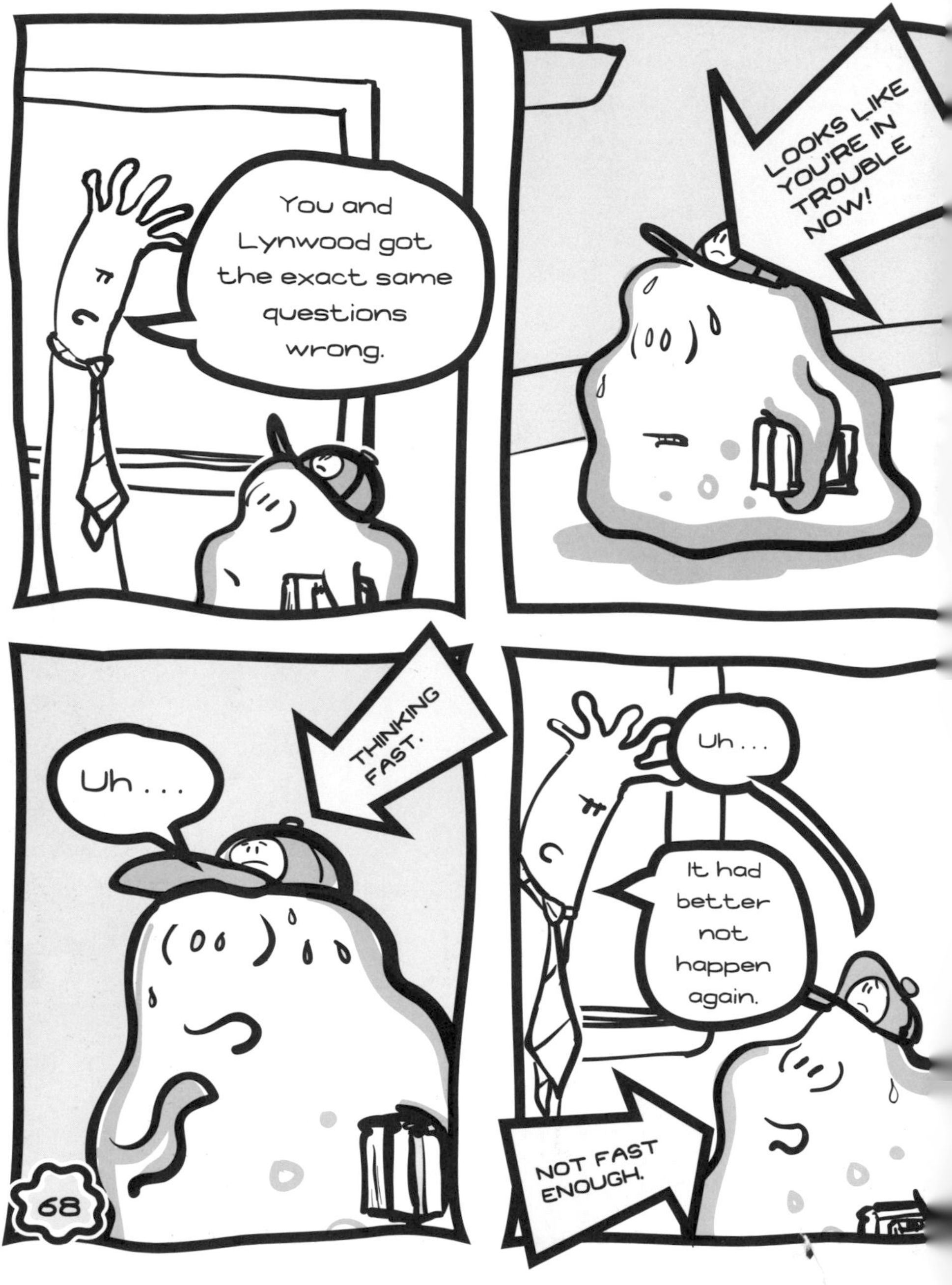
You and Lynwood got the exact same questions wrong.
LOOKS LIKE YOU'RE IN TROUBLE NOW!
Uh . . . .
THINKING FAST.
Uh . . .
It had better not happen again.
NOT FAST ENOUGH.

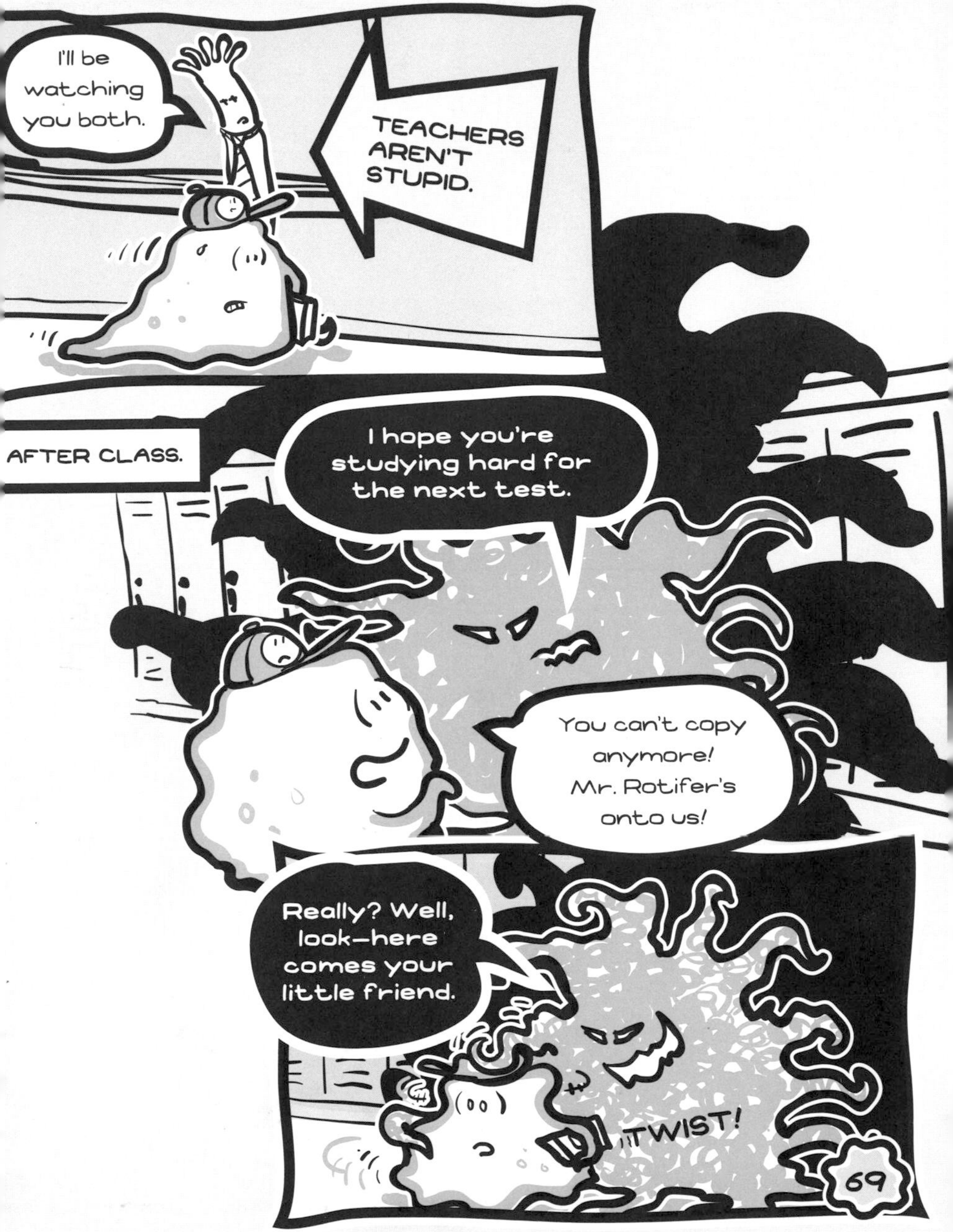

I'll be watching you both.
TEACHERS AREN'T STUPID.
AFTER CLASS.
I hope you're studying hard for the next test.
You can't copy anymore! Mr. Rotifer's onto us!
Really? Well, look—here comes your little friend.
TWIST!

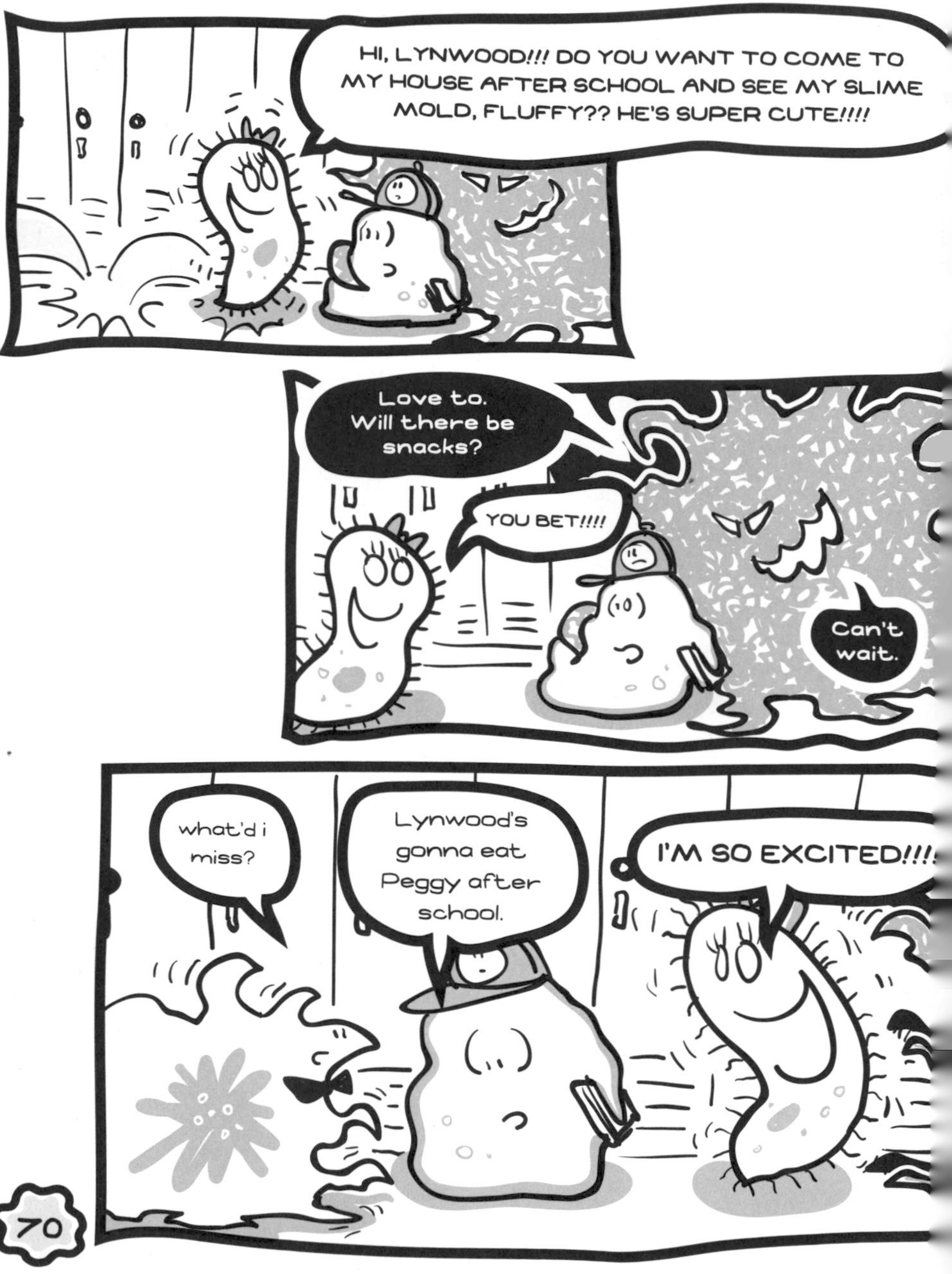
HI, LYNWOOD!!! DO YOU WANT TO COME TO MY HOUSE AFTER SCHOOL AND SEE MY SLIME MOLD, FLUFFY?? HE'S SUPER CUTE!!!!
Love to. Will there be snacks?
YOU BET!!!!
Can't wait.
what'd i miss?
Lynwood's gonna eat Peggy after school.
I'M SO EXCITED!!!!

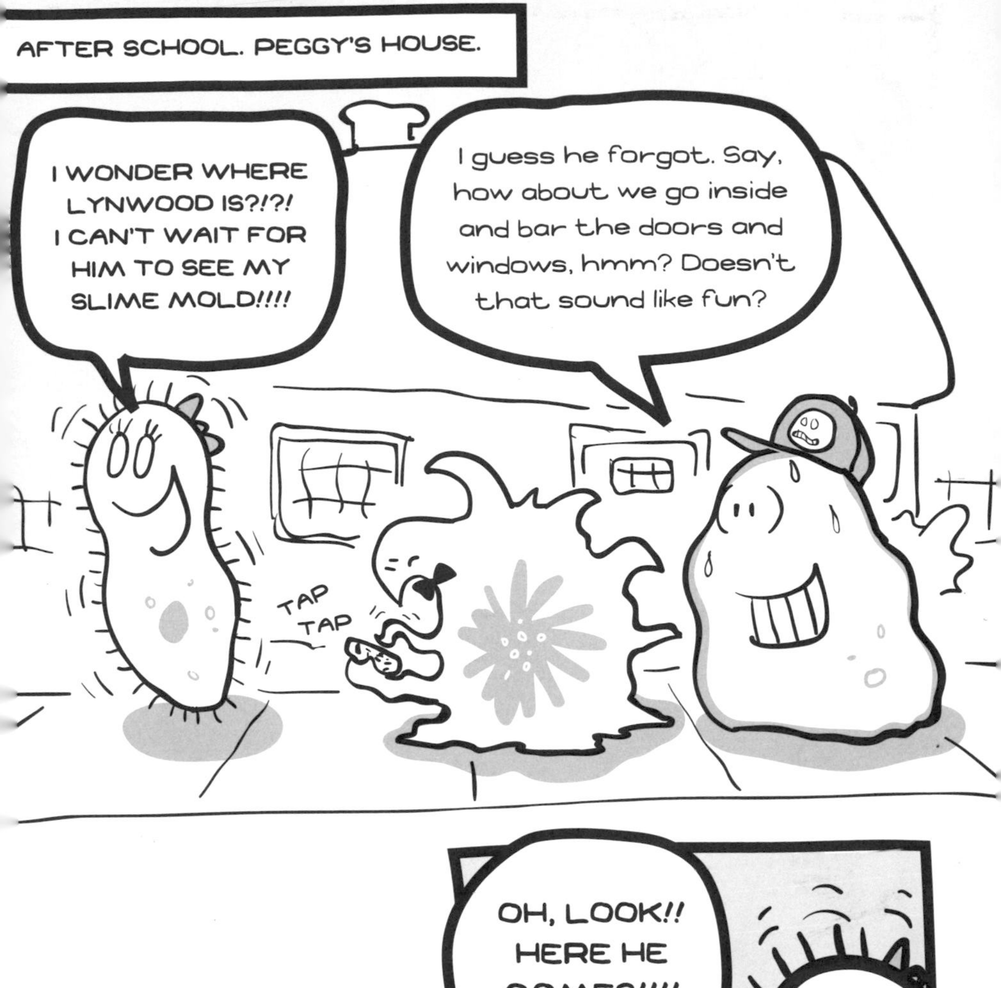
AFTER SCHOOL. PEGGY'S HOUSE.
I WONDER WHERE LYNWOOD IS?!?! I CAN'T WAIT FOR HIM TO SEE MY SLIME MOLD!!!!
I guess he forgot. Say, how about we go inside and bar the doors and windows, hmm? Doesn't that sound like fun?
TAP TAP

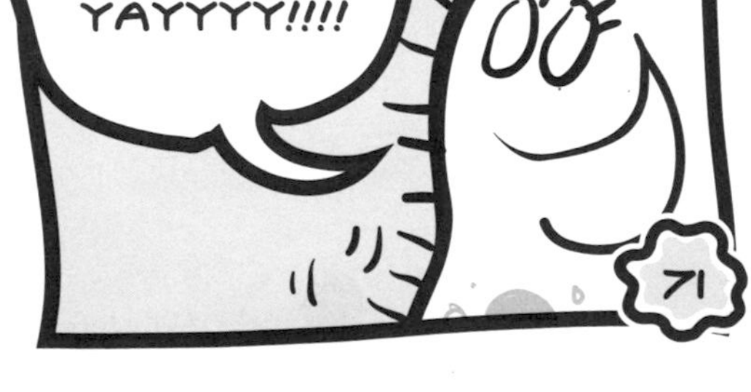
OH, LOOK!! HERE HE COMES!!!! YAYYYY!!!!

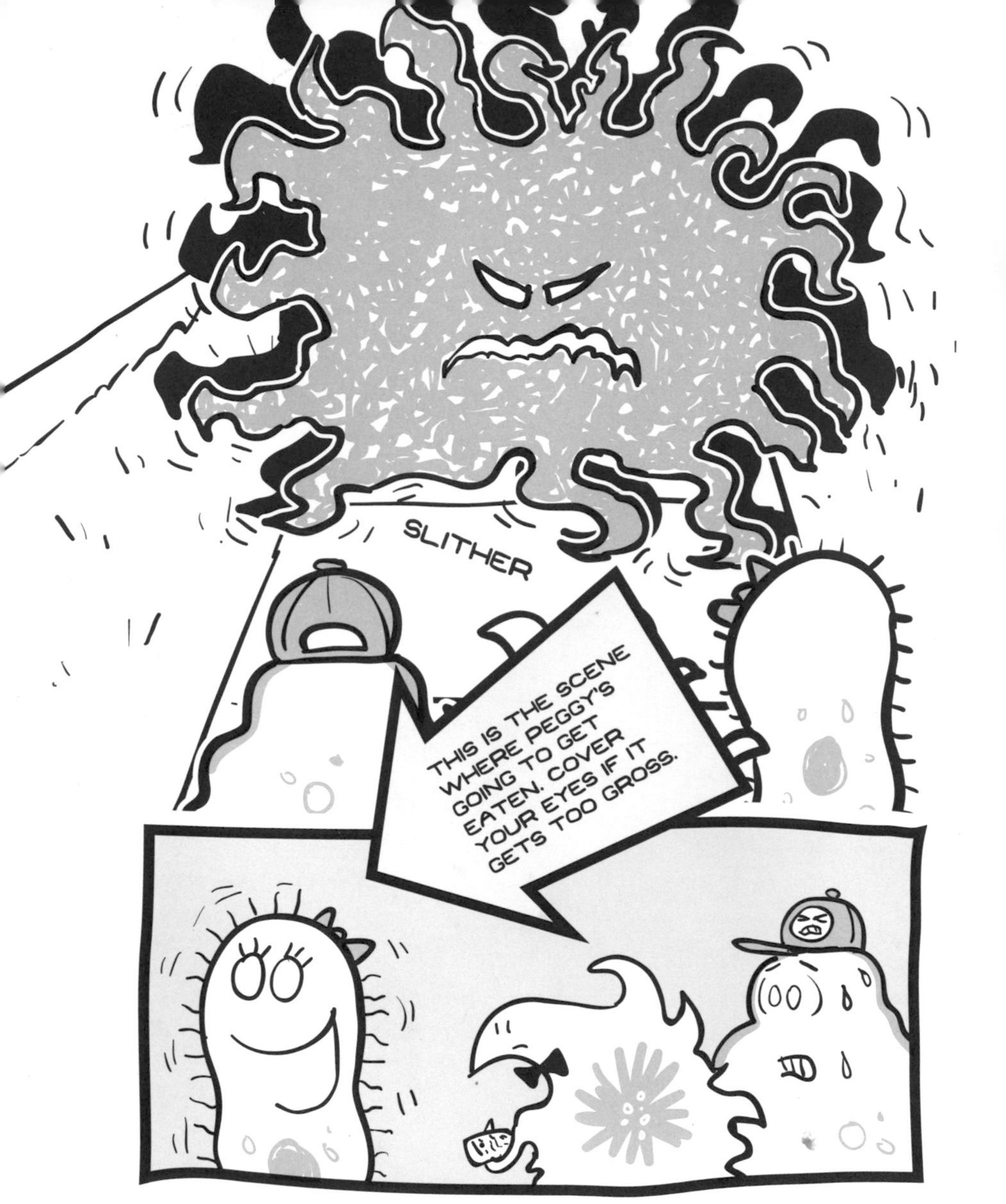
SLITHER
THIS IS THE SCENE WHERE PEGGY'S GOING TO GET EATEN. COVER YOUR EYES IF IT GETS TOO GROSS.

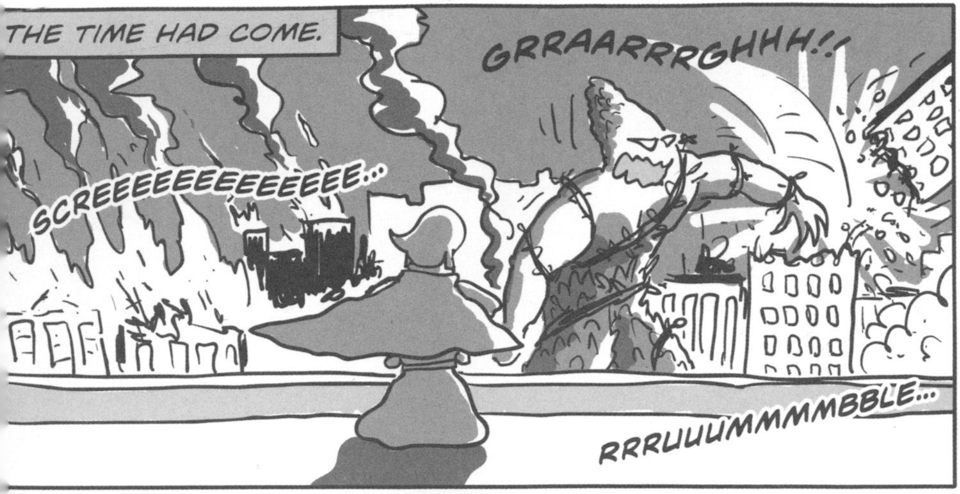

THE TIME HAD COME.
GRRAARRRGHHH!!
SCREEEEEEEEEEEEEE...
RRRUUUMMMMMBBLE...

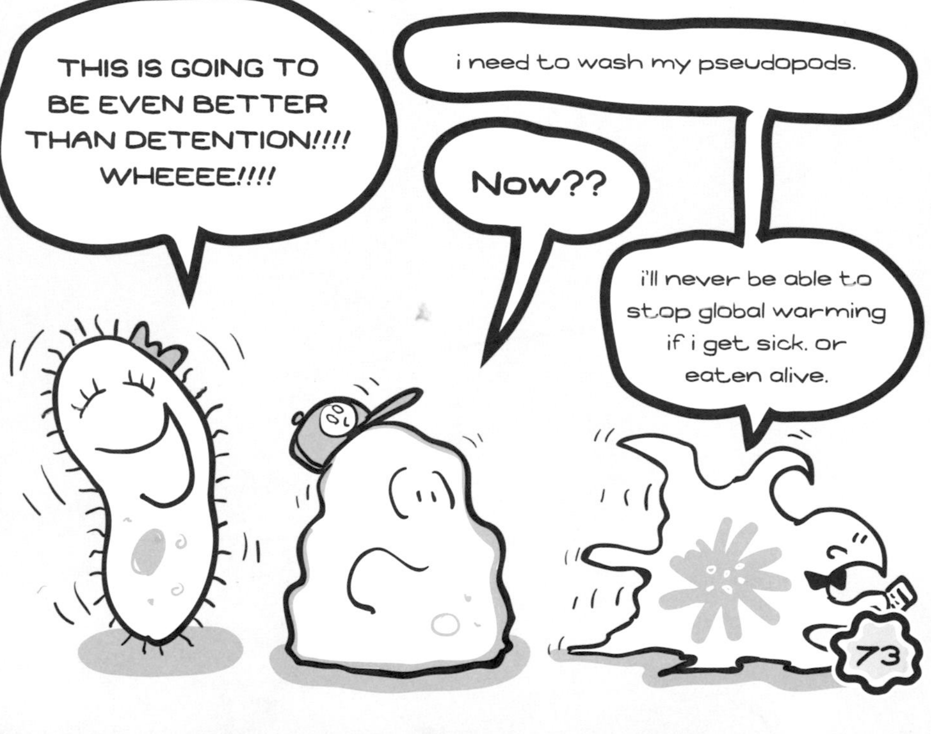

THIS IS GOING TO BE EVEN BETTER THAN DETENTION!!!! WHEEEE!!!!
Now??
i need to wash my pseudopods.
i'll never be able to stop global warming if i get sick. or eaten alive.

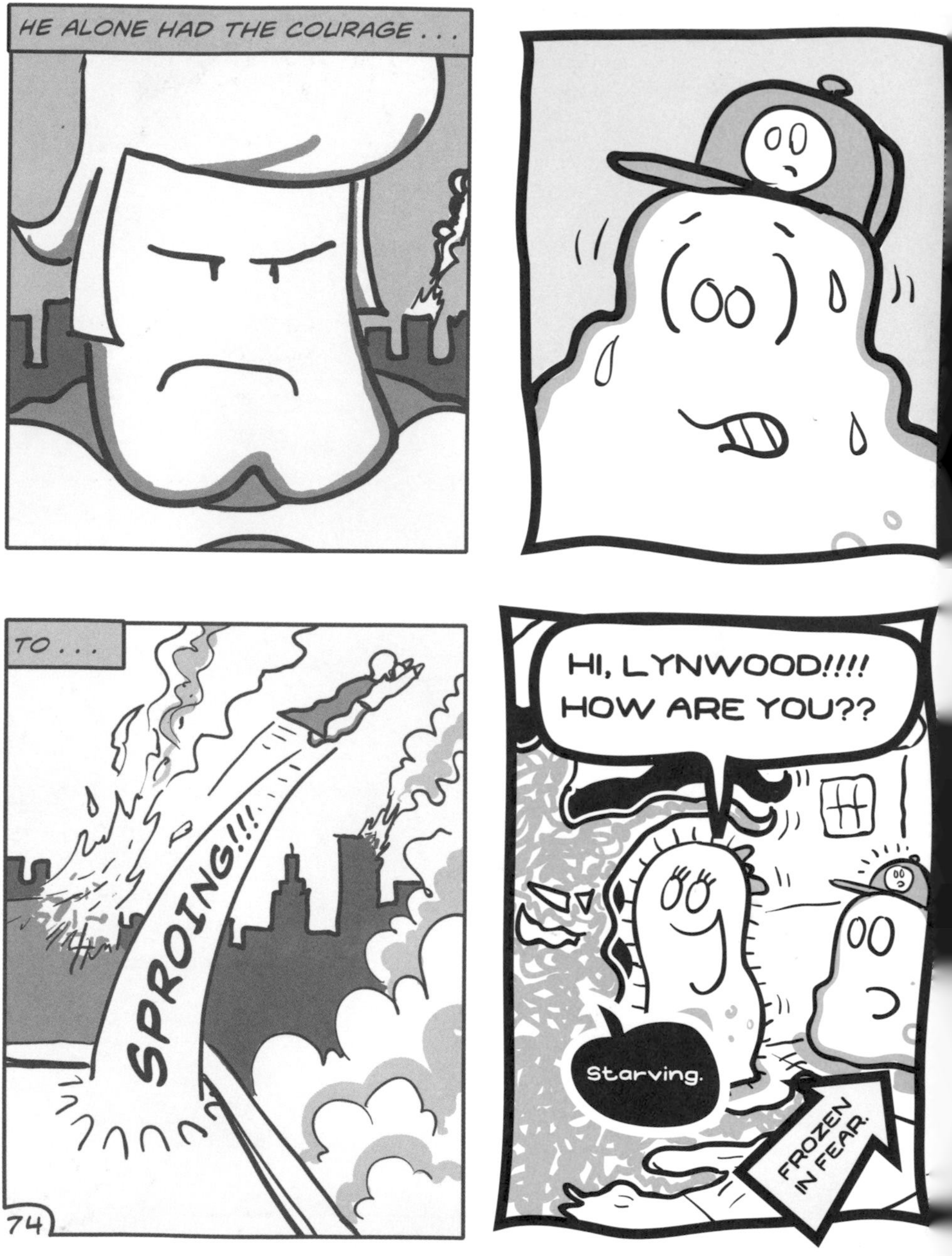

HE ALONE HAD THE COURAGE . . .
TO . . .
SPROING!!!
HI, LYNWOOD!!!! HOW ARE YOU??
Starving.
FROZEN IN FEAR.

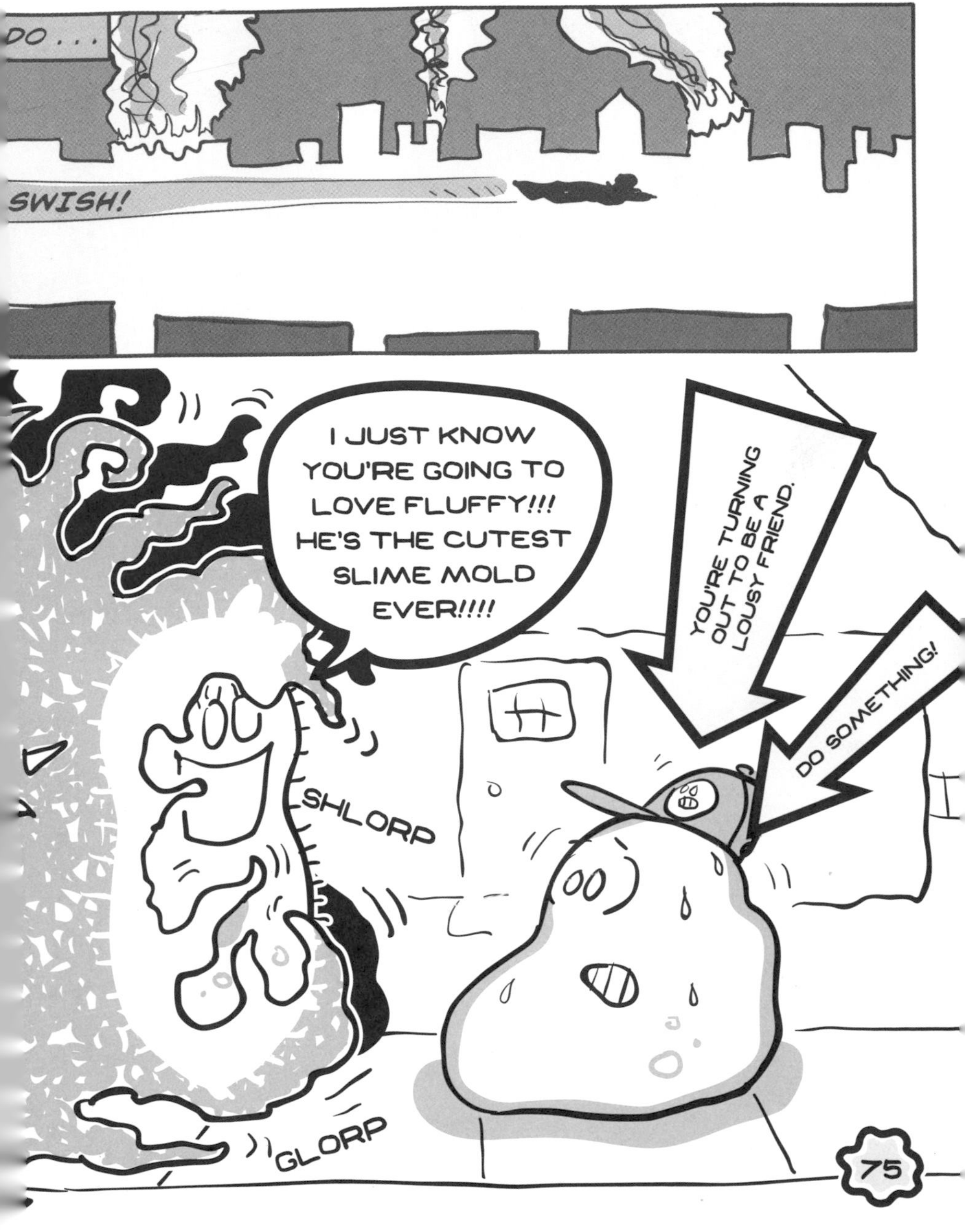
DO . . .
SWISH!
I JUST KNOW YOU'RE GOING TO LOVE FLUFFY!!! HE'S THE CUTEST SLIME MOLD EVER!!!!
YOU'RE TURNING OUT TO BE A LOUSY FRIEND.
DO SOMETHING!
SHLORP
GLORP

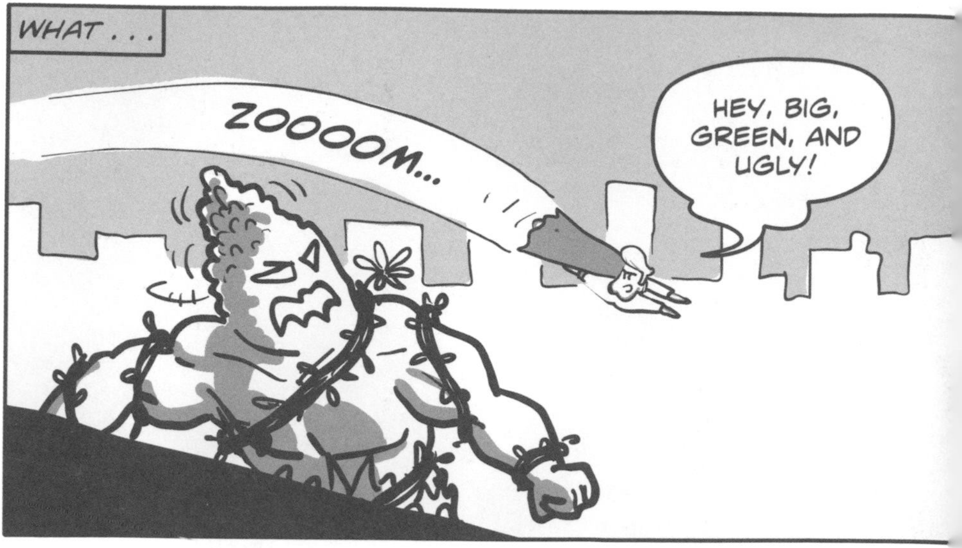
WHAT . . .
ZOOOOOM...
HEY, BIG, GREEN, AND UGLY!

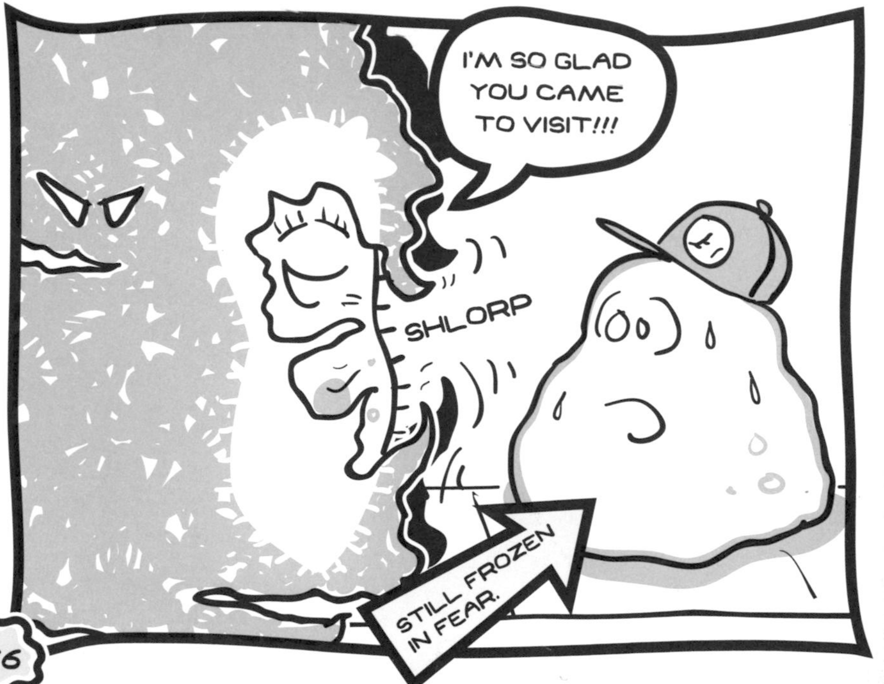
I'M SO GLAD YOU CAME TO VISIT!!!
SHLORP
STILL FROZEN IN FEAR.

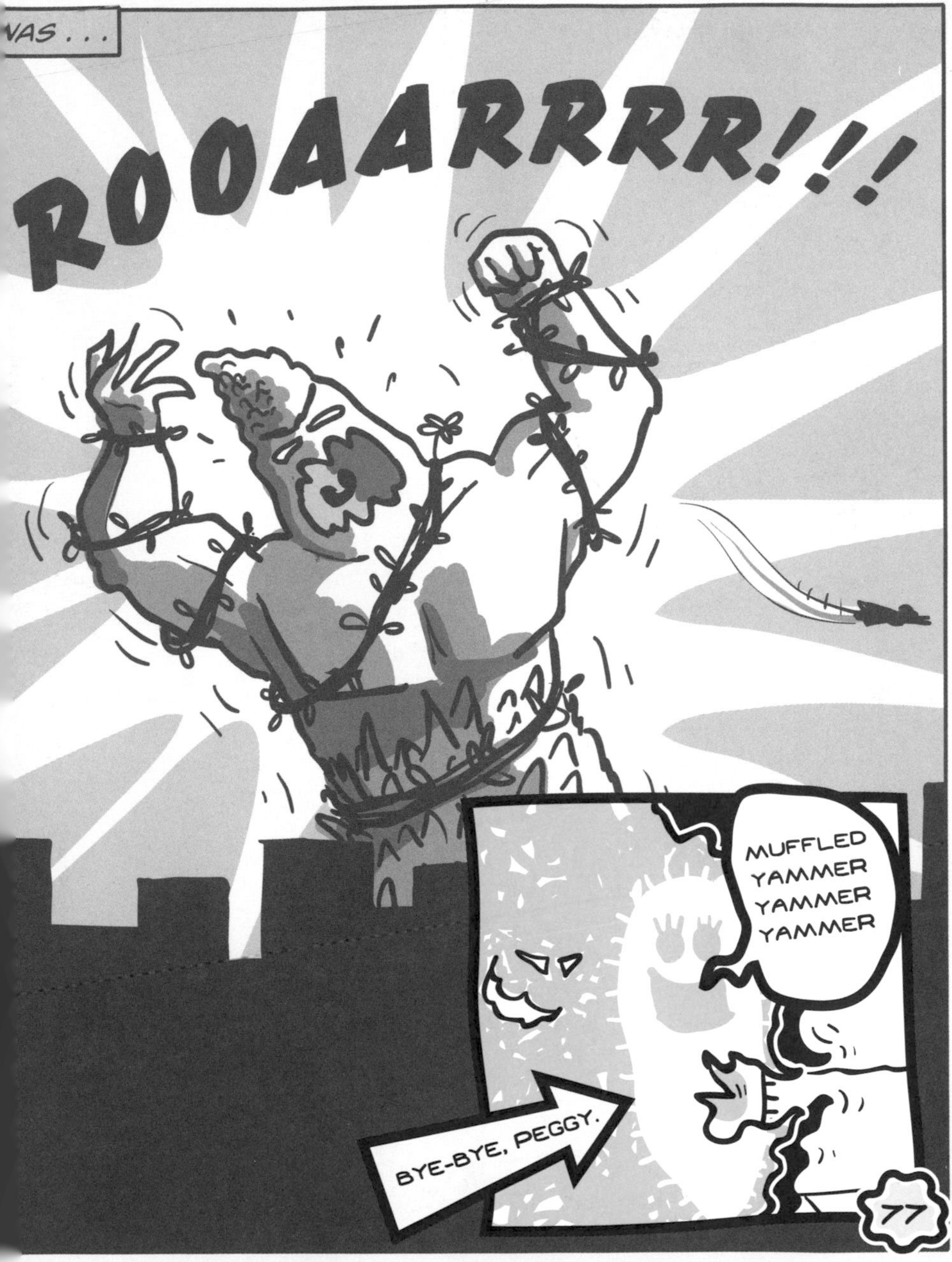
WAS . . .
ROOAARRRRR!!!
MUFFLED YAMMER YAMMER YAMMER
BYE-BYE, PEGGY.

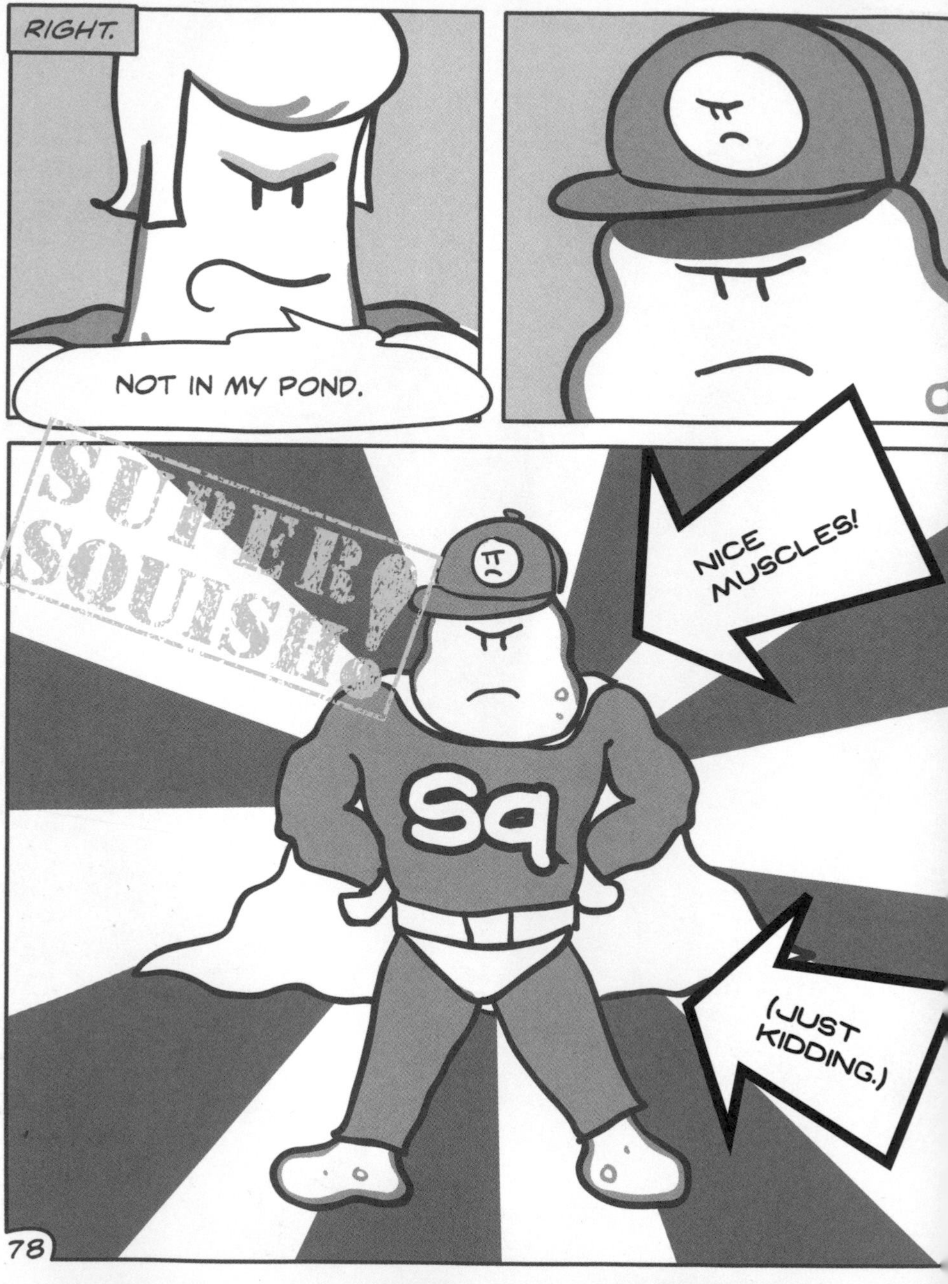
RIGHT.
NOT IN MY POND.
SUPER SQUISH!
NICE MUSCLES!
(JUST KIDDING.)

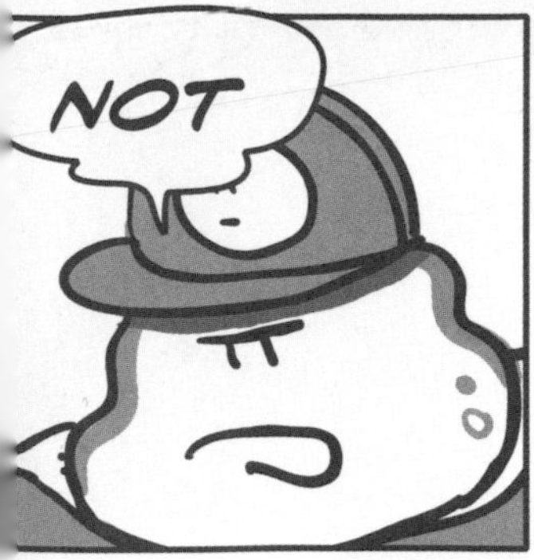
NOT

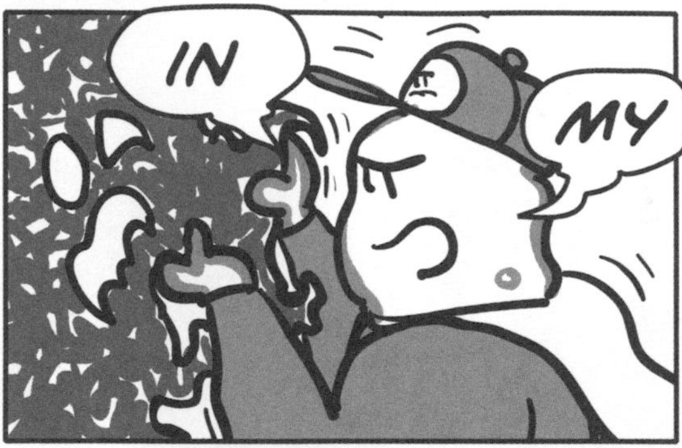
IN
MY

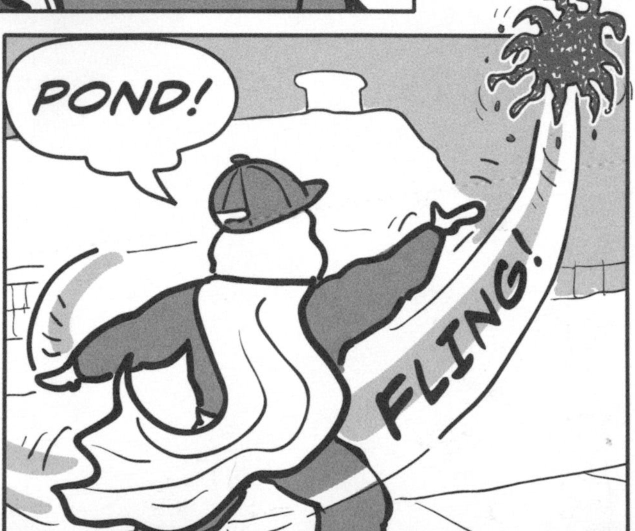
POND!
FLING!

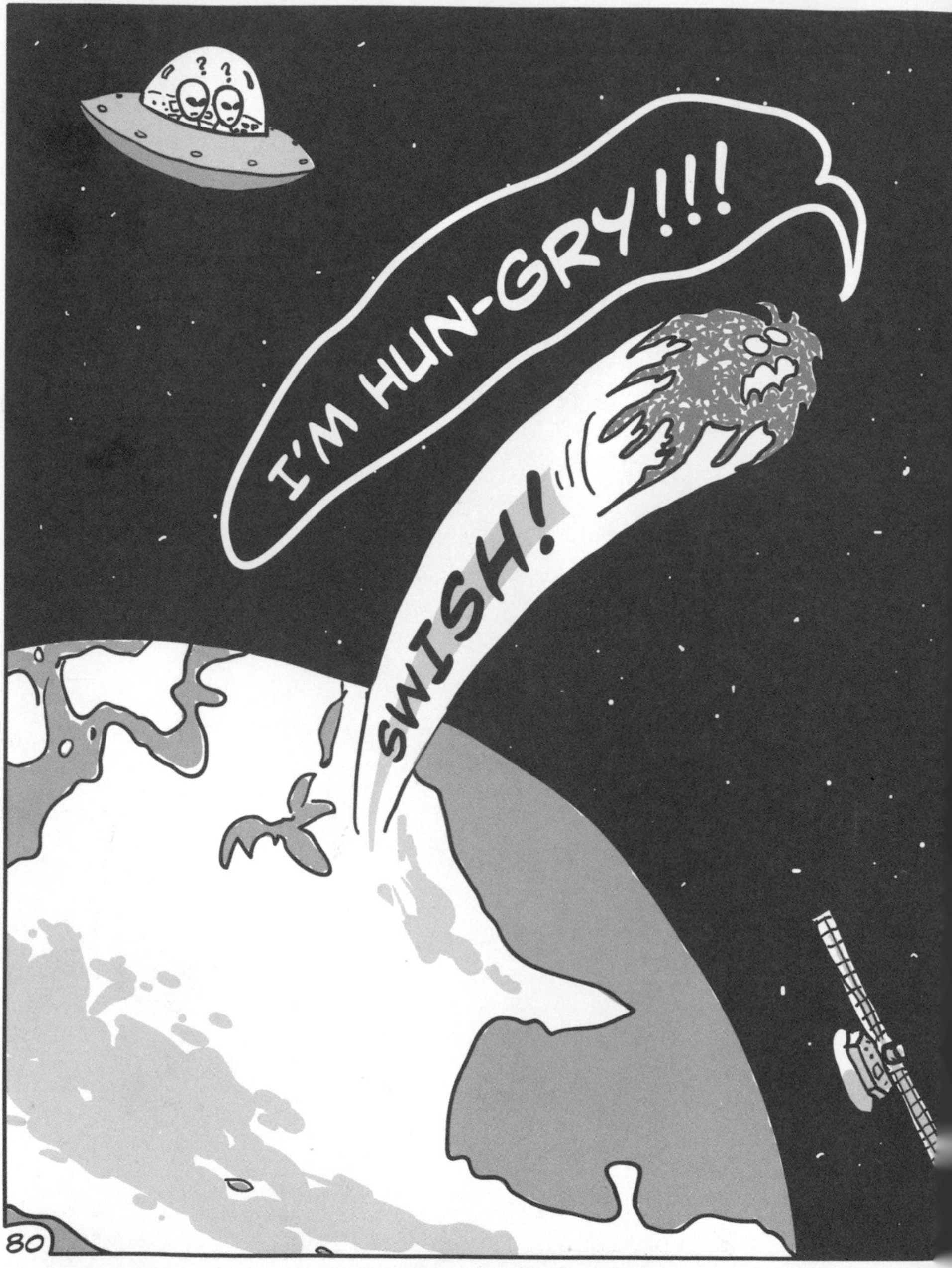
I'M HUN-GRY!!!
SWISH!

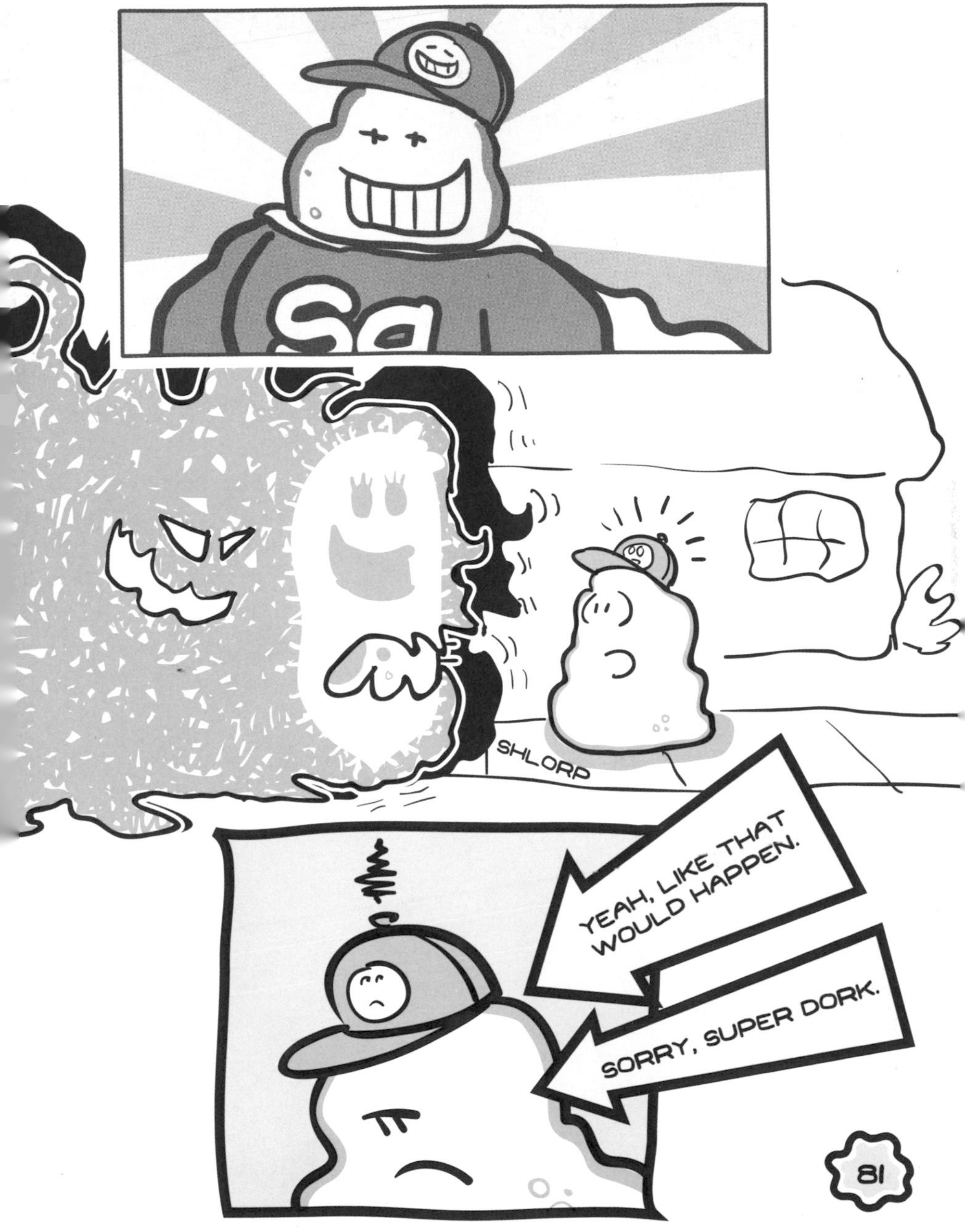
SHLORP
YEAH, LIKE THAT WOULD HAPPEN.
SORRY, SUPER DORK.

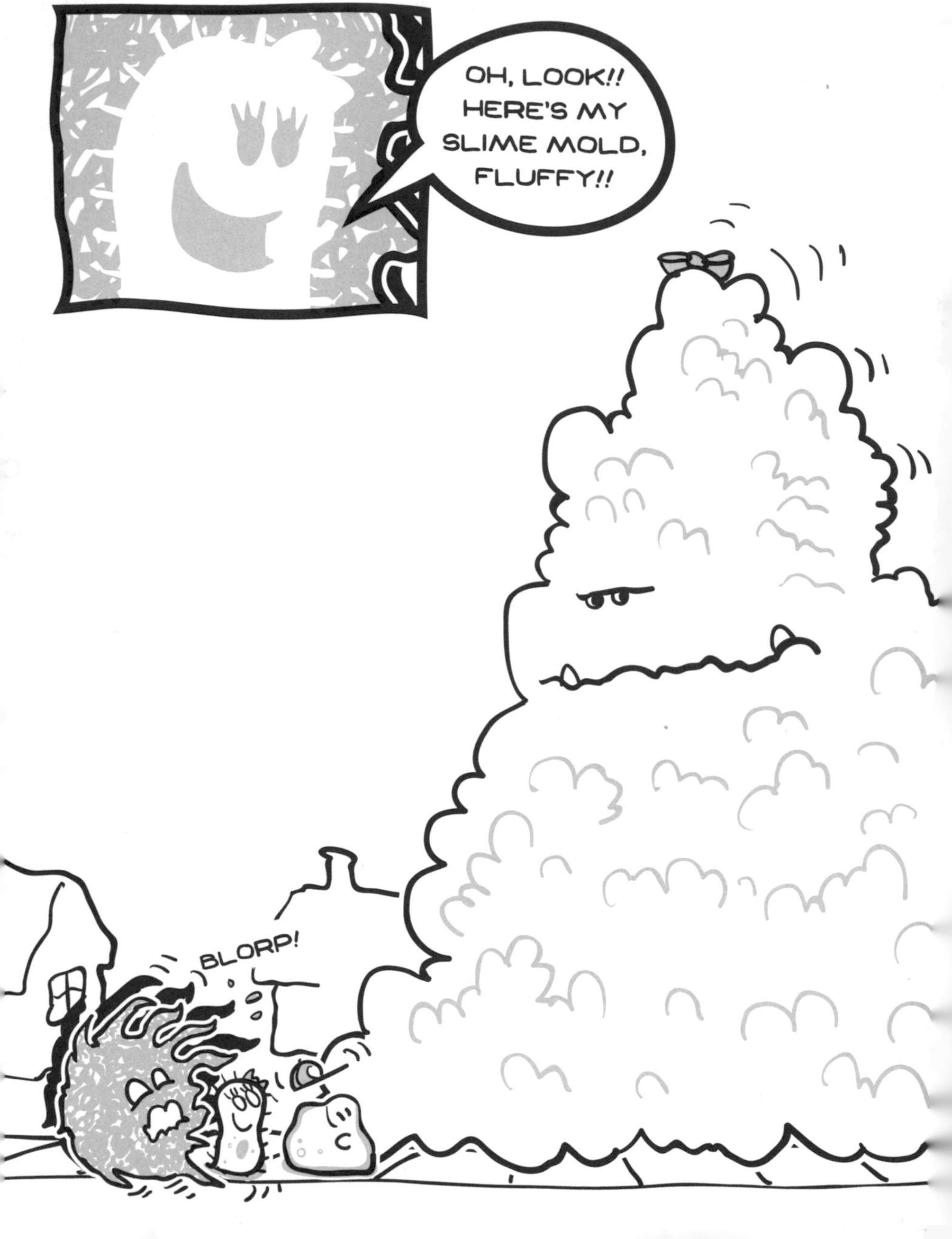
OH, LOOK!! HERE'S MY SLIME MOLD, FLUFFY!!
BLORP!

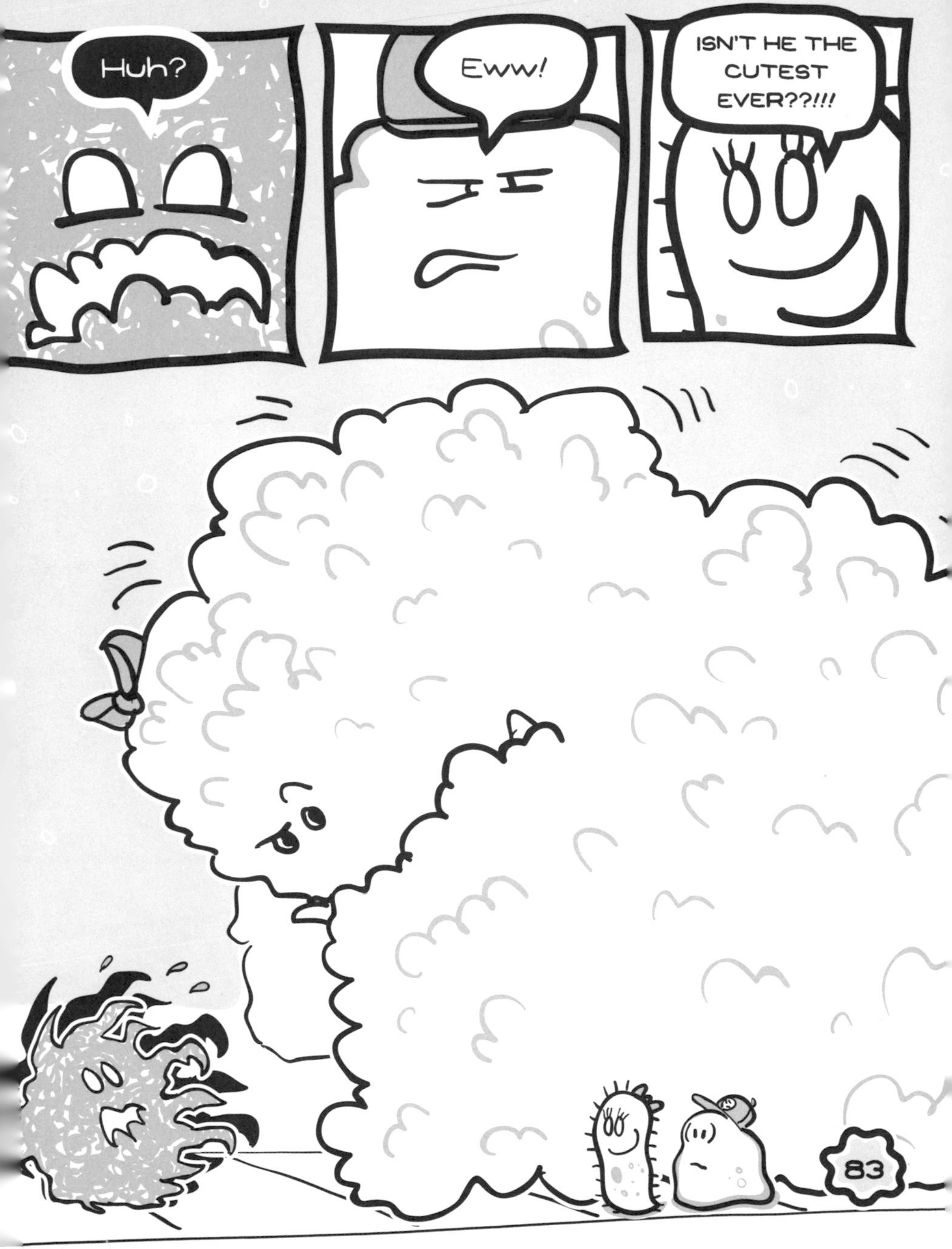
Huh?
Eww!
ISN'T HE THE CUTEST EVER??!!!

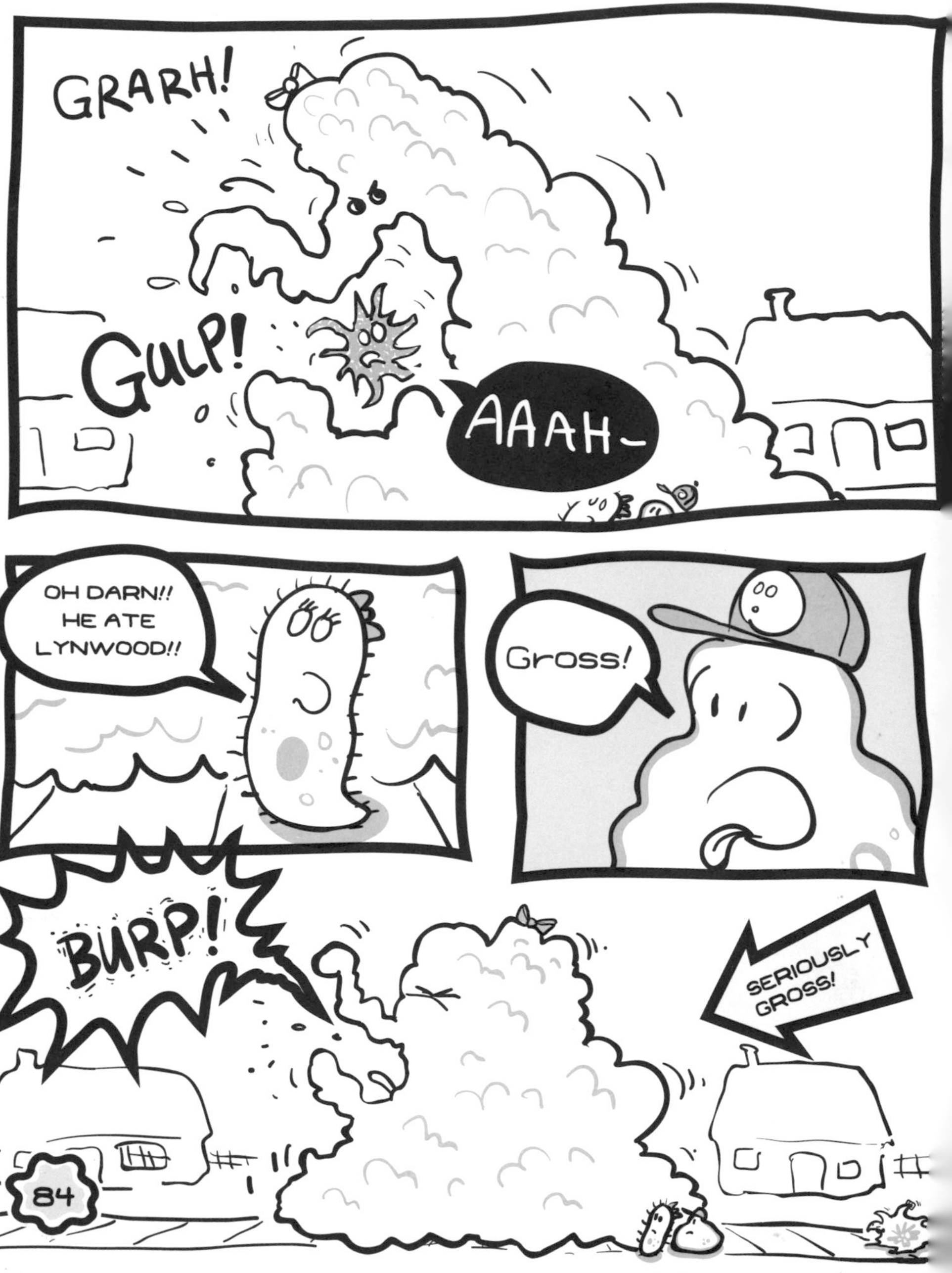
GRARH!
GULP!
AAAH-
OH DARN!! HE ATE LYNWOOD!!
Gross!
BURP!
SERIOUSLY GROSS!

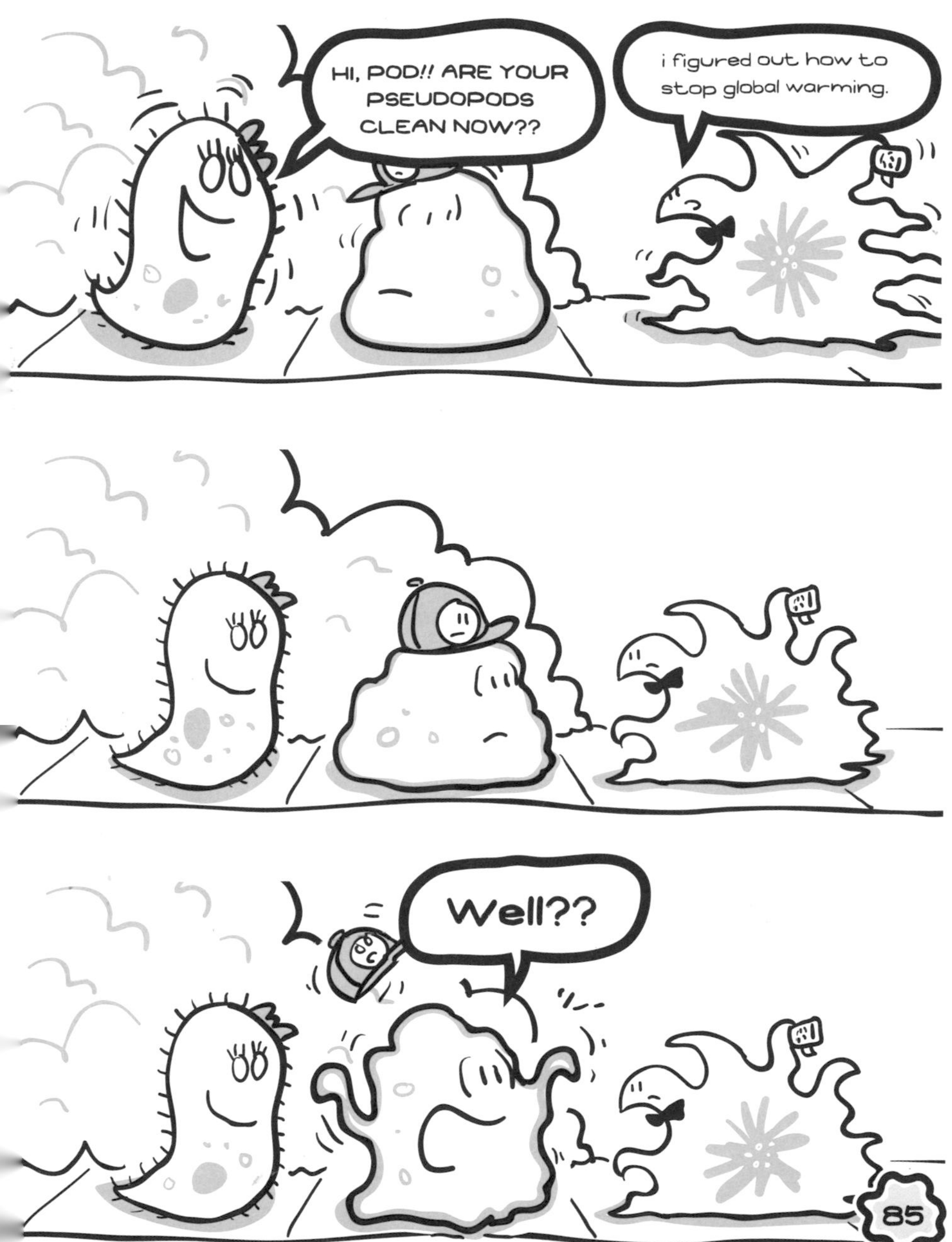
HI, POD!! ARE YOUR PSEUDOPODS CLEAN NOW??
i figured out how to stop global warming.
Well??

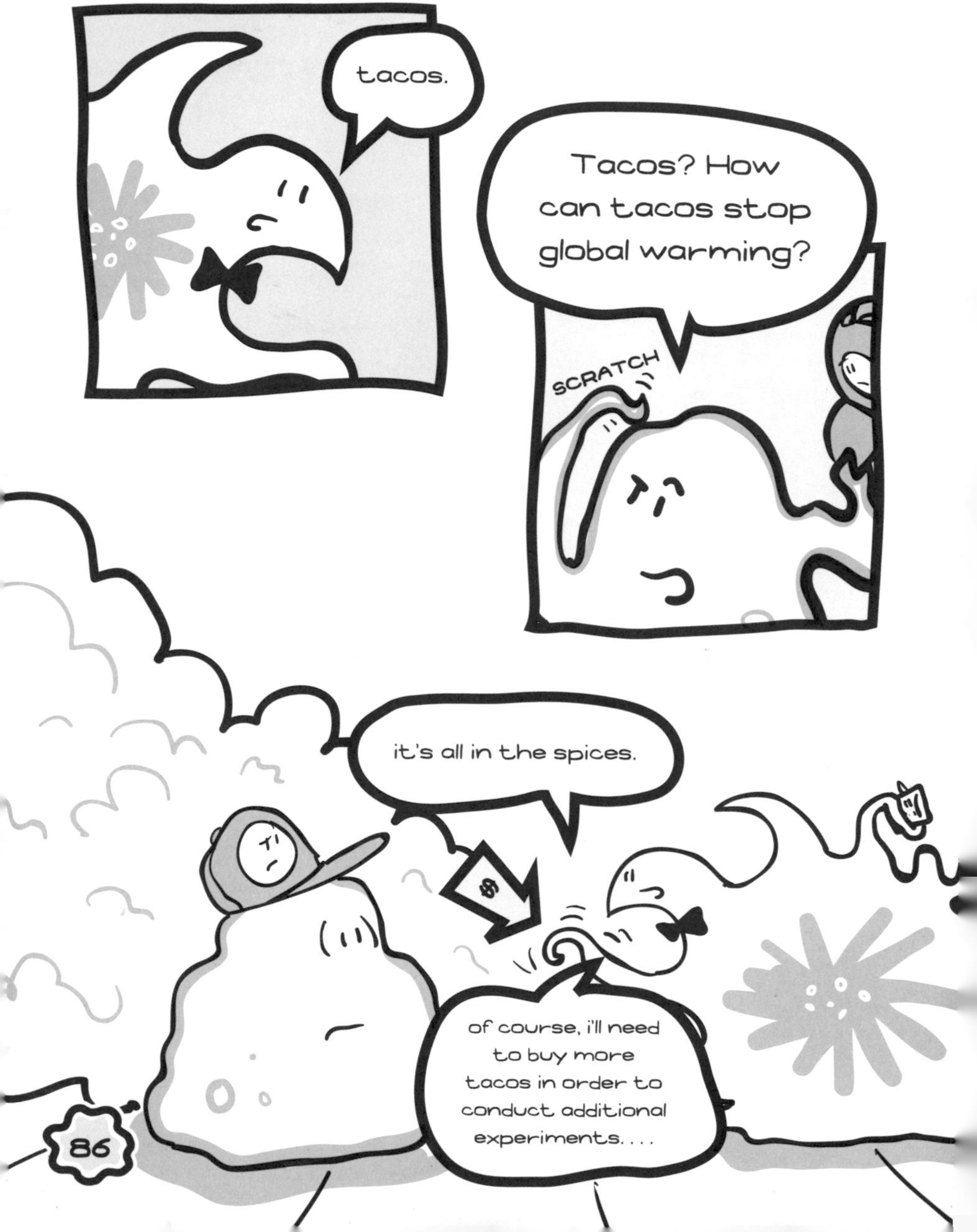
tacos.
Tacos? How can tacos stop global warming?
SCRATCH
it's all in the spices.
of course, i'll need to buy more tacos in order to conduct additional experiments. . . .

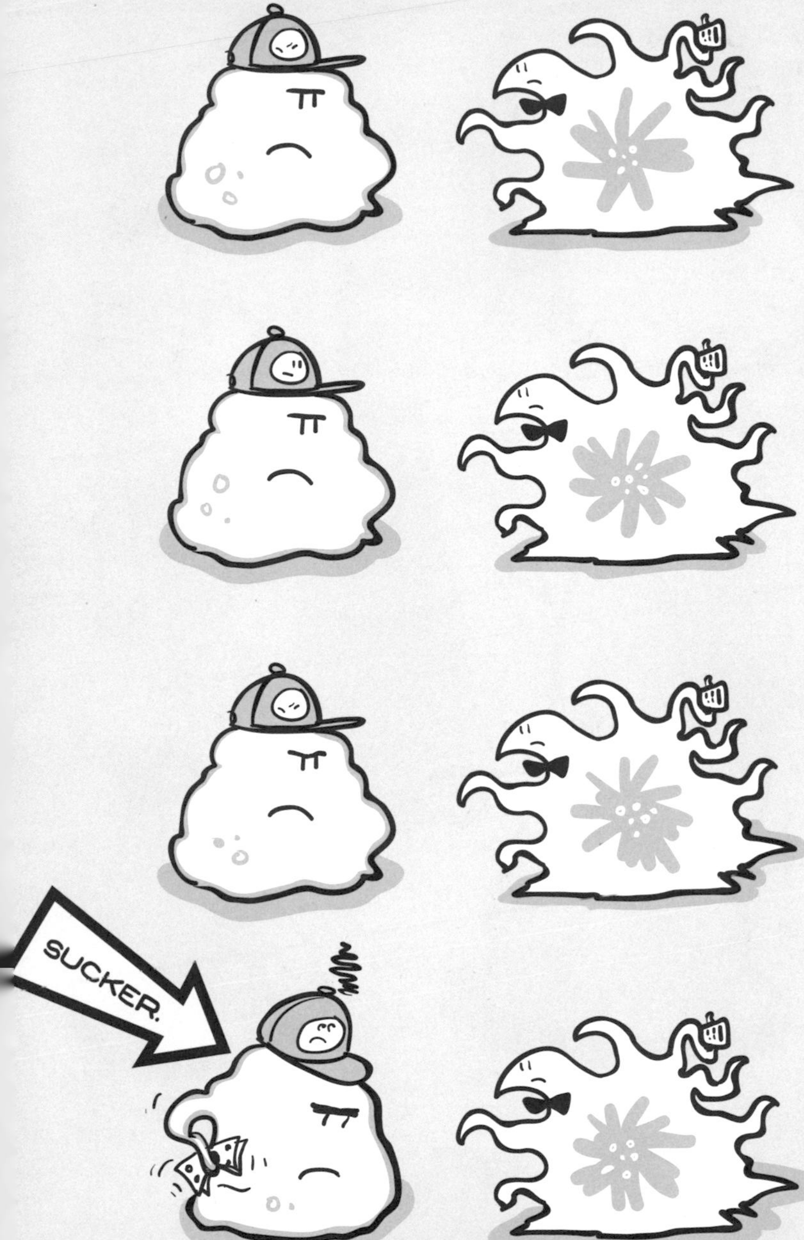
SUCKER.

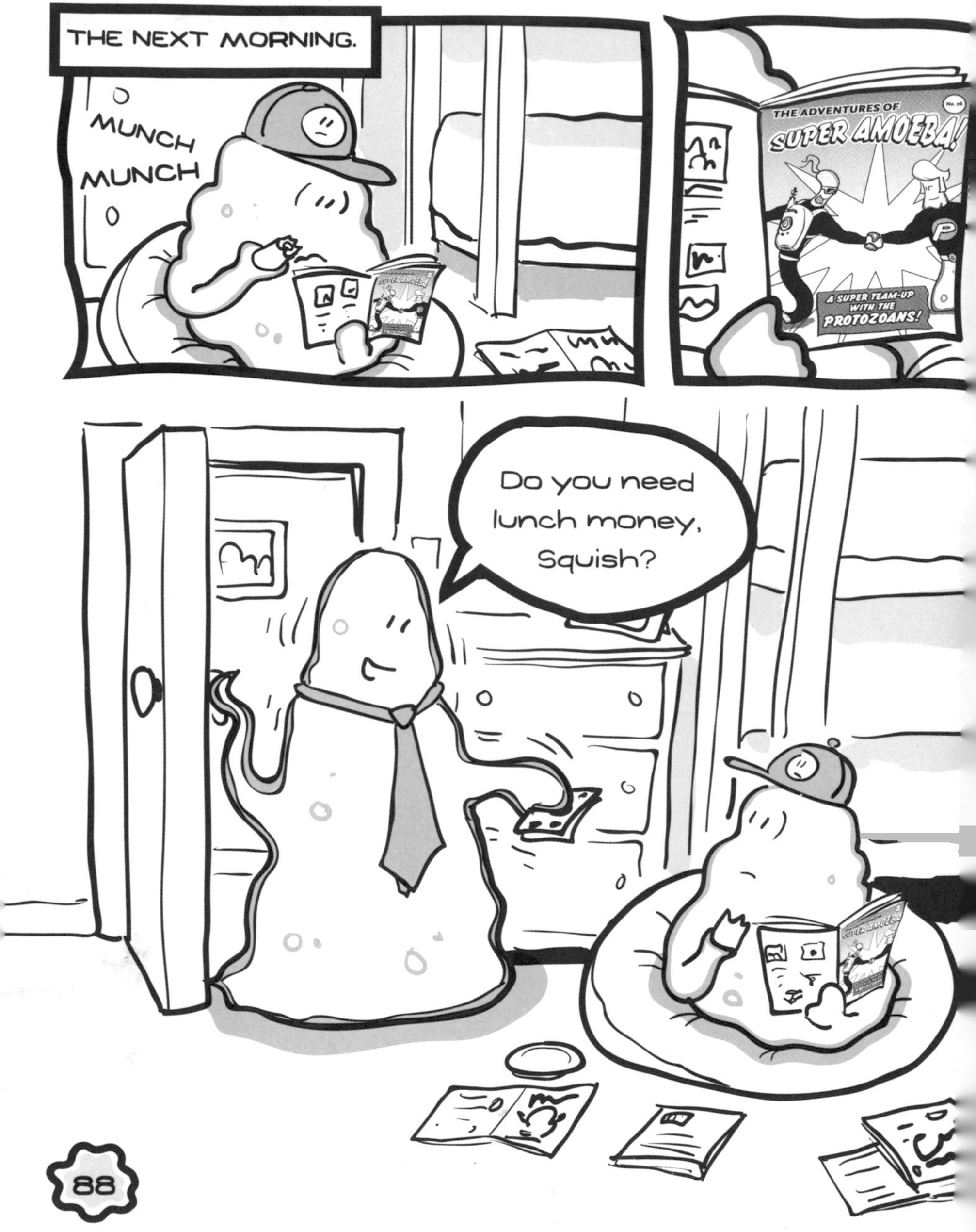
THE NEXT MORNING.
MUNCH MUNCH
THE ADVENTURES OF
SUPER AMOEBA!
A SUPER TEAM-UP WITH THE PROTOZOANS!
Do you need lunch money, Squish?

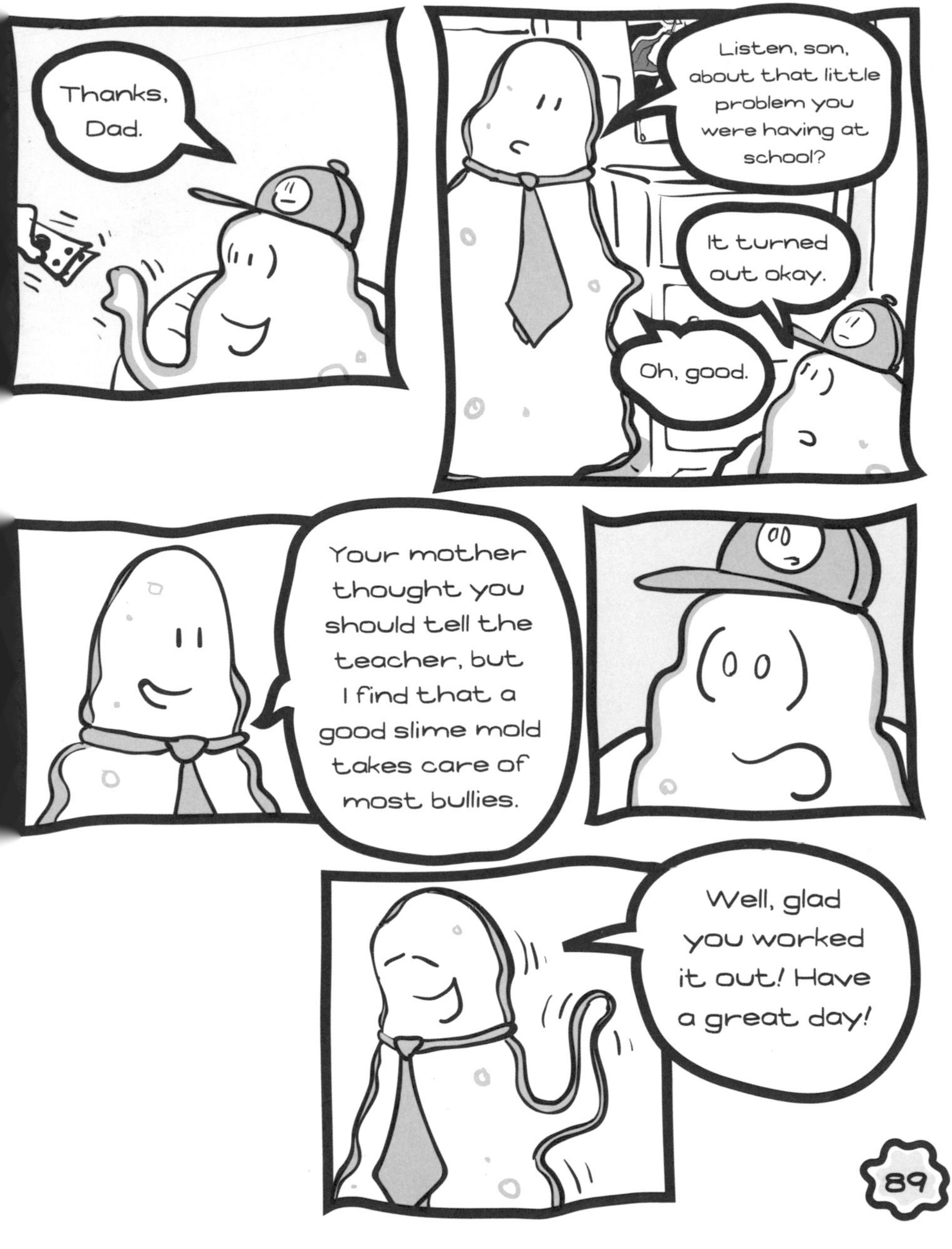
Thanks, Dad.
Listen, son, about that little problem you were having at school?
It turned out okay.
Oh, good.
Your mother thought you should tell the teacher, but I find that a good slime mold takes care of most bullies.
Well, glad you worked it out! Have a great day!

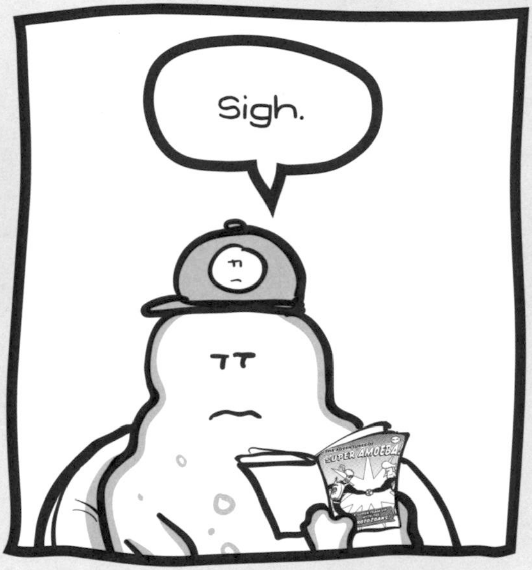
Sigh.
THE ADVENTURES OF
SUPER AMOEBA!

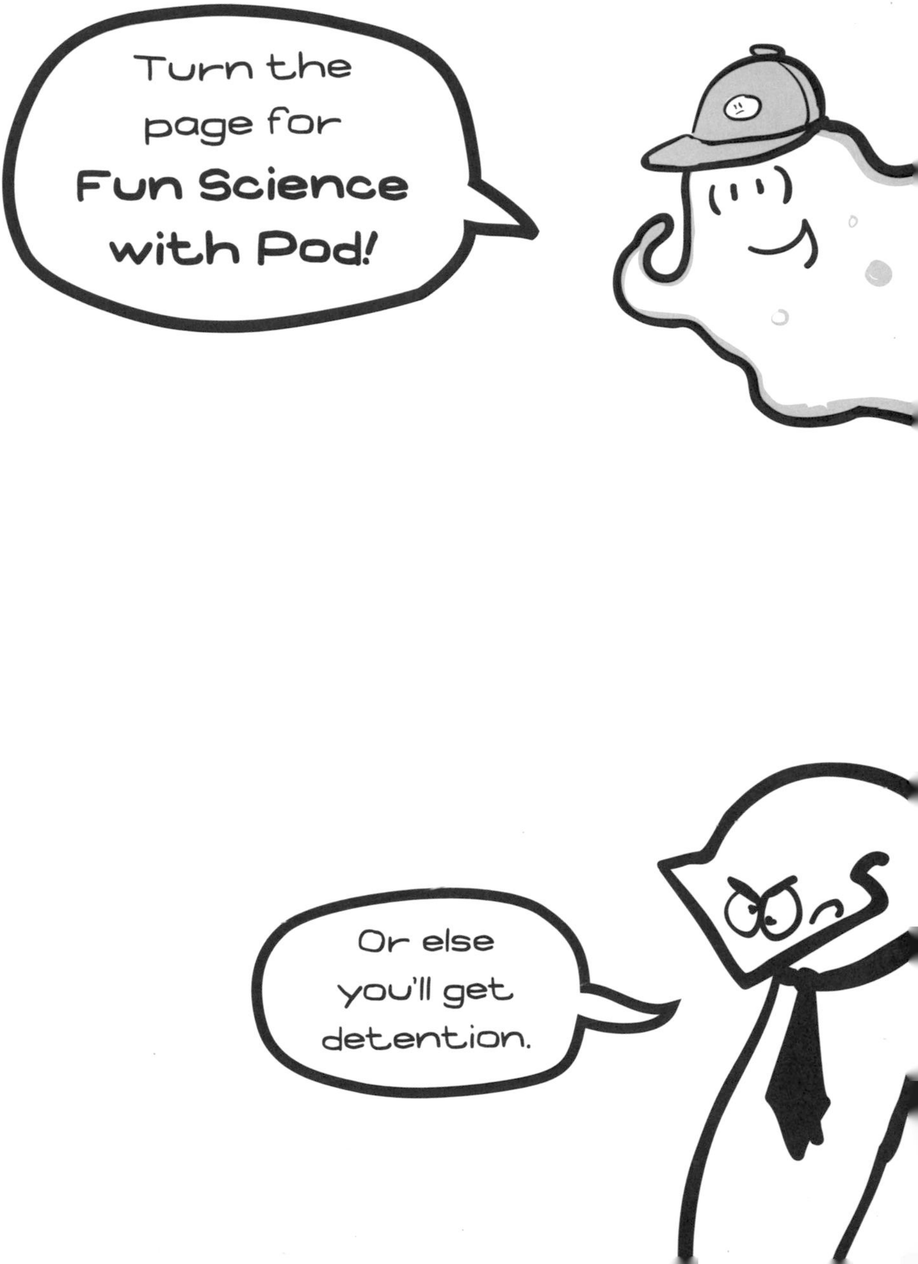
Turn the page for Fun Science with Pod!
Or else you'll get detention.

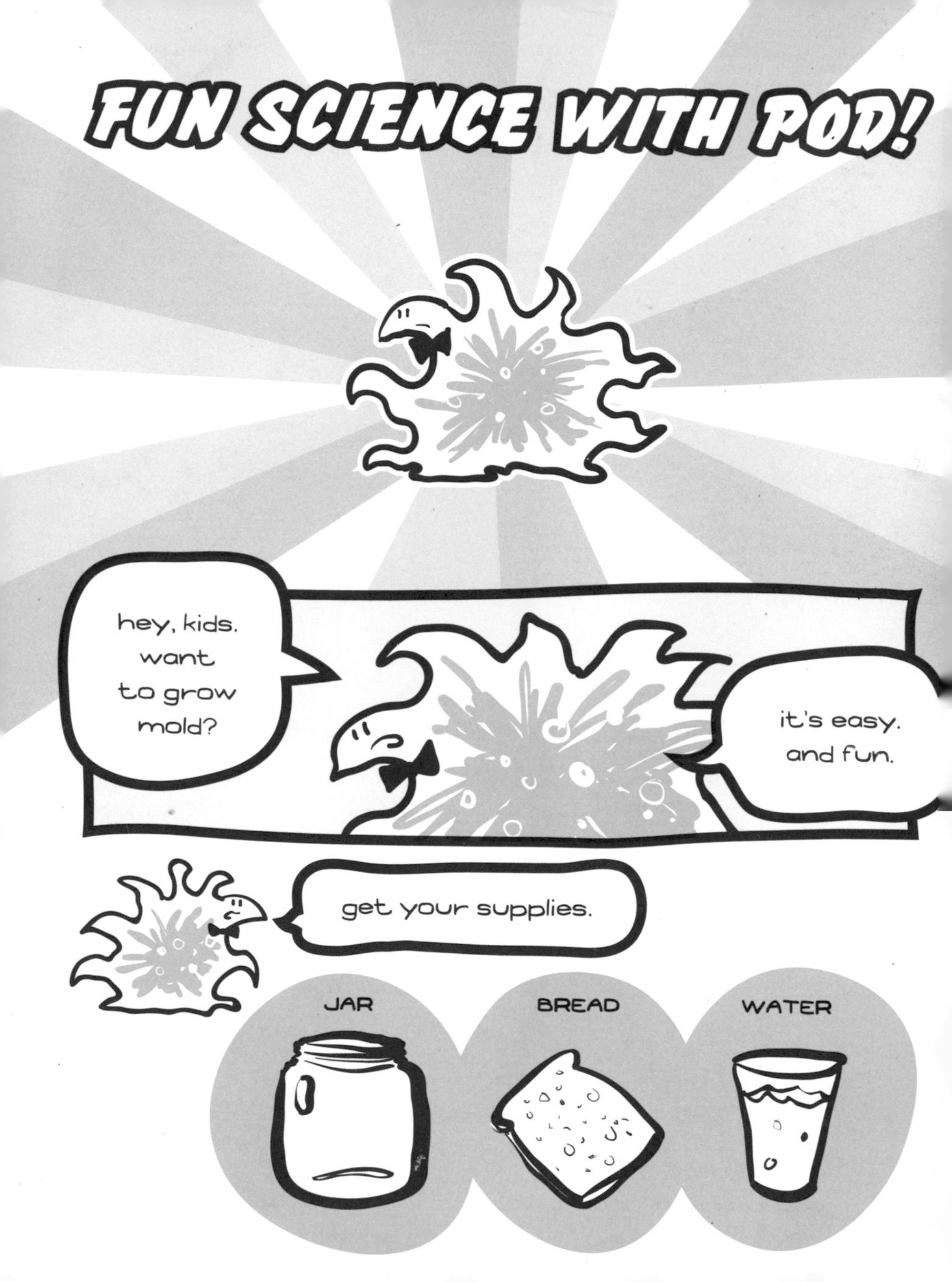
FUN SCIENCE WITH POD!
hey, kids. want to grow mold?
it's easy. and fun.
get your supplies.
JAR
BREAD
WATER

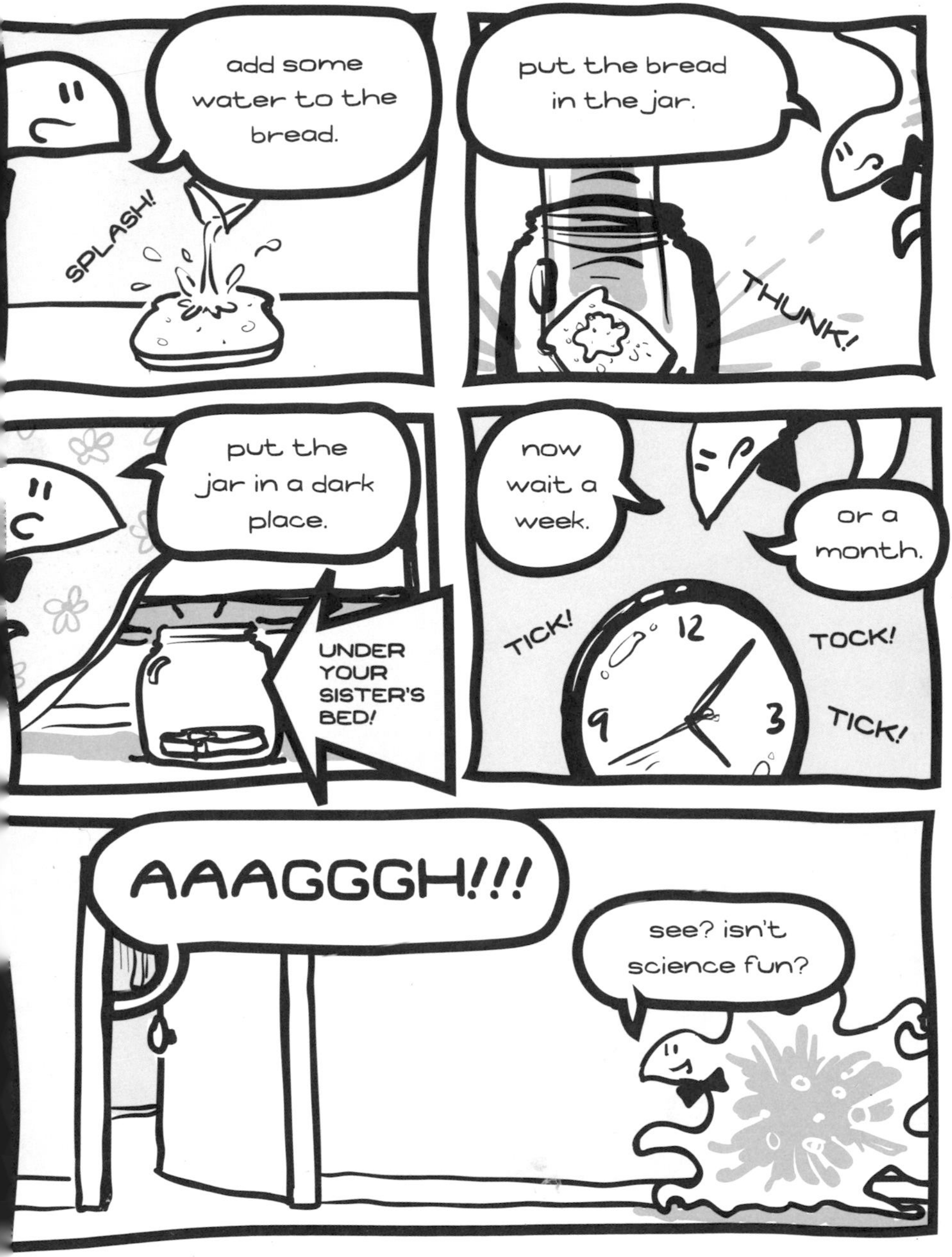
add some water to the bread.
SPLASH!
put the bread in the jar.
THUNK!
put the jar in a dark place.
UNDER YOUR SISTER'S BED!
now wait a week.
or a month.
TICK!
TOCK!
TICK!
AAAGGGH!!!
see? isn't science fun?

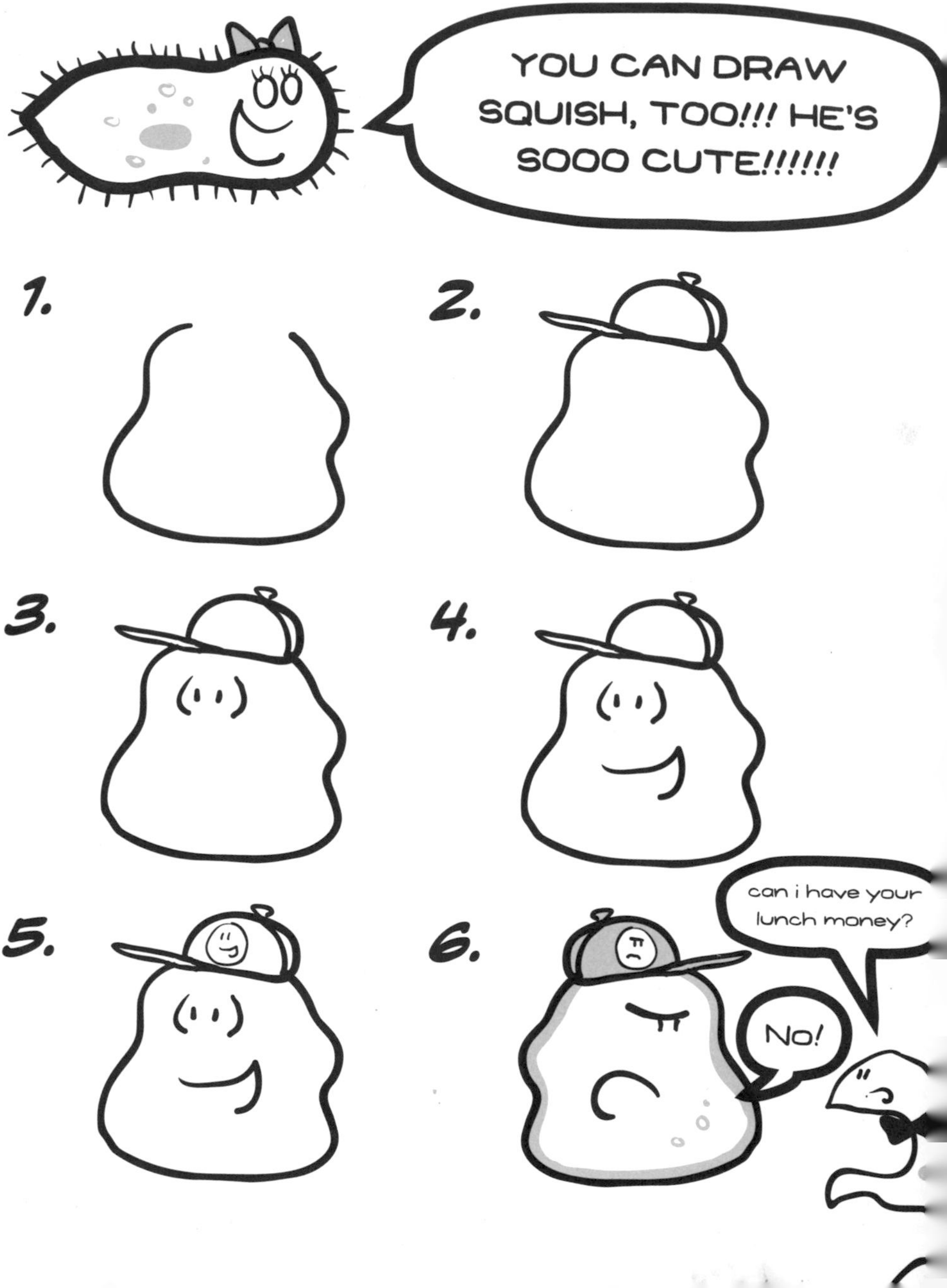
YOU CAN DRAW SQUISH, TOO!!! HE'S SOOO CUTE!!!!!!
1.
2.
3.
4.
5.
6.
can i have your lunch money?
No!

IT'S GREEN...
IT'S BLOBBY...
IT'S GROSS...

IT'S squish!

DON'T MISS SQUISH'S NEXT *AMAZING, ACTION-PACKED ADVENTURE!*

COMING IN SEPTEMBER 2011!

squish
BRAVE NEW POND NO. 2

FROM THE DARING DUO WHO BROUGHT YOU *BABYMOUSE!*
JENNIFER L. HOLM & MATTHEW HOLM

I am
NOT
a blob!

IF YOU LIKE **SQUISH**, YOU'LL LOVE **BABYMOUSE**...

#1 BABYMOUSE: Queen of the World!

#2 BABYMOUSE: Our Hero

#3 BABYMOUSE: Beach Babe

#4 BABYMOUSE: Rock Star

#5 BABYMOUSE: Heartbreaker

#6 CAMP BABYMOUSE

#7 BABYMOUSE: Skater Girl

#8 BABYMOUSE: Puppy Love

#9 BABYMOUSE: Monster Mash

#10 BABYMOUSE: The Musical

#11 BABYMOUSE: Dragonslayer

#12 BABYMOUSE: Burns Rubber

#13 BABYMOUSE: Cupcake Tycoon

#14 BABYMOUSE: Mad Scientist

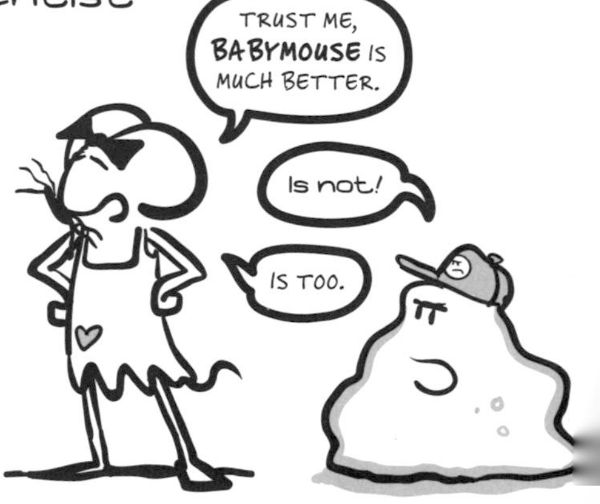
TRUST ME, BABYMOUSE IS MUCH BETTER.
Is not!
IS TOO.